THE GOAT

The
Goat
Lady's
Daughter

Rosella Leslie

NEWEST
PRESS

Library and Archives Canada Cataloguing in Publication
Leslie, Rosella M., 1948-
The goat lady's daughter / Rosella Leslie.

(Nunatak fiction)
ISBN-13: 978-1-897126-06-6
ISBN-10: 1-897126-06-9

I. Title. II. Series.

PS8623.E847G62 2006   C813'.6   C2006-902961-X

Editor for the press: Lynne Van Luven
Cover image: Rosella Leslie
Cover and interior design: Ruth Linka
Author photo: Betty C. Keller

 Canada Council for the Arts **Conseil des Arts du Canada** Canadian Heritage Patrimoine canadien edmonton arts council

NeWest Press acknowledges the support of the Canada Council for the Arts and the Alberta Foundation for the Arts, and the Edmonton Arts Council for our publishing program. We also acknowledge the financial support of the Government of Canada through the Book Publishing Industry Development Program (BPIDP) for our publishing activities.

NeWest Press
201–8540–109th Street
Edmonton, Alberta, T6G 1E6
(780) 432-9427
www.newestpress.com

NeWest Press is committed to protecting the environment and to the responsible use of natural resources. This book is printed on 100% post-consumer recycled and ancient-forest-friendly paper. For more information, please visit www.oldgrowthfree.com.

1   2   3   4   5   09   08   07   06

PRINTED AND BOUND IN CANADA

This book is dedicated to my friends in the Quintessential Writing group: Maureen Foss, Dorothy Fraser, Gwen Southin, and my mentor Betty C. Keller. Thank you for nudging me to go back and back again, until I got it right.

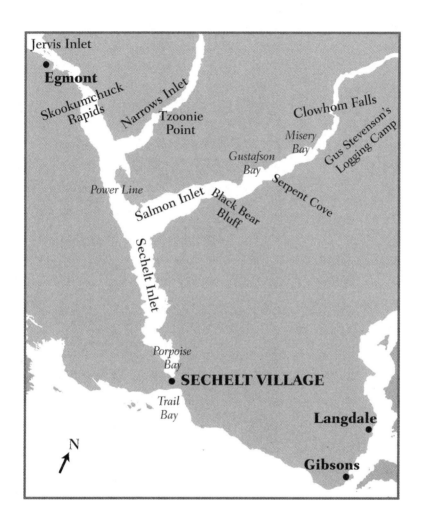

CHAPTER ONE

No smoke rose from the chimney of the floathouse moored in Anchor Bay, yet Mag Larson knew that the girl had to be home. Even from her goat yard at Serpent Cove, a full half mile away and across the other side of the inlet, Mag could see that the girl's rowboat, upturned and covered with snow, had been pulled up onto the edge of the float. She narrowed her dark brown eyes until they were mere slits amid the creases of her face. "Damn!" she said and stomped back to her goat shed.

Mag had built the shed out of boards scrounged from a dumpster in the village of Sechelt, twenty-five nautical miles to the south. She had nailed the boards vertically onto a lopsided framework so that their length dictated the height of the building. Now, though she was only five foot two, her hat scraped the ceiling as she shovelled goat dung and fouled hay from the floor into a large plastic bucket. "Hippies," she snorted, curling stiff fingers around the bucket handle. "Crazy damned hippies."

As she added the dung to a growing mountain of refuse and hay behind the shed, a lock of salt and pepper hair teased her weathered forehead. She pushed the offending curl under her worn felt hat, then grabbed a water bucket and trudged toward the creek. Her gait was masculine, her posture slightly crouched as if she was climbing a mountain rather than walking on level ground. Though a path had been beaten down through the snow, it was icy wherever the water from her daily trips to the creek had slopped out of the buckets and frozen, and she placed each foot with care.

Her sister Florrie had been asleep when Mag went out to do the chores, and Mag knew she could stay that way for hours. *Never even know if I fell an' broke somet'ing.* She edged her way down to the slight embankment. *Time she found me, I'd be froze to death.* The sisters had dammed the pool a few years back. Now it was almost covered with ice, and there was only one deep spot still free. Using a bucket stowed near the creek, she crouched, knees against the bank, and scooped water into her pail. When it was full she climbed painfully to her feet, paused until the cold arrows shooting through her knees subsided, then trudged back along the trail to the cabin.

The warmth from the wood fire enveloped her as she entered the main room. Mag hung her hat on a hook by the door, but left her coat on. "No smoke from the hippie's house," she announced to the huge mound buried beneath the quilts on the bed nestled in a dark corner of the room.

The mound stirred, and Florrie's plump face peered over the top of the quilt.

"Boat's still there," Mag went on. "Somet'ing's wrong."

Florrie propped her head on her hand, elbow against the pillow. "You joost better go see," she advised, yawning and displaying two gaps where teeth were missing on either side of the top gum. Although she was only fifty-one, three years younger than Mag, Florrie appeared much older. She sat up and pushed a stray wisp of grey hair back into the thick braid that reached to her waist.

Mag dumped some of the water from her bucket into a large aluminum pot and set it on the stove. Then she shoved a few sticks of alder into the firebox. Smoke billowed from the opening, filling the room, and sending Florrie into a fit of coughing.

"I'm not going alone," Mag said. "Not when it's like this out there. Don't figure she's cleared any snow off the deck of that floathouse."

"Maybe she's dead," Florrie warned, grasping at anything that might discourage her sister from going out on the water. "Shooer could bring trouble if the cops come."

Mag frowned. Two RCMP officers had arrived at the cove several years ago looking for a whisky still. The officers had refused to listen when Mag and Florrie insisted they wouldn't know a still from a jackrabbit. The officers had torn the Larson house apart and left it in a shambles—as if it wasn't worth putting back together. Mag had complained at the Sechelt headquarters, but the sergeant in charge just laughed and said the place was a mess before they started looking. Now she walked heavily to the window and squinted out through the only pane free of frost and dirt. Between the trees she could just make out the top of the floathouse. Still no smoke.

"There's a kid," she said finally, straightening and plodding back to the stove. She took down the cup that rested on the warming oven above the main cooking surface, poured black coffee from a pot at the back of the stove, and carried the cup to a wooden table in the centre of the room. "You better get dressed."

A sharp easterly wind was whipping the water into frosty waves. Though the sun was shining when they set out, its feeble rays did little to warm the inlet. The boat's steering cable had come apart again, and Mag had to navigate from the stern, using the handle of the outboard. It meant half-standing to see over the windshield and exposing herself to the cold. The wide brim of her hat shielded her eyes, but the wind cut through her coat like it wasn't there. Florrie huddled near the bow, a woollen blanket wrapped around her.

The snow covering the girl's float had not been disturbed, which meant nobody had visited or departed in the past three days.

"Maybe somebody picked her up before it snowed," Florrie offered hopefully as Mag slowed the motor and searched the edge of the float for a place to tie up.

"There was smoke day before yesterday," Mag said. She found a scrap of boom chain attached to one of the logs that supported the float's floorboards. It would mean getting her hands wet to fasten the stern line around it, but she had no choice. As soon as the line was secure, she shoved her hands back into her wool gloves, wincing from the pain in her finger joints.

"Wait here," she told her sister, knowing it would be a major job for Florrie to climb onto the deck. Florrie pulled the blanket closer. Mag brushed some of the snow from the float's edge and heaved herself up. As she looked at the closed cabin door, a heaviness enveloped her. She'd seen lots of dead creatures on her trapline and on hunting trips. She'd even seen dead men. There was the guy she and Florrie fished out of the inlet that time—and there was Florrie's boss, Schwabby. But a baby was different. Mag wasn't so sure she was up to seeing a dead kid.

She gave the door two sharp kicks, sparing her icy hands from further pain. Receiving no response, she turned the door handle and pushed inward. It took a moment after she stepped over the sill for her eyes to adjust to the gloom, and her nose to the smell. *Shit* was the word that came to mind, but it was more than that. It was something unhealthy. Vomit.

A bed sagged against the cabin's far wall. The girl was lying on it, clutching the edge of the tattered sleeping bag that covered her. Mag walked closer. Lying beside its mother, the baby had a bluish tinge but seemed to be breathing. At Mag's approach it began to cry, filling the cabin with angry shrieks. The girl tried to sit, but partway up she began to cough—deep, dry, convulsive heaves that tore through her whole body.

"Help us, please . . ." she gasped between coughs. "She's hungry." Grey-faced, she collapsed back against the pillow.

Mag looked around the room helplessly. Nothing here that would fix a cough. Although she hated hospitals and medicine, Mag had to admit that this girl needed a doctor. She found a coat hanging on a nail near the door and brought it to the bed.

"Put this on," she ordered, pulling back the covers. She was glad to see the girl was dressed in jeans. "Where's the kid's clothes?" The girl motioned to a black plastic bag near the bed. Mag rummaged through an assortment of baby things, found something that looked like a sleeper, and started to stuff the baby into it. Only then did she realize the child's diaper was dripping urine.

"Shitah," she muttered, using Florrie's childhood adaptation of "shitter," the name their father gave to the outhouse. Her eyes burned from the stench of urine. She'd never had a child of her own, and she'd maintained a safe distance between herself and Florrie's babies, so it took a moment for her to figure out how to unfasten the pins to remove the offensive diaper. The baby girl's bottom was red and blistered. Mag flung the diaper aside and stuffed the child into the sleeper, then clumsily fastened the front zipper. A child-sized quilt rested on the end of the bed. She wrapped it around the screaming infant, grabbed an empty bottle that was lying where the quilt had been, and shoved it into the folds of the blanket.

At Mag's approach, Florrie moved clumsily to the stern. Her sister dumped the child into her arms. "Keep her warm," she commanded. She returned to the cabin, helped the girl finish putting on her coat and boots, grabbed the sleeping bag, and guided her to the door. When they reached the boat, Mag faced a new problem. The girl didn't have the strength to stand on her own while Mag got in, and she certainly couldn't get in by herself. Finally, Mag heaved her over her shoulder, pulled the boat tight against the float, climbed over the side, and dumped the girl onto the floorboards as she would have tossed in a bale of hay.

"She dead?" Florrie shouted over the baby's screams.

"Not yet," Mag grunted. She started the motor, untied the boat, and headed across the bay to the cove. There she stopped just long enough to deposit Florrie and the baby on the dock. Then, confiscating Florrie's blanket, she wrapped it around the girl.

"What'll I do with the kid?" Florrie protested.

"Feed it!" Mag called back over the engine noise as she headed out again.

It usually took sixty minutes for Mag to make the trip to Sechelt. Today, two hours after leaving Florrie and the baby at Serpent Cove, she was still in Salmon Inlet, fighting a sea not meant for a motor and a vessel as old and weathered as her Sangstercraft. The east wind and waves pushed against the fibreglass hull, tossing it forward and back, rolling it from side to side, so that they made little headway. Mag steered first with one hand and then the other, warming the resting one against her belly under her fleece-lined coat. It was the only way she could tolerate the pain. Her face was stiff with cold. Occasionally she glanced at the girl huddled in the bow. At least she was out of the wind, but she hadn't moved since they started out.

"Probably dead," Mag muttered and began worrying about what she would do with the body. For a moment she contemplated dumping it overboard. Nobody but Florrie would know—and she wouldn't say anything. She lifted her head just enough to peer under the brim of her hat. Billy Thom's *Squawk Box* was creeping toward her up the inlet.

She could dimly see his outline in the wheelhouse. A small, wiry man with a shaggy mane of grey hair and toothless grin, Billy was the son of a transplanted Nova Scotia fisherman and a Sechelt Native woman. Taken from his parents at the age of five, he had been raised at the Sechelt Residential School, a time that he frequently and bitterly described as his "prison sentence". To make up for his forced confinement, he had spent the past thirty years on the move, roaming the waters of Jervis, Narrows, Salmon, and Sechelt inlets in his old fish packer, collecting and selling the metal scrap he salvaged from beaches and abandoned logging camps.

Mag discarded all thoughts of dumping the body. Billy would see for sure, and Billy couldn't keep nothing to himself. "What's he doing heading out in a storm like this anyways?" Inlet squalls could come up without warning when north and south winds collided and turn the sheltered waters into frothy seas in a matter of moments.

At last, making a wide sweep around Nine Mile Point, Mag's Sangstercraft entered Sechelt Inlet. Far to the south she could see the village, a cluster of tiny houses crowding the isthmus that connected the Sechelt Peninsula to the mainland. Roughly a thousand metres wide, the isthmus separated Sechelt Inlet from the less sheltered Georgia Strait. Mag could remember when there was nothing but cedar trees lining the inlet shore and one rickety old dock. That was back in the days when she and Florrie would row to town and back on the same night because Florrie liked to go dancing, and Mag had to go along as a chaperone. Not that it did much good because Florrie had a way of slipping in and out of the hall so fast Mag couldn't keep track of her. When Florrie's escapades finally landed her with a swollen belly, their dad had blamed Mag for not keeping a sharper lookout.

The anger she felt at the memory drove some of the chill away from her face. Their dad had always favoured Florrie—that is, until she had that kid—because she was the pretty one with her blond curls and blue eyes. Not like Mag with her brown mop that always seemed to be a nest of tangles.

Mag scowled. It wasn't as if she hadn't had the same feelings for the opposite sex as Florrie had. But the men Mag had knocked on their butts for bothering Florrie when they were boys weren't interested in a romantic liaison with their attacker. And when it became evident that she wasn't going to find her own lover, Mag had pushed those softer feelings into distant recesses of herself. The same recesses in which she stowed her pity for the animals she killed and her yearning for the sweet soap smell of her mother.

Debris in the water thumped against the bow, drawing Mag out of her reverie. She shook herself. She couldn't let the cold take over her mind, yet even as she struggled to stay alert her thoughts returned to that earlier time. It was finding the kid in the floathouse, Mag supposed, that made her remember the worst failure of her life. She had promised their dying mother she would look after her little sister. Less than a year later she'd broken that promise.

Mag gripped the wheel and forced her attention back to the water. The wharf was close now, but the curve of Porpoise Bay sheltered the boat from the wind, enabling her to dock with less trouble than at the girl's float. She pulled back on the throttle, and they bumped alongside.

Only when she had secured the lines did she turn to the girl. "Well, we got here," she said loudly. There was no response from the bundle. Mag made her way to the bow and crouched down. "You alive, girl?" She pulled the blanket away from the girl's face. The air frosting near her mouth was the only sign that she was still breathing. She didn't open her eyes and she didn't speak. Mag replaced the blanket. "I'll get a taxi," she said.

Someone had shovelled a path through the snow as far as the ramp. Mag hobbled stiff-legged to the top, then turned left to the pub and restaurant next door. They let her use the telephone to call the taxi and sold her a cup of coffee while she waited. She thought of taking coffee down to the girl in the boat then dismissed the idea. Instead, she sat down in the warm room, letting the coffee penetrate her chilled body.

The taxi came too soon. Reluctantly, Mag went back out into the cold.

"Where you goin', Mag?" Stu Phelps, the taxi driver, asked. He was the long-haired type with a beard and a carefree manner, but Mag liked him. He wasn't a talker. He'd been called to the wharf to pick her up many times and had even given her a lift when she couldn't pay.

"I got a passenger for you," Mag said. "She needs a ride up to the hospital."

She led the way down to her boat and climbed in. Stu looked at the blanketed figure. "You should'a called an ambulance, Mag. I don't think . . ."

Mag lifted the girl and blankets and staggered to the stern with them, thrusting the bundle toward him so he either had to grab the girl or let her fall into the water. "Ambulance will call the cops," Mag said. "I don't want cops."

Climbing out of the boat, Mag helped him carry the girl up the ramp and tuck her into the back seat of the taxi.

"You should sit with her," he told Mag.

She shook her head. "I gotta go back," she said firmly. Without giving him a chance to argue or ask about the fare, she spun on her heel and stomped down the ramp. He stared after her, then shook his head and got into the cab. As he drove away, Mag was already easing her boat back into the wind.

It was almost dark when Mag returned to the float at Serpent Cove. Her hands and face were numb. It was all she could do to loop the bow rope around the mooring post. She didn't bother about the stern—she'd send Florrie down to do that.

A faint yellow glow emanated from the kitchen window. Mag stumbled along the frozen path, hobbled up the two steps, avoided the broken board on the porch, and pushed open the kitchen door. Florrie turned from the stove, where she was pouring grease from a frying pan into a can that once held tomatoes. "I got bacon cooked," she said. For the first time all day Mag felt hungry. She closed the door and sagged down onto a wooden chair.

"Did she make it?" Florrie asked. She lowered the frying pan to the stove and reached for a bowl of eggs.

Mag closed her eyes as pain from her thawing hands and feet coursed through her body. Her lips were so stiff it was hard to form words. "Coffee," she managed.

Florrie lowered the eggs. She brought the coffee pot to the table and filled the cup Mag had used that morning. Setting the pot down, she lifted the cup to her sister's lips. "You're half froze!"

The coffee burned Mag's lips and mouth, but she swallowed it anyway. She began to shiver. Florrie stood in front of her, still holding the coffee cup. She was so used to her sister being in charge, she couldn't think of what to do. Hesitantly, she brought the cup back to Mag's lips, but her shivering spasms made the coffee slop over Florrie's hands.

"Shitah!" Florrie muttered. She pulled another chair closer to the stove, helped Mag over to it, then plodded heavily to a cupboard behind the door where a small bottle of whisky was hidden in an old metal coffee pot. She poured some into Mag's coffee and held the cup while Mag drank several swallows. When the cup was almost empty, Mag was able to hold it herself.

"You need to eat something," Florrie said with a show of confidence belied by the worry lines on her forehead.

The bacon grease was smoking now. Florrie cracked four eggs into it, giving each a liberal dose of salt and pepper. She left them to cook while she pulled a plate from the cupboard, and a knife and fork from the cutlery box. After flipping the eggs over once, she dumped them onto the plate, added five strips of bacon, and buttered two thick slices of bread. Her mouth watered as she carried the meal over to Mag. Still hunched over her coffee and shivering, Mag made no move toward the food. Florrie hauled the table toward the stove along with her own chair. Sitting in front of Mag, she forked some egg and bacon into her sister's mouth. While Mag slowly chewed, Florrie helped herself to a mouthful and then another.

It was close to an hour before Mag had warmed enough to take off her coat and tell Florrie about the girl. It was only then that she remembered the baby.

"Where's the kid?"

Florrie's expression softened. She nodded toward a large cardboard box she'd placed beside the stove. The infant was asleep, thumb in mouth. Dark pincurls of hair framed her thin face and her forehead was creased in the middle as if she was working out a difficult problem.

"Joost about six months," Mag guessed. The hippy had been gone from Anchor Bay around the end of the summer, and that's when she must have had the kid. "She cry long?"

"Soon as I fed her, she stopped," Florrie said proudly. She pointed at a pot half-filled with oatmeal porridge sitting on the warming shelf. "She ate a whole bowl of mush."

Mag retrieved her coffee cup from the table. "I thought babies drunk milk."

Florrie held up a quart sealer with less than a cup of goat's milk left in it. "She drunk all this. She was half-starved."

"I was going to coddle that milk," Mag said sharply. She glared at the child in the box. "Tomorrow we'll take her to the Welfare."

Florrie's chin lifted and Mag knew her sister was about to get stubborn. "We kin look after her, Mag."

"No." Mag's chin also lifted. "Her mother's probably dead and we got trapping to do." She pushed away from the table and refilled her cup with coffee, giving herself time to think. She knew Florrie was remembering the three kids she'd born. Bastards, all of them. "Kid needs a family, Florrie. Welfare will find her one."

"A kid needs its mother," Florrie said harshly.

Mag responded with a humourless laugh. "Well, yer not its mother, and we got no place fer a kid."

Florrie's chin dropped back into the folds of her neck. "You talk joost like our dad and Schwabby," she complained. "I kin look after her. I could'a looked after the others. . . ."

"Goddamn it!" Mag shouted, slamming down her cup. "We got no room and we're shooer not keeping that kid." Startled awake, the child began to scream.

"You made her cry," Florrie accused.

"She'd have woke up anyways," Mag growled.

Florrie picked up the naked child and rocked it gently against her chest. The infant's head almost disappeared between the mounds of her large breasts, and Mag marvelled that it could even breathe there. The screaming eased and finally stopped, and the baby resumed sucking her thumb. Her large sea-green eyes solemnly surveyed Mag. Then she peed, the urine running down Florrie's arm and onto the floor.

"She don't even have a diaper on!" Mag snorted. "That's how much you know about kids."

"Don't have no diapers," Florrie said defensively. "You didn't bring 'em and she peed on that thing she was wearing."

Mag stomped into the cabin's only other room, which served as her own sleeping quarters and a general storage area. She rummaged through several cardboard boxes and piles of black plastic garbage bags until she found an old sheet and a child's woollen sweater. She ripped the sheet into large squares. Returning to the kitchen she searched through the cutlery box, tossing knives, forks, spoons, and larger utensils this way and that.

"Got no pins," she said finally. "You'll have to tie it on."

Florrie carried the baby to her own bed and clumsily fashioned a diaper from one of the squares. She tried to place it on the child, but when the fabric rubbed against the red blisters that covered her bottom, the infant screamed.

"That kid's gonna make me deaf," Mag complained.

"She's sore," Florrie said. Mag studied the blisters for a moment, then retrieved a tin of Bag Balm from the window sill. "Rub this on her," she said. "Works on the goats' tits."

Florrie slathered the yellow salve over the blisters while the child twisted and screamed. She fastened the diaper with a knot and pulled the sweater over the baby's head. It was too large and the sleeves buried her hands until Florrie rolled them up. "Where'd this come from?"

"Box of rags I got outside the thrift store," Mag said. She nodded approvingly at the outfit. "Fits her good."

The child stopped screaming when Florrie handed her to Mag.

"You sit with her while I make a new bed," she said. She nodded toward a wooden rocking chair crammed between the cardboard bed she'd made for the child and a cluttered old sofa. She'd rescued the rocker years earlier from the Sechelt dump and normally it was kept on the porch where Florrie liked to sit when it was warmer. The end of the right runner was broken, and two slats were missing from the back. Still, it rocked.

"Got no room for that thing in here," Mag groused, but she sat in the rocker because it was close to the stove.

"We got room fer all yer stuff," Florrie fumed under her breath as she rummaged through a tangle of sheets, towels, and other debris piled on the sofa. She was still smouldering over Mag's refusal to consider keeping the baby. *I kin look after a kid as good as anyone,* she told herself. She pulled a large towel, part of an old quilt and a stained feather pillow from the clutter and fashioned a new bed in the box. When she turned to take the baby, however, the child was sleeping, thumb in mouth, head tucked against Mag's shirt.

$\mathcal{T}$he temperature dropped during the night and the cove froze over. At dawn, Mag hobbled down the wharf. With a pick axe, she hammered at the ice around the boat, but there was no way she could break through such a thick layer without damaging the hull. It could be weeks before the cove thawed enough for them to take the kid to the Welfare office.

"Damn," she muttered. "Damn!"

Although she had lived all her life on the inland sea, Mag had never lost her awe of its impetuous moods, even if that mood blocked her path as it did today. Once, when she was purchasing a hunting licence, the government agent had shown her a map of the inlet system. Although she had stared long and hard at it, Mag really couldn't fully grasp the relationship between the one-dimensional drawing and the waterways that she knew as intimately as her own hand. "Don't look nothing like the inlets."

"Well, that's Jervis Inlet there at the top," the agent had said, pointing to the body of water at the northern end of the Sechelt peninsula. He ran his finger along a waterway that stretched in a northeasterly direction from the Georgia Strait. "And see here?" he indicated a channel between the north end of the peninsula and the mainland. "That's the Skookumchuck where Jervis joins Sechelt Inlet. It's only a thousand feet wide there, and the currents can get up to twelve knots at tide change."

"Oh, shooer." Having fought her way out of whirlpools created by those very currents, Mag didn't need to be told how fast they travelled. She pointed to another patch of blue, branching northeast of Sechelt Inlet.

"That's Narrows Inlet," the agent said. "And this . . ." He indicated Salmon Inlet, just south of Narrows Inlet and also running in a northeasterly direction. "This is where you live."

Mag was still shaking her head when she left the agent's office.

Now, chilled by an icy gust of wind, she shouldered her axe

and stomped up the trail. From habit, she looked beyond the house toward the path that meandered to a storage shed and two makeshift shelters, one of them her goat shed, the other accommodating two dozen chickens. Though their father had carved a large clearing in the flatland between the shoreline and the heavily forested slope behind the house, Mag and Florrie had been unable to control the relentless advance of salal, salmonberry, and thimbleberry bushes, mountain ash, and alder. Had it been summer, when the brush and trees were in full leaf, the animal sheds would have been invisible from where she stood.

She clomped noisily up the steps of the house, opened the door, and stuck her head inside. Florrie was still in bed, the fire unlit. "You gonna sleep all day?" Mag asked loudly, then slammed the door again and headed for the storage shed. The traps she needed to run her line along the creek were lying amid a jumble of empty coffee tins, mildewed magazines, old hand tools, rusting crosscut saws, broken outboard motors, and other hoarded bits of junk. Every winter she vowed she was going to store the traps where she could find them easily, and every spring she ended up tossing them among the debris to be searched for later. "Next spring I'm gonna do different," she promised herself. As the shed was windowless, she used the light from the open door and a kerosene lantern to guide her search, and by mid-morning she had located and repaired fifteen rusty leg traps which she stuffed into a canvas pack.

When Mag returned to the house, Florrie was feeding the baby a slimy mixture of oatmeal porridge and goat's milk. While she spooned it in, she told the baby how—as little more than babies themselves—she and Mag had travelled with their parents on a big ship from Norway to Canada. They rode for days and days on a train across the prairies and mountains to reach Vancouver. There Helga and Frederick Larson had secured a homestead on an inlet neither of them had ever heard of. "Gosh, there was nutting here but trees," Florrie said, unconsciously broadening the mild Norwegian accent that affected both sisters' speech. "Oh, shooer, he and Mother built this cabin. Cut all the boards themselves!" She was so lost in the

14

story, she didn't notice the child happily squishing bits of porridge between her fingers, smearing them over her head and sweater. Nor did she notice that she was standing on the soiled diaper that was lying on the floor.

Mag ignored her sister's chatter. She warmed herself with two cups of strong coffee and a bowl of oatmeal, then grabbed a slab of bacon that had been left on the counter overnight. Mice had nibbled one end of it, leaving tiny teeth marks in the fat.

"We gotta set traps," she said as she hacked walnut-sized pieces from the slab. "This cold is gonna send the critters down the mountain." She placed the bacon bits in a small plastic bag and crammed it into the pocket of her coat. Stepping outside, she shoved the rest of the bacon into a refrigerator that stood in a shady spot near the steps. There was no electricity to run it, but the box protected the food from wildlife.

When she returned to the kitchen, Florrie was thrusting another spoonful of porridge into the baby's mouth. "What about Jen?"

Mag stared at her. "Who?"

Florrie waved the spoon at the child. "Her. She's gotta have a name," she explained. "I t'ink 'Jen' sounds pretty. Like a bird . . ."

"She's already got a name," Mag said impatiently. "Welfare'll find out what it is. No sense confusing her."

"Gotta call her somet'ing," Florrie said, her chin rising. Mag decided to drop the matter.

"Put her in a backpack," Mag said. "She kin come with us."

Florrie shook her head. "You can't put a baby in a pack!"

"Indians used to."

"But, Mag, she don't got clothes for going outside." She dipped the spoon into the porridge and brought it up to the baby's mouth. "You kin set them traps by yerself. You done it before."

Mag knew it suited Florrie just fine to be sitting in a warm cabin while she beat her way through the brush along the creek to set traps. She scowled at the child. "Soon's the ice is gone, that kid's out of here."

She stomped outside, leaving the door for Florrie to close.

Florrie carried the child to the door and closed it with her foot. "All she ever does is work," she grumbled as she resumed feeding the baby. "Joost like our dad."

It was mid-February before the cold front moved on and the rains came again. By the time the ice was soft enough for the boat to break through, Mag had gathered four otter skins, two beaver, and three martin. "Enough to get me a new pair of boots," she said with satisfaction. "And maybe some left over."

Florrie was playing with the baby on the bed. She gurgled as she grasped Florrie's index fingers and let herself be pulled into a standing position. Her chubby legs wobbled unsteadily. "Gosh, maybe we kin get Jen some shoes, too. She's almost walking."

"I guess not. Welfare'll get her what she needs."

Florrie hugged the girl protectively. "She shooer can't go all the way to town, Mag. She don't have clothes!" Florrie had found some small T-shirts among the thrift store rags, but the nighties she'd fashioned out of them were far too big for the baby.

"There's a whole bag of 'em in the girl's shack," Mag said firmly. "I'm going over there to get 'em, and right after we're heading into town and the Welfare."

"Maybe her mother didn't die," Florrie protested. "We gotta check at the hospital."

"Welfare'll do all that, Florrie. We got no more business with her or her mother."

Mag finished tying up the parcel of furs, then grabbed her coat. "You be ready when I get back." She could feel Florrie glaring at her as she stepped outside. "Don't make it harder than it's gotta be, Florrie!" She slammed the door and headed for the boat. The thing had to be done.

A light rain was falling. The snow remaining on the deck of the young woman's float was so saturated with moisture that its weight had pushed one end of the structure underwater, making the house tilt at a thirty-degree angle. Mag clambered onto the float, then dug the sharp prong of her pike pole into the wood and used the handle to balance herself as she inched her way across the deck to the house.

Nothing had been touched inside the building, though it smelled worse, but Mag was too intent on finding clothes for the child to pay any attention. There were several more sleepers and a collection of cloth diapers in the black plastic bag, which she grabbed. On the kitchen table a small woven backpack yawned open, and Mag could see there was a wallet inside. Disappointed that it held no money, she tossed it back into the pack. An unopened envelope with a handwritten address also lay on the table, but while Mag could read simple printed words, handwriting was beyond her. Still, the letter looked important. *Might tell the Welfare who she is.* She shoved both the pack and letter into the plastic bag.

As she guided her boat back through the floating ice chunks, Mag felt pleased with herself. The kid would soon be gone and the house would get back to normal. The last few nights had been hell as the child kept waking and screaming. She wouldn't shush unless Florrie rocked and sang to her. Trouble was, Florrie only knew one lullaby that their mother used to sing, and Mag was sick to death of hearing it.

With blankets Mag had hauled down from the house, the two women made a bed for the child in the bow. By the time they left Serpent Cove and headed out into the open water of the inlet, the little girl was asleep. She was still sleeping more than an hour later when Mag tied the boat to the dock in Sechelt. Leaving her with Florrie, Mag walked up to the restaurant to call the taxi.

A short, plump girl was waiting tables. "Hey, Mag. Where you been hiding?"

"We was iced in," Mag said. She chose a seat near the window where she could watch for Stu. The girl plunked a mug in front of her and filled it with coffee.

"Florrie come with you?"

"Yeah." Mag sipped the coffee. It felt extra hot against her cold lips. A radio behind the counter was blaring the latest news about the launch of Apollo XIV transporting Captain Alan Shepard and two other astronauts to the moon. Mag preferred music. She wished the girl would turn it off. "You got the paper?" she asked loudly. This was the day the local weekly was published, and she liked to check the want ads in case there was something offered for free. She'd got a rabbit that way once. Made a real nice stew.

"Just came in," the waitress said, dropping the paper on the table.

Mag didn't usually bother with the news items—reading the want ads took all the concentration she could muster—but today the front page picture caught her attention. It was the young woman from the floathouse. With her index finger, Mag began tracing the words accompanying the picture, struggling to make sense out of them. When the waitress came with more coffee, Mag thrust the paper at her.

"What's it say here?"

The waitress nodded at the picture. "That? She's a real slick one. Even came in here and tried to pawn one of them bad cheques off on me. But I knew better'n to take it."

"Where's she now?" Mag tried to keep her voice casual.

"Who knows? If she's smart she's caught the ferry out've here. Cops are looking all over for her." She glanced out the window. "Hey, there's your taxi."

In her haste to leave the restaurant, Mag took the paper with her. She caught up to Stu Phelps just as he was backing off the pier.

"Thought maybe you decided to walk into town," he told her as she climbed in.

"I was having coffee," Mag said. "Florrie's still down on the boat. We gotta pick her up." As Stu drove to the end of the pier, Mag showed him the paper.

"Yeah, I read it," he growled. "Should've left the little bitch in the snow. She's been nothing but trouble since they let her out've the hospital. Stiffed me for thirty bucks. Drove her all the way to the ferry and she run off without paying me."

"Figured she was dead," Mag said.

"Nah. You owe me for that one, Mag. Cops been bugging me about her for weeks."

Mag tensed. "What fer?"

"Hospital told them I brung her in. They wanted to know where she come from."

"What'd you say?"

Stu grinned. "Told them I picked her up at the wharf. Didn't figure they needed to know who else was with her."

As a dark mountain suddenly lumbered up the ramp, Mag jumped out of the car. "Florrie—"

"We been freezing down there!" Her sister yanked open the cab's back door. "Yer sitting here blabbing while me an' Jen are freezing!"

Stu turned to stare into the back of the cab as Florrie positioned herself and the baby on the seat.

"What the hell—?"

"Florrie's got her grandkid staying with us," Mag said loudly, with a meaningful look at her sister. "Her girl Elsie's kid. Right, Florrie?"

A puzzled expression flitted across Florrie's face. "Yeah?"

"Oh shooer. Her mother's gone away fer awhile so Florrie's looking after the kid." Mag was as close to babbling as she had been in her whole life.

"Didn't even know you had a kid, Florrie," Stu said.

Florrie glared at him. "I got t'ree," she snapped.

Mag had Stu drive them to the Seawind Café on the north corner of the village's main street and the Sunshine Coast Highway. Still angry, Florrie climbed out with the baby and stomped into the restaurant to get herself some coffee, while her sister walked on down the street to the post office.

From the Larson's mailbox, Mag extracted a tight bundle of envelopes and newspapers which she dumped on the counter. Two big envelopes had come from Promotion Sweepstakes, and she pawed impatiently through the brightly printed pieces of paper inside them. Her brow furrowed as she searched the envelopes once again, but the cheque they had promised to send was definitely not inside. She was studying a card with a gold sticker on it, reading just enough to know it had something to do with the prize, when the door to the post office opened and a tall, bearded man entered. On his black corduroy bill cap were the words JOHN DUNCAN CHARTERS printed in a circle around the white, embroidered image of a boat. "You counting up your winnings, Mag?" he asked cheerfully as he passed the counter.

"Ah, gosh, they don't give me nothing," Mag complained. "They're supposed to send me money, but I don't see no cheque here." She pulled out the card with the gold sticker and thrust it at him. "What's it say to do?"

John glanced at the card. "They want you to send them another twenty bucks. I told you the last time that's what they'd do."

"But what else does it say?" she persisted. "When am I gonna get my prize?"

"You aren't, Mag. It's a gimmick. They just want your money." He moved on into the main part of the post office where the wickets were.

Lyin' bugger, Mag thought angrily, tucking the sweepstake papers into her backpack. She'd figure them out when she got back to the cove. She was about to sweep the remaining flyers and advertising brochures into her pack as well when she spotted a small, white envelope with 'Mag Larson, Sechelt Post Office' scrawled on the front. There was no return address. Mag picked it up and turned it over several times. She didn't often get letters. Finally, she tore the end off the envelope and pulled out a single sheet of writing paper.

John Duncan came out of the office while she was still trying to read the message scrawled in a spidery handwriting that seemed somehow familiar. She handed him the letter. "What's it say?"

He read it silently at first, then aloud. "'Dear Mag, I owe you for saving me but I've got to get my life straightened out. Please don't take Lisa to Welfare or I'll never get her back. I'll come and get her as soon as I can. Yours truly, Sue Drummond.'"

John said the name again, his expression thoughtful. "Sue

Drummond. Isn't that the dame that's been passing bad cheques all over town?"

"I don't know nutting about cheques," Mag said coldly. She snatched the letter from him and peered at it suspiciously. "You shooer that's what she says?"

He grinned and nodded. "This Lisa her kid, Mag? She big enough to help with the chores?"

Mag scowled. "She's a baby."

He laughed out loud. "A baby? God, that I'd like to see. You and Florrie wouldn't last two days looking after a baby!"

"Already lasted three weeks," Mag snapped. "Few more won't matter."

John grew serious. "No way, Mag. What if she gets sick? You two don't know a thing about what a baby needs."

Mag's jaw stuck out. "No different than looking after a goat kid." She shoved the letter into her pack. "You got time to take me over to the feed store? I need some oats an' hay fer my goats."

Florrie's face was wreathed in smiles when Mag met her in the café and told her they were keeping the child a while longer. "You hear that, Jen?" she said happily to the child on her lap. "You get to stay!"

"It's joost 'til the girl gets back," Mag said sharply. "If she don't come soon, the kid goes to the Welfare."

But Florrie didn't hear her. She was already heading out the door on her way to the thrift store. Jen needed shoes and some more baby clothes. Maybe she might even find a toy for her there.

Susan Drummond didn't return in a few weeks or even a few months. Winter rolled into spring, and Mag was too busy harvesting cascara bark, planting the garden, and tending to the newborn goats to do anything about the baby. During the summer, Mag spent most of her days on the water beachcombing for logs that had slipped away from Gus Stevenson's log booms at the head of Salmon Inlet. By then, Jen was crawling and getting into everything within reach. Florrie barricaded the outside door with chairs and boxes, but it did little to keep the child inside. Twice she followed Mag through the barricade and tumbled down the steps into a pile of boat motors, crab traps, and fishing gear.

"She's gonna kill herself," Mag warned after returning Jen to the cabin, having rescued her from a tangle of netting. Her sister spied the hole that Jen had used to escape the barricade. "Gosh, it don't matter how I fix it up, she finds a way out," she said forlornly, taking the squirming child from Mag. Jen looked unrepentant; as soon as Florrie put her back on the floor, she made her way back to the barricade.

"Joost no stopping her when she puts her mind to something," Mag agreed. There was a grudging admiration in her tone. She shoved the boxes aside with her foot and slammed the door, shutting out the daylight. Jen shrieked with indignation. Mag laughed, which made the girl angrier.

"You scared her!" Florrie scolded. She tried to pick the child up, but Jen fought her off.

"Better'n having her drown," Mag said calmly, then escaped outside, leaving Florrie to cope with the tantrum.

By September Jen was walking, making it even harder for the sisters to keep track of her. She followed Mag like a shadow and howled whenever she was shut inside. Mag didn't mind her tagging along when she was tending the goats or chickens, but she put her foot down on taking the child to town, unless Florrie came too.

The first part of November was wet, cold, and windy—perfect weather for the pine mushrooms that grew in the woods above Misery Bay. Early one Monday morning, Mag loaded her boat with large plastic buckets and headed for a patch she'd found the previous fall. Although there were no other boats on the inlet, she took the precaution of landing almost a mile down the beach from a deer trail that wound up the hill to the patch. *Damned hippies'll dig up the whole damned mountain if they find my patch*, she groused as she clambered over the rocky shore to the trail. Her buckets banged noisily against the rocks.

It took her an hour to reach the grove of trees that sheltered the large, flat-headed mushrooms. She knelt and gently cleared the moss away from the largest fungi, and as she pulled it free, the air around her filled with its distinctive sweet, spicy aroma. After depositing the mushroom in the bed of moss she'd made in the bottom of her bucket, Mag pushed the dirt back into the hole it had left in the ground, so the lingering roots and spores would generate a new plant next season. Close by, she spied a white mound just protruding from the same patch of moss. Swiftly she uncovered a "button"—a pine mushroom just barely formed. She grinned delightedly and exercised special caution as she placed it in her bucket. Buttons were treasured by all mushroom harvesters because they brought the highest price.

A light rain fell around her, the soft pattering on the nearby salal leaves providing a soothing accompaniment as one by one she removed the mushrooms from their beds and laid them between layers of moss in her buckets. The ground was soft against her knees, but her pants were soon soaked through. Her back ached and her fingers cramped painfully. *Joost one more*, she told herself again and again as she moved from patch to patch. By late afternoon she had exhausted her territory, filling four of her five buckets. She paused just long enough to wolf down the bacon sandwich Florrie had made for her, then toted the containers, one at a time, over the rough trail to the boat. It was almost dark when she finished—too late into the day to take the mushrooms to the buyer in town.

"I'll take 'em in the morning," she told Florrie, as she hung her wet coat and hat by the stove to dry. "Got to get feed fer the goats anyways."

Jen crawled out from under the table. "Ag-ag!" Florrie scooped the child into her arms.

"No Flowie! Ag-ag!" the child screamed.

"Mag's tired," Florrie said as she plunked Jen in the high chair they had rescued from a dumpster that summer. Mag had replaced its broken leg with a two-by-four. Though it still wobbled, it kept the child secure, even now as she squirmed and screamed in protest.

Mag pulled several small, smooth stones from her pocket and

clattered them onto the table, successfully diverting Jen's attention. "They was in the creek," she said gruffly. "I t'ought maybe they'd keep her from squawking."

"Oh, gosh," Florrie worried as Jen put one of the rocks into her mouth. "I t'ink she might eat them."

Mag shrugged, more intent on the coffee she'd poured for herself than on the child. "If she do, she'll shit 'em out."

A strong southeasterly wind made it a slow, cold trip to the Sechelt wharf. Once there, Mag hired Stu Phelps to take her and the four buckets of mushrooms to Pete Saari's warehouse, a mile east of Sechelt.

Mag had no use for the Saaris. Pete's dad, Erik, had come up the inlet one winter day when she and Florrie were girls. He was half frozen, his clothes ragged and torn, and his face swollen and battered. When their mother set a plate of bread and goat cheese in front of him, he had wolfed the food down as if he hadn't eaten in days. Afterward, he begged for work in exchange for board and a place to stay. Little did he know how much he would regret it later, their dad hired him and asked no questions.

Mag scowled, as the taxi sped along the highway. Erik Saari had turned out to be a liar and a cheat. The harm he had done to their family was something she would never forget nor forgive, and as far as she was concerned, Pete Saari was no better than his dad. "Them Saaris is terrible peoples," she complained to Stu. "Always grabbing money from other folks' sweat." Mushroom buying was just one of Pete's businesses and, because he was the only buyer on the coast, she had to deal with him. Her scowl darkened as the taxi wheels crunched onto the gravel drive and pulled up beside the garage he had converted into a grading room.

"I'll walk back to town," she told Stu, not wanting him to see how much she was paid for her cargo. "Joost wait 'til I empty these buckets. You might as well take them back to the wharf fer me." She carried her cargo into the shed, gently lifted the moss and mushrooms from the buckets, and laid the bundles on the sorting table. A few minutes later, she stowed the empty buckets on the taxi's back seat and gave Stu a five-dollar bill to cover the fare to Saari's. It did not cover the cost of returning the buckets.

"But . . ." Stu began, then shook his head. "Takes more time arguing than it's worth," he muttered. Leaving a shower of gravel in his wake, he drove out of the yard, while Mag returned to the shed to begin sorting her mushrooms. On a shelf above the table were bins for various types and grades of fungi, and she put most of hers in the highest grade bin, grudgingly depositing the few broken ones into the second highest bin.

"Now, Mag, you know I'm not paying top dollar for bruised mushrooms," Pete Saari boomed as he entered the shed. A tall, burly man with dark hair combed straight back from his brow, he nudged Mag aside and redistributed her mushrooms to lower grade bins.

"Them buttons don't got a mark on 'em," Mag objected, returning the mushrooms to the first bin. "You're shooer not gonna cheat me this time, Saari."

"I'm not paying top dollar for day-old mushrooms either," the buyer said calmly. "You don't like the grade I'm giving, go somewheres else."

Mag glared at him. "You know I got no way of going to town," she growled, but this time when he shifted the mushrooms around, she didn't stop him. Neither did she thank him when he handed her a twenty-dollar bill for her efforts. "Damned cheating bugger," she grumbled, stuffing it into the worn billfold she kept in the front pocket of her jeans. She stomped outside, then remembered that she needed to find someone to take her to the farm supply store and haul the two sacks of feed she was buying to her boat. She dismissed the idea of asking Saari, knowing he'd charge her more than Stu Phelps, and turned instead to the picker who had just arrived in a battered pickup. She waited until Saari had paid him for his mushrooms then asked, "You going back through town?"

"Sure," he said easily. "You need a ride?"

On her way out of the sorting shed, Mag saw Pete Saari shift her mushrooms into higher grade baskets, but since they were mixed with the new seller's stock, there would be no way to prove ownership. She kicked angrily at the gravel as she followed her driver to his truck. When they reached the village, she let him know they needed to stop at the feed store before he took her to her boat.

The wind that had slowed Mag's trip down the inlet was still blowing hard when she headed home. By the time she rounded Nine Mile Point it had turned into a gale. Frothy waves washed over the bow of the Sangstercraft, slowing her progress even more so that dusk was already settling over the inlet before she finally reached the cove. The tide was ebbing, leaving just enough water in the bay to dock the boat, a task made harder by the wind that kept blowing the stern toward the mud. With one hand holding the boat to the dock, she secured the stern line, then crawled out and fastened the bowline. She looked up to see Florrie hobbling down the ramp, her hair blowing wildly about her face.

"Jen's gone!" she yelled over the wind. "She's drowned! I can't find her nowheres!"

Mag got to her feet and put a hand on her sister's shoulder. "What happened?" she demanded.

"I was making cookies," Florrie blubbered, gesturing frantically. "I heard the door banging and I knew she'd got out again, but I looked and looked and I can't find her!"

"You check the chicken shed?" Mag demanded and Florrie nodded. "I looked everywhere!"

"How long's she been out?"

"A long time!" Florrie wailed. "Least an hour or more! She's gonna be froze!"

Mag was cold from the boat ride, but she could take the chill. Florrie wasn't as hardy. "Go back inside, Florrie, and build up the fire. I'll look fer her."

Florrie seemed about to protest, but the expression on Mag's face stopped her. She turned and hobbled back up the ramp. It began to rain as Mag lugged sacks of feed up to the wheelbarrow she'd left on the shore. *Letting the rain ruin two good bags of oats won't do the kid any good*, she reasoned as she wheeled them to the shed. Still, she wasted no time. Although she hadn't told Florrie, Mag was worried about more than Jen's exposure to the weather. A bear had recently decided that their clearing was a handy place for a meal. Twice in the past week, she had found refuse from the compost heap scattered around the yard and a large pile of purple feces peppered with salal berry seeds. At this time of year the animals were preparing for hibernation, eating everything they could find. A child as defenseless as Jen would be easy prey.

Outside of the shed, Mag put her fingers to her lips, whistled hard, then listened. She heard only the wind howling through the trees that surrounded the clearing and the crash of waves against the shore. Even if the child was crying, it would have been impossible to pick the sound out from the noise of the storm. Making the same rounds she did every morning, Mag searched the places where she usually paused to inspect the goat pen and the netting that enclosed the chicken yard. As she pushed her way through the brush at the far end of the chicken fence, she realized it was getting too dark to see and started back to get the flashlight. She was passing the shed when she stumbled over a small, soft mound. "Shitah!" The child was shivering, and when Mag picked her up Jen's shirt and pants were oozing icy water.

Heat was pouring from the stove and the kettle was steaming as Mag burst into the cabin with Jen in her arms. "Found her behind the shed," Mag said, dumping her into Florrie's arms.

"She's turned all blue!" Florrie gasped.

Mag squinted at the child. Her eyes were closed and she didn't seem to be breathing. "You get her outta them clothes. I'll get the tub and some water." Grabbing two buckets, she picked her way along the dark trail to the creek. She returned with the water, dumped it into the metal tub she and Florrie used for bathing, and went back for two more buckets. The kettle full of boiling water, that always sat at the back of the stove, brought the tub water temperature up to a little better than lukewarm. Florrie had stripped off Jen's sopping clothes and was rubbing her plump limbs, trying to restore circulation.

"She hasn't made a sound since you brung her in."

Mag lowered the child into the tub. "Boil up more water," she ordered. Soaking her own shirt sleeves, she leaned Jen back so that all but her face was underwater, and continued rubbing her limbs as Florrie had done. Jen's eyes were still closed as if she was asleep.

"Saw this done at a camp up Jervis," Mag explained. "Pulled a guy out've the water, almost dead from cold." She didn't tell her sister that the guy had died anyway. Mag's swollen hands were rough and hard, and as she massaged the child's limbs the blue changed to red. Florrie placed more pans of water on the stove. When they were close to boiling, Mag lifted the child up while Florrie emptied them into the tub, gradually increasing the heat. For more than two hours Mag knelt beside the tub, holding the child, taking turns with Florrie massaging her.

"It's joost no use," Florrie moaned finally, sinking into a chair, exhausted after a round of massaging Jen's limbs. "She's not gonna wake up."

"She'll wake," Mag said, rubbing harder than ever. As if on cue, Jen's eyes opened. For a full second she stared up at Mag. There was a peacefulness about the child's eyes that scared her. Then suddenly Jen opened her mouth and screeched with indignation. Mag winced and wondered why she had just worked so hard to save such a noisy creature. She lifted the child from the tub and wrapped her in the biggest towel they had. Pulling her chair close to the fire, she held Jen against her chest.

"She'll be needing some food now," she said

Florrie's smile filled her whole face. "Porridge," she said. "With lotsa sugar." By the time she'd made it, however, both Jen and Mag were sound asleep in the chair. Florrie wrapped a blanket around them, then covered the porridge and stoked up the fire. She collapsed into her bed, too exhausted to bother undressing.

The third winter that the girl was with them, Mag decided Florrie was no longer going to use her as an excuse for not doing her share on the trapline. The morning Mag brought the subject up was bitterly cold and the trails were icy. They'd had snow and freezing weather for a week, followed by a day of rain, and back to freezing. Even Mag wasn't anxious to head out, but they needed the cash the furs would bring. As she pulled on her boots, she glanced at her sister making the morning porridge.

"You coming?"

Florrie shook her head and edged closer to the stove. "I can't." She looked meaningfully down at Jen who was building some kind of structure with a pile of kindling stacked near the stove. The child's auburn hair was loosely fastened in a single braid like Florrie's, but with so many wisps sticking out that the braid seemed about to fall apart. She was skinny and her cheeks were red and chapped, but she was a quick mover. Mag had tried to catch her once after she threw her bowl on the floor in a tantrum. The girl was out the door and into the woods before Mag even started.

"She kin come too," Mag said. "She'll manage fine."

Jen looked up, her expression hopeful. She had been pestering Mag for weeks to take her on the trapline, but Mag always refused. Wouldn't work, she'd said, without Florrie coming to keep an eye on her.

Florrie stirred the porridge vigorously, partly to hide her anxiety. The bush, an intricate part of Mag's life, had become alien to Florrie. Besides, it was difficult for her to walk any distance because her right hip hurt continuously now, and since the summer she had developed a limp. "I can't," she repeated, exaggerating the limp as she carried the porridge pot to the table. "My leg's hurting too bad."

Mag snorted disbelievingly. "Wasn't hurting you yesterday."

"I joost never spoke of it," Florrie said. "It's been hurting worse every day."

Mag finished tying her boots. She glanced at the door where Jen was hauling out her own rubber boots. "Where do you t'ink yer going, girl?"

"Me go wif Mag," Jen said firmly.

Florrie plopped a large spoonful of porridge into Jen's bowl, sprinkled brown sugar over it and poured in some goat's milk. "I'd slow you down, Mag, but Jen could help you. I was younger'n her when our dad took you and me with him."

Mag grunted. "Yer the one could help me," she said shortly, "instead 'a sitting in here burning up the wood I cut." As Jen shoved her bare feet into her boots, Mag scowled. This wasn't the result she had intended, but she said gruffly, "Git some socks on," then went outside to feed the animals.

The trail was treacherous. Although Mag cut herself a stout limb to use as a walking stick, she still slipped and twice she almost went down. At first Jen kept up with her, chattering about what they were going to find in the traps, whether it would be a mink or a martin or an otter, and why she would prefer one over the other. The chattering stopped after they came to the second trap. The snow around it was stained with blood, and in its jaws were the bloody remains of a white paw. The weasel it had belonged to was gone. Mag released the foot and tossed it into the bushes. When she had reset the trap, she glanced at the girl. Jen had rescued the mangled foot and was studying it intently. "Where weaso?" she asked finally.

"Critter chewed it off," Mag snapped, annoyed to have lost a prime fur.

Jen stared at her. "She eated her feet?" she asked, her expression horrified.

"Only way she could get free." Mag hoisted the pack on her shoulders and grabbed her stick. Jen followed slowly.

"Weaso hurted?"

Mag focused on manoeuvring her way down an icy slope. She trudged on, only partly aware that the girl had fallen behind, but when she reached the next trap, she realized that the child was no longer with her. "Damn." She debated whether to go back and find her, then she tightened her lips. Girl had to learn. Same as she and Florrie learned. She dropped her pack and knelt down to free the raccoon corpse locked in the trap, but as she searched her mound of bacon for just the right piece of bait, she kept glancing down the trail. She was adjusting her pack on her shoulders when she heard a childish voice mutter, "Shitah" from around the corner. Mag waited just long enough to see Jen's red jacket, then headed for the next trap.

It took longer than usual to do the trapline, and by the time Mag finished she was chilled to the bone. Jen must have been even colder, but the girl hadn't complained. She never said much of anything, even when they returned to the house.

"Gosh, her tongue must've got froze," Mag joked when Florrie questioned the girl's silence. Florrie had made an extra effort with supper, cooking a venison roast, boiled potatoes, and gravy. She even opened a can of peas. Jen ate little. When the meal was over, she crawled up on the bed and went to sleep.

"Walk done her in," Mag reasoned, as she sat fleshing out the new pelts. Turning each hide inside out, she fastened it to a board, then with a sharp razor blade cut away bits of flesh and tissue until the inside of the skin was smooth. "Won't be yakking about coming along no more."

Florrie was at the table studying the pictures in a magazine Mag that had rescued from the post office wastebasket on her last trip to town. "Walking don't scare Jen," she said. "She'll go again."

Mag didn't believe her, but the morning proved Florrie right. Jen ate her breakfast rapidly and was ready to return to the trapline when Mag finished with the animals. Mag didn't like being slowed down, but she had to admit the girl was company, even if she did refuse to touch the traps or the animals Mag collected. And it wasn't long before Jen was moving as fast as Mag along the trail.

By the following summer Mag had stopped worrying about the child getting lost or hurt. Like one of the creatures in the Norwegian stories Florrie was always telling, Jen would disappear for a while, then suddenly burst from the bushes as she rushed to show Mag a new bug or an odd-shaped rock. One day in late August, Jen amused herself by climbing a cascara tree while Mag picked salal nearby. Used by florists across the continent, the branches were currently fetching top prices.

The patch she was working was almost as large as her goat pen. The sturdy, ovate salal leaves varied from what she called the "hurting" green of the new leaves to a dark green and occasionally reddish-brown of the old growth. It was easy for Mag to lose herself in this task. She developed a rhythm as she broke a forked branch from a bush, expertly ran her hand down the stock, and pulled off any damaged or extraneous leaves. Sliding the branch behind several smaller ones in her left hand, she turned back to the bush, selected another cluster, and began again. When her fist was full, she paused long enough to wrap a wire around the stems, deftly tightened the loop with a small hooked twister, then tossed the bundle onto the trail. By the time it landed, she was back in rhythm, snapping a branch for her next hand.

"What's these?" Jen demanded, wriggling into the patch. She thrust a fist full of dark black berries at Mag's face, knocking the salal from her hand.

"Watch what yer doing, girl!" Mag pushed Jen aside and retrieved her branches. "Won't get nothing fer these with you tramping all over 'em!"

Undaunted, Jen asked again. This time Mag took a moment to peer at the berries, and at the purple stains on the child's mouth

"Them's shitty berries. Don't eat 'em."

Jen's brow furrowed. "How come? Is they bad?"

"They joost ain't good fer eating."

"Humph," Jen snorted in a perfect imitation of Mag. She wriggled back out of the salal patch. A few moments later, Mag saw the cascara trees swaying. *Should'a made shooer she don't eat 'em*, she thought, but dismissed the idea. *Might be best if she did. Then she'll learn to listen to folks what know best.*

When she called out to the child to say she was heading home, Jen took longer than usual to catch up. The purple stain around her mouth had grown darker.

As she walked, Mag bent forward under her load of salal—fourteen bundles tied together at the stems, seven facing one way, and seven the other, with the centre straddling her shoulders. Beside her Jen moaned quietly. "Told yer not to eat them berries," Mag said without breaking her stride.

Suddenly Jen gasped and dove behind a salal bush to relieve herself. Mag continued to walk on, albeit at a slower pace. The girl soon caught up to her, but she was still moaning. She suffered two more attacks before they reached the cabin, then she went straight to her cot, refusing the treats, and later the supper Florrie offered her.

"You shouldn't have let her eat them berries," Florrie scolded.

"I told her to let 'em alone," Mag said gruffly. "Now she's learned."

CHAPTER THREE

People got used to seeing the two sisters on the streets of Sechelt, or doing their shopping with the child between them. As the years passed, Mag's hair became completely grey, her face more wrinkled, while Florrie grew heavier and her limp became more pronounced. In contrast, Jen was lean and strong and bursting with energy, though too shy to venture far from their sides. Her clothes were often soiled and her hair unruly, but the trio was never in the village often enough or long enough for the local busybodies to make a fuss about her care, or for the authorities to question the sisters' guardianship.

"She's our kid," Florrie said one summer evening as she sat in her rocker on the porch.

From her seat on the bench beside her, Mag watched the seven-year-old clamber over a mound of rocks on the beach. "She belongs to her ma," she growled, refusing to accept ownership that wasn't of her own choosing.

Florrie shrugged, knowing she was never going to change her sister's mind. "She's gotta go to school come fall," she said.

Mag frowned. "She don't gotta go nowheres."

"John Duncan says she's gotta learn to read and stuff, Mag."

"Jen's none of Duncan's business," Mag snorted. "She kin learn them t'ings here, joost like we done."

Florrie laughed so her whole frame shook. "We didn't learn nutting, Mag. We was always out in the bush."

Mag remembered how mad their dad would get when he came back from his trapline and found they hadn't done the lessons he'd left for them. He'd yell and stomp around the cabin, sending everything flying. Their mother hadn't been able to control them, and they would head for the bush as soon as he left for the day.

"Mother wouldn't put nutting on the table 'til he stopped shouting," Florrie said. Her face sobered as she remembered how hard their mother had tried to teach them to read. But although

Helga Larson could read and write Norwegian, she had never mastered English. "Guess you can't learn someone somet'ing you can't do yerself."

Mag thought of the mail and the newspapers she could barely read. Maybe it would have been better if they'd gone to a regular school for a year or two.

"I'll t'ink about it," she said.

A week later, the sun was shining as they walked from the public wharf into the village and by the time they reached the end of Cowrie Street, even Mag was sweating. She shifted her pack to her other shoulder as she and Florrie and the child walked past the totem pole and the sign that read CEDAR BAY ELEMENTARY SCHOOL. Jen clung to Florrie's hand, edging so close to her side that she almost disappeared in the folds of Florrie's floral print dress. At the bottom of the steps the trio stopped, forming a wedge which caused a temporary split in the stream of children and parents going in and out of the building.

"Oh, shooer. It's gotta be in here," Mag said finally. "These kids look about Jen's size."

"Don't look the same size to me," Florrie said. She put a protective hand on Jen's shoulder. The child peeped out from among the folds. Her auburn hair was fastened in two clumsy braids that threatened to break away from the elastic bands holding them. She had no waist or belt to keep her blue jeans in place, so they were gradually sliding down. Florrie hoisted them up and stuffed the tails of Jen's checkered shirt into them. "Told you they was too big for her," she said accusingly to Mag.

"She'll grow into 'em," Mag said, starting up the steps.

They followed two of the smaller children into the building and down a set of stairs to a classroom which held at least twenty youngsters and almost as many adults. Mag pushed her hat back and scratched her head.

"Which one's the teacher?" Florrie whispered as they stood blocking the doorway.

"Damned if I know." Mag took a step into the room and poked a finger at a blond lady who was transferring notebooks and pencils from a plastic bag to a box. The way she was dressed and had her hair styled made Mag think of the mannequin in the thrift store window.

"You the teacher?" she asked loudly.

The woman paused. Her gaze went to Mag's stout boots, travelled slowly up her faded denims to her checkered work shirt, and then to her face, half-hidden beneath her battered felt hat. Her scrutiny took so long Mag wondered if she didn't understand English. Finally, the woman shook her head and pointed to a brunette near the centre of the room.

"That's the teacher," she said. The woman she identified had her hair tied in a ponytail. She was dressed in a blue jumper and a long-sleeved white blouse.

"Looks more like a kid," Mag grumbled. She led Jen and Florrie across the room to the teacher who was instructing another parent on where to place her child's school supplies.

"You the teacher?" Mag demanded, breaking into their conversation.

The ponytail swished softly as the woman turned. "I'm Miss Gresham," she said primly.

"Then who's the teacher?" Mag asked impatiently. "I got a kid here to go t'school." She grabbed Jen's arm and pulled her away from Florrie's side, thrusting her at the teacher. "This is Jen."

Miss Gresham looked down at the child. For a moment her expression softened. "What grade are you in, dear?"

Jen's face reddened. She stared at the floor without speaking.

"She don't got a grade," Mag said. "She's joost starting."

"Is she registered?"

Mag looked at her blankly.

Miss Gresham's voice grew impatient. "Have you taken her to the office?"

Mag shook her head. "I brung her here. If yer the teacher, then Florrie an' I'll be getting on our way." She turned to go, followed somewhat reluctantly by Florrie. In a flash Jen was at Florrie's side, grasping her hand.

"You gotta stay here, Jen," Florrie said quietly. Before she could pry the child's hand free, the teacher caught up to Mag.

"Excuse me, ma'am, but you cannot leave this child here. You *must* register her at the office."

"I brung her here," Mag said coldly. "Now Florrie an' me's going."

"No. You must register at the office!" Miss Gresham's voice was growing shrill. "The child cannot stay if you don't register her!"

Florrie put a comforting hand on Jen's shoulder. The girl was hiding in the folds of her skirt again, though occasionally she turned her head so she could watch the other children in the classroom. But when one small boy stuck his tongue out at her, Jen burrowed even deeper into the folds. She didn't look out again.

Mag reached the door before she realized Florrie was still standing in the middle of the room with Jen.

"Where we gotta go?" Florrie asked the teacher, refusing to look at Mag.

"Over to the new building," Miss Gresham said with obvious relief. "Go inside the first door, down the hall, and to your right. You can't miss it."

There was pandemonium in the school office. Phones rang, people rushed in and out, and a line of impatient parents with fidgeting children in tow waited in front of the main service window, while a woman with a megaphone voice harangued the office clerk. "I will not have Erica in the same class as her brother! I made that perfectly clear last year."

Mag ignored the lineup. With Florrie and Jen close behind, she marched into an adjoining office. A woman was typing, the rapid clack-clack of her keys adding to the din. She looked up when Mag loomed over her machine.

"I got a girl starting school," Mag said. "Teacher told us to bring her here."

The typist managed a faint smile. She pointed to the queue of parents outside the office. "If you line up there, someone will help you as soon as they can," she said.

Mag shook her head. "No. Florrie an' me's gotta go."

The woman smiled. "Of course you do. But first you must stand in line like everyone else."

"We got hay to get," Mag said, refusing to move.

"And I have this notice to get out."

The door of an inner office opened, and a tall, balding man came out. "What's going on, Miss Struthers? Where's that notice?"

The typist's cheeks grew red. "I'm sorry, Mr. West, but this lady says she needs to register her child. She won't leave."

He looked sternly at Mag and Florrie. "Why not?"

"We gotta get hay," Mag said stubbornly. "Duncan's waiting to give us a ride."

Putting a hand on her shoulder, he tried to guide Mag toward the door. "Well, if you get in line now," he said smoothly, "I'm sure someone will help you soon."

Mag resisted the pressure of his hand and stayed where she was. "No. We got no time fer lining up."

The stream of staff entering and leaving the office continued, only now it was hampered by Mag and Florrie and their bulky packs.

"I could fill out the registration," Miss Struthers offered helpfully.

The man shook his head. "No. You keep working on that notice." He looked around, but everyone else was busy. "All right," he said impatiently to Mag. "Come into my office and I'll fill out the form."

There were only two visitor chairs. Florrie took the one in the corner, and the child stood next to her. Mag hauled the remaining chair close to the desk.

The principal pulled a form toward him. "The child's name?"

"Jen," Mag said.

"I need the spelling. And her other names."

Mag looked at Florrie who shrugged.

"It's joost Jen," Mag said.

"No," he said slowly. "Her surname."

"Oh, shooer," Florrie said proudly. "Jen's the name I give her."

He scowled. The top of his forehead where the hair was receding grew red. "I mean," he said, deliberately spacing his words, "what names did you use to register the child when she was born?"

Mag began to feel uneasy. "Don't remember," she said. "We joost call her Jen."

"Well, you must know your own last name!"

Mag grinned. "Oh, shooer. Larson."

He let out a relieved breath. "Okay. Jen Larson. Now, what's her birthdate?"

"She's seven, I figure," Mag answered promptly.

"I see. And when was she born?"

Mag frowned. "Why you gotta know that?"

"It's the law." He turned to Florrie, "You must know her birthdate?"

Florrie looked helplessly at Mag.

"Florrie and me don't pay much mind to such t'ings," Mag said.

The principal's eyes narrowed slightly. "I'm sorry," he said. "I've seen you around town so I just assumed one of you was the child's mother." When neither sister responded he looked closely at Florrie. "So you are not the mother?"

"Oh, shooer . . . sorta," Florrie mumbled. She pulled Jen closer.

"She's the girl's grandma," Mag said. "She's been looking after her since Jen was a kid."

"Where's her mother?"

Mag shrugged. "She took off."

The principal stared down at the form and shook his head. "This is very confusing." He looked at Mag. "Do you have papers to verify that you're the child's guardian?"

"What kinda papers?" Mag asked suspiciously.

"Legal documents. Birth certificate . . ."

"Oh, shooer. We got 'em at home," Mag lied.

"That's great. You bring them in tomorrow and we'll finish filling out this form. Meanwhile, we'll get Jen settled into Miss Gresham's grade one class. You can pick her up at two-thirty this afternoon."

To prevent Jen from clinging to Florrie any longer, Mag took the child's hand. They followed the principal back to the older school building. As soon as he opened the classroom door, Mag gave the child a firm push forward then turned and walked outside.

"You gotta be tough with her," she scolded Florrie as they trudged down the street to the business section of the village. "Way you keep spoiling her, she won't be good for nutting."

Florrie sniffed loudly and swiped at her nose with her sleeve. She was too frightened to care that Mag was bossing her. "Where we gonna get them papers he wants?"

Mag hitched her pack to a more comfortable angle. "We'll get 'em," she said.

The girl was in high spirits when they met her at the school gate. She babbled all the way to the wharf about what she'd done all day. Florrie listened to every word, almost as excited as the child.

"We singed a song," Jen told them, "all about morning time. An' we drawed a picture of what it was like."

The sisters had been busy while Jen was in school. The boat was filled with boxes of groceries, bags of feed for the goats and chickens, and two bales of hay. Jen hopped in first, then helped Florrie over the gunwale. She stood back as Florrie squeezed past the hay to the front passenger seat. Meanwhile, Mag was hauling a rope out of the water. At the end, weighted down by two rusty links of boom chain, a small fishnet held a plastic bag with two cartons of fresh eggs and three quart sealers filled with goat's milk. She stowed the dripping bundle near the stern. Jen perched on top of the hay.

"Don't seem like you did much learning," Mag observed, untying the mooring ropes. "What about reading and writing?"

Jen shook her head. "We didn't do none of that, but there's tons a books and pencils there." She rummaged through her pack and pulled out a crumpled sheet of paper. "Teacher says I gotta bring all this stuff tomorrow."

Mag steered the boat away from the dock and out into the harbour before she looked at the paper, holding it close to the windscreen so it didn't blow away. "What's all these t'ings fer?" she blustered, to hide the fact that she couldn't read half of the items on the list. "Pencils and books? What's the matter with all them books yer teacher's already got?"

"Those are her books," Jen explained patiently, but there was a worried note in her voice. "And the pencils and stuff was brung by other kids. Everybody's gotta bring some."

"Well, we're not bringing them tomorrow," Mag said firmly. "That kinda stuff costs lots of money."

Florrie took the note. She stared at the printing for a long time, but it made even less sense to her. "If she's gotta have it, we gotta get it," she said finally.

Mag snorted. She steered the boat toward a cluster of summer homes that dotted the waterfront on the west side of the inlet. Halfway along, a large speedboat cut across their path. As Mag turned sharply to avoid a collision, Jen screamed and toppled backward, landing hard on the bag containing the eggs and milk.

"Shitah!" Florrie yelled. Mag fought to steer over the other vessel's wake and, as the boat steadied, Jen crawled to her feet. She rubbed her bruised leg. "I broked the eggs," she said remorsefully.

Mag shook her fist at the man piloting the speedboat. He had pulled up to a private dock in front of one of the summer homes, and as he climbed onto the wharf, his laughter floated across the water. "You could'a kilt us, Saari!" Mag shouted, but that only made him laugh harder.

Jen removed the egg cartons from the plastic bag. Every egg was either broken or cracked. She was about to toss them overboard when Mag stopped her. "Leave 'em be."

Mag steered toward a distant dock at the bottom of a long slope, cutting her speed as she drew closer. When the boat bumped gently against the wharf, Jen held the bull rail while Mag fastened the mooring ropes. After helping Florrie out of the boat, the child grabbed the bag of milk jars and they clanked together as she jumped onto the wharf. Mag grabbed the bag away from her. "Way yer crow-hopping, girl, these'll be busted joost like them eggs!"

Sylvia Lower met them at the top of the path and, although she smiled, there was a mild reprimand in her greeting. "It's fortunate that you stopped by today. I'm almost out of milk."

"I brung you three jars," Mag retorted, tolerating Sylvia's bossy tone only because the middle-aged widow was one of the few people who would buy milk and eggs from the sisters. They both waited while Florrie puffed her way up the hill, occasionally pushed from behind by Jen.

"We had eggs but they broke," Jen said. "I felled on them."

"I saw Pete Saari's boat cut you off. It's a miracle he didn't hit you." They reached the top of the hill and Sylvia led the way into a white clapboard cottage. She paused in front of the mirror in the entranceway to smooth her dark, shoulder-length hair and straighten the lacy collar of her blouse. "I have tea and cookies all ready," she said as the others trooped in behind her.

"I'd shooer like some coffee," Mag said.

Sylvia frowned. "I told you before, Mag. I serve coffee in the morning and during emergencies. In the afternoon, I serve tea." She put the three jars in the refrigerator. "I do wish I wasn't so allergic to cow's milk. Or that someone else sold goat's milk that is as good as yours."

Florrie collapsed into a chair at the table and mopped at the sweat pouring from her brow, while Mag, ignoring her sister's panting, took the seat next to her. From her post near the door, Jen smiled shyly at Sylvia.

"Would you like a cookie?" Sylvia asked her.

Jen nodded, but she glanced hopefully toward the living room where Sylvia had a treasury of knick-knacks—all souvenirs of places she'd visited.

"Yes you may, Jen," she said. "It's all still there. Just as you left it."

Jen took a cookie and slipped silently out of the room, as Sylvia sat in a chair at the head of the table. "She looks so much like my little sister Cassie," she murmured as she poured tea from an ornate

China pot into equally ornate cups nestled on dainty saucers. "We used to come here when we were little girls to visit our grandmother. If we behaved ourselves, Grandmother would permit us to play with some of those very same treasures." A shadow passed momentarily over Sylvia's face. "That was just after the war, so Cassie would have been about Jen's age." She set the teapot back on its matching trivet. "She's about six now, isn't she?"

"I t'ink she's seven." Mag spooned sugar into her tea, then wrapped both gnarled hands around the cup, raised it to her lips, and drained the contents. The cup clattered back onto its saucer.

Sylvia winced.

"We took her to the school today," Mag said. "They want a paper saying somet'ing about where she was born."

Florrie chewed noisily on a cookie. "Gosh, we don't have nutting like that," she said sadly.

Sylvia's expression grew thoughtful. "Do you still have the letter her mother wrote to you?"

Mag shrugged. "Oh, shooer. It's somewheres I t'ink. But a birth paper—I dunno about that."

"It wasn't with her mother's things in the floathouse?"

"All them t'ings got wrecked when Saari burned up her floathouse." Florrie said.

"Son-of-a-bitch didn't want us getting it," Mag added.

"He said he was joost renting it to Jen's mother," Florrie chimed in, happy to be distracted, "but he was lying. That was Billy Thom's shack. He give it to Jen's mother, and he was gonna haul it back to Sechelt, but that Saari was so miserable he burnt it."

Sylvia had heard the story before. "Surely you would have noticed if her birth certificate was with the letter," she said crisply, bringing them back to the birth documents.

Mag's eyes narrowed slightly. "That's somet'ink I joost can't remember."

"And you never heard anything more from Jen's mother?"

"I guess not. That little bugger never wrote or nothing," Mag snorted. "Should'a taken her kid to the Welfare like we was going to."

Sylvia frowned. "It's a little late to be thinking of that now, Mag. The issue at hand is whether or not you have the documents to prove you have the right to be her parents."

As Mag's jaw hardened, Florrie said swiftly, "Gosh, she's like my own kid. She's real good at helping, too, when she isn't chasing off after Mag or playing in the bush. She brings me rocks and flowers and—"

"Florrie's gotten used to her," Mag cut in harshly. "She's gonna feel real bad when they take the kid away."

"Don't be ridiculous, Mag," Sylvia said tartly.

A sound made them turn toward the living room. Jen stood in the doorway, a stricken look on her face. Mag bit back the retort she was about to make, and Sylvia smiled reassuringly at the girl.

"What about you, Jen?" she asked softly. "Do you like living with Mag and Florrie?"

The child looked at her solemnly, then slowly nodded.

"Well, we'll just have to see that you continue doing so." Sylvia turned back to Mag. "Do you have anything besides the letter her mother wrote to you? Something that would say when Jen was born, and where?"

"There was that pack," Mag admitted grudgingly.

Sylvia waited.

"I got it from her shack after I brung the girl to the hospital," Mag continued finally. "Didn't have no money in it, but I t'ink I remember a letter."

"Who was it from?"

"Gosh, I don't know. I couldn't read none of it."

"Well," Sylvia said, "my late husband was a lawyer in Ontario. He maintained that bureaucracy was merely a test of a man's patience, not an invincible wall. However, if there's to be any hope of clearing this mess up, Mag, you must find out the name Jen was registered under. You will also need her birthdate and the place where she was born."

"Maybe it'll be in that letter," Florrie said hopefully.

"If it's still around," Mag warned. But Florrie wasn't worried. Mag never threw anything out.

Before heading home, Mag detoured to the dock where Pete Saari had moored his speedboat. As she came alongside, she cut the motor and made her way to the stern where Jen left the broken eggs. Florrie grinned, knowing full well what her sister was up to, but Jen wasn't so sure. "You gonna give them our eggs, Mag?"

"Oh, shooer." Mag opened the first carton and one by one tossed the cracked eggs at the speedboat. Several landed inside, but most of them hit the foredeck, forming a large yellow pool on the dark blue paint. When she'd emptied both cartons, she met Jen's solemn gaze.

"Now we're even," Mag said coldly.

Gale force winds that swept up the inlet the following day, prevented the sisters from taking Jen back to school. Mag used the time to look for the pack she had taken from Susan Drummond's float shack seven years earlier.

"Gosh, I guess it's in them cupboards," Florrie said, indicating the wall of six broad shelves near the outside door. Over the years, the rough wood that framed the shelves had grown black from wood smoke, dust, and grease, while the contents of each shelf had increased in bulk and variety. Chains for Mag's power saw mounded over a pile of old spark plugs from the outboard and Florrie's battered straw hat cradled a chipped China teapot she had found in the thrift store.

Mag eyed the shelves doubtfully. "I don't t'ink it is," she said. "I'm shooer I put it in a box in my room."

"No. It was cold that day, remember? You don't put nutting in your room when it gets cold."

"Cold don't mean nutting to paper, Florrie," Mag contradicted.

Jen was sitting on the floor by the stove, creating a forest with dried moss, shells, and fir-cone animals.

"You kin come and help me," Mag told her. For the rest of the day they investigated the contents of every box in her room. In the end, all they found were piles of old, musty-smelling clothes, magazines and newspapers, and a nest of baby mice. Jen saved the tiny pink creatures from being tossed into the firebox, by hiding them in a hollow log near the edge of the woods.

"They'll joost die slower that way," Mag told her when she returned to the house. "Or get eaten by somet'ing."

Jen didn't believe her, but when she went to look later that afternoon, the mice were gone.

The wind blew hard through the night and all the next morning. Mag and Jen milked the goats, fed the chickens, then went back to their search. This time they hauled everything out from under the beds. When that search also yielded nothing, Mag finally tackled the shelves near the outside door. In the late evening she pulled the pack from under a pile of old gloves and sweepstakes circulars. One end of the bag had been chewed by mice, but the envelope and the wallet didn't seem to be harmed. As she removed the letter, a torn yellowed newspaper photo of Jen's mother fell onto the table, but Mag was only interested in the letter. She held the page close to the oil lamp on the table and studied the writing but could make no sense of it.

Florrie was in bed watching her. "Sylvia will know what it says, Mag. We kin take it to her tomorrow."

The worst of the storm hit that evening. The trees moaned, the sea pounded against the shore, and the old cabin shuddered as the wind buffeted it from every direction. Mag went out twice to check the boat but, though it was slamming hard against the rubber bumpers, the mooring ropes were holding. Close to dawn the wind suddenly died and, by the time Mag rose to look after the animals, the inlet was calm.

"We'll head fer town after breakfast," she announced.

The schoolyard swarmed with children. It was recess time, and each child seemed to be competing to see who could make the most noise. Jen took one look at the chaos and ran back to Florrie. "I want to go home," she announced.

"You gotta go to school, Jen," Florrie said. "We're heading off to the drugstore to get them things yer supposed to be bringing."

Jen looked slyly at Mag. "It's gonna cost a lot."

"Oh, shooer it will," Mag agreed easily. "We should joost go back home. You kin clean the chicken shed and I kin split some firewood."

Jen hesitated. Mag knew the child hated cleaning the chicken shed, but even this threat didn't deter her. "Okay," she said solemnly, turning her back on the schoolyard.

"Gosh," Mag remarked as they walked slowly in the direction of the wharf. "Shooer gonna be hard to live with being called a scaredy britches."

Jen glanced at her sideways. "I ain't scared."

"Seem scared to me."

Florrie followed behind them. "I shooer was hoping you'd learn to read," she said sadly. "I got that book from the thrift store with that fat little bear and that pig. Gosh, I t'ought you was gonna read it to me."

The girl stopped, turned, and studied Florrie solemnly. Then she let out a long breath. Squaring her shoulders, she marched past Florrie and back to the schoolyard. She didn't look back and she didn't slow down as she went up the steps and disappeared into the building.

Mag and Florrie spent the morning tracking down a goose offered free to a good home. A waitress at the restaurant read the ad to Mag, but by the time the sisters reached the goose's owner the creature had already been given away.

"Aw," Mag said, disappointed. "That goose would have tasted real good."

"We got that chicken the raccoons kilt," Florrie said absently. She was more interested in getting Jen's school supplies. "I t'ink we should get them at the drugstore. Jen's teacher said we should go there."

"Humph," Mag grunted, but she started down the street toward the store. "Need to get more salve fer my hands anyways." The clerk helped them gather the supplies on Jen's list. Before they took them to the counter, Mag eliminated items that she thought were unnecessary. "She don't need twelve pencils," she told Florrie. "And she don't need a case fer crayons. I got a box at home she kin have."

Late in the day, having collected Jen at the school gate, they stopped at Sylvia's cottage. After they were seated around the table with tea, milk, and cookies, Mag gave Sylvia Susan Drummond's pack.

She studied the envelope first. "This must have been written by Jen's mother," she said. "But it was returned because it didn't have enough postage." She removed the letter and read it aloud. "'Dear Mom and Dad, you probably don't want to hear this, but your first grandchild was born on July 16th. I've named her Lisa Marie Drummond, after Grandma.

Luke Hamlyn isn't with me anymore. He said he wasn't ready to have a family yet. Like I had a choice! If you could send me a few bucks for bus fare, I could come down for Christmas and bring Lisa Marie. Maybe I could get my job back at the deli and take some night classes to finish high school. I'm trying to get my life together here, but it's real hard with a kid to look after. Lisa's a good baby. She's got your smile, Daddy, and Mom's eyes. You can't help but love her. Love, Susan.'"

The room was silent when Sylvia finished reading.

Then Mag spoke. "Kin you get the birth paper with that?"

Sylvia took the wallet from the pack. In the folds were a driver's licence and social insurance card. Behind them lay Jen's birth certificate. "I don't need to," Sylvia said, holding up the certificate. "But we have a new problem."

"What?" Mag demanded.

"This is the birth certificate, but it's for Lisa Drummond, not for Jen Larson. If you take it to the school, they're going to ask why."

Florrie said firmly, "She's Jen. That's the name I gived her."

Sylvia tapped the envelope thoughtfully. "What did you tell them when they asked about Jen's parents?"

"We joost said she was Florrie's grandkid," Mag answered. She added bitterly, "They don't know the Welfare stole Florrie's other babies."

"Probably not," Sylvia agreed.

"Gosh, you t'ink they would steal Jen from me?" Florrie asked, anxiously twisting her napkin into knots. "Shooer, I t'ink I did everyt'ing right this time."

"You've been a very good mother to her," Sylvia agreed, but hesitated before she added, "I know the school principal, Gordon West. He probably won't question it if I bring the certificate in to him and explain that you'd prefer Jen to go by Larson rather than Drummond."

"And they won't steal her?" Florrie asked again.

"No, they won't steal her, Florrie. They're overcrowded and understaffed in that school. If they can find a good reason for leaving things as is, that's what they'll do."

Jen wandered in from the living room where she had been playing with Sylvia's knick-knacks. She picked up the newspaper photo of Susan Drummond that was lying on the table. "Why'd she go away, Mag?"

Mag started to say, *because she was a crazy damned hippy with no brains,* but something in the child's expression stopped her. "She was looking fer somet'ing better," she said instead. "Guess she joost got lost on the way."

Florrie reached out and took Jen's hand. "Gosh, I t'ink she shooer felt bad leaving you."

The girl looked back at the picture. The captions had been torn away, but the photo was intact. "Kin I have this?"

"It's yers," Mag said.

Sylvia refilled the teacups and poured another glass of milk for Jen. "So how are you doing in school?" she asked.

Jen looked down at the floor. "Okay, I guess."

"She's only been two times," Florrie said. "That bad storm kept us from bringing her in 'til today."

Sylvia frowned. "What's going to happen this winter when the inlet gets really rough?"

Mag shrugged. "She'll have to get her schooling when the weather's good, I guess."

"Absolutely not," Sylvia snapped. "She needs to be in school every day."

"Then she kin stay here with you," Mag said slyly.

"Don't be absurd! I have trips planned—" Sylvia's reproach held a hint of panic that was echoed by Florrie's frantic protest. "No! She's too little. And she hasn't never been away from me. Not since she was a baby."

Jen tightened her grip on Florrie's hand.

"She's real good at chores," Mag persisted, liking the idea that Florrie would be free once more to help with the trapline.

"She kin learn at home," Florrie said, wishing she'd never suggested Jen should go to school. "Joost 'cause she can't get to school, don't mean she can't keep learning." Her alarm increased as Sylvia's expression grew thoughtful.

Jen's face reddened with embarrassment. She moved as close to Florrie as the chair would allow.

"She don't eat much more'n a bird," Mag added.

Sylvia shook her head, and Mag marvelled that she could do so without disturbing the hair that wedged her face. "It just wouldn't work. . . ."

"Maybe during the week," Mag prompted.

"She's too little," Florrie insisted again, but Mag dismissed that notion with a wave of her hand. "I guess not," she said, then added firmly. "The girl's gotta stop hiding in yer skirts anyways. She kin come back on weekends."

Mag watched as Sylvia studied Jen then turned and looked out the window. For a full moment it seemed as if they were no longer in the room. Finally she nodded. "We could try it," she said slowly, "for a while."

Florrie tried desperately to think of a new argument, but she was afraid if she protested too loudly, Mag would take Jen to the Welfare as she still occasionally threatened to do. With growing sadness she listened to her sister and Sylvia spar with each other as they worked out the details. By the time they left, Mag had arranged to drop Jen off at the public wharf on Monday morning and pick her up there on Friday.

"She can walk to my place along the woods trail with that boy the Duncans adopted," Sylvia said. "I'll arrange it with John."

CHAPTER FOUR

The first week Jen was away from Serpent Cove, Florrie spent most of her time in bed. "I'm sick," she maintained when Mag urged her to get up to make a meal. But when Mag tried to determine what was wrong, Florrie had no specific ailment to offer.

"Yer joost mad about the girl staying in town," Mag snorted. She refused to admit that she, too, missed the little shadow following her about the yard. Most of all, she missed the meals Florrie had taken to preparing since the girl had come into their lives. By Thursday morning Mag had exhausted any empathy she might have felt for her sister. "Get out've that sack and start helping!" she ordered. "Or I'll stay home Friday instead of getting the girl."

Knowing Mag would keep her word, Florrie got out of bed and dressed. "Shooer don't make sense cooking anyt'ing when there's no one to eat it," she sniffed, stoking the fire to make breakfast.

"What the hell you mean, 'no one'?" Mag demanded indignantly, but Florrie was too caught up in her own misery to answer.

On Friday afternoon, Florrie insisted on travelling to Sechelt to collect Jen, even though the boat was already full of salal which Mag had spent the week cutting and bundling. Florrie was forced to sit with a bundle on her lap, but she was too concerned about Jen to complain. She even helped Mag hoist the salal onto the evergreen buyer's wharf and carried a fair share of bundles up to the packing shed.

"Gosh, maybe she won't want to come back home," she worried when they finally headed to the school. But the child who tore out of the school building and down the walk to the two sisters brushed Florrie's worry aside. She hugged both of them in turn and chattered non-stop about the things she'd done in school and how Sylvia had given her a room all to herself.

"It's all blue, Florrie, an' there's a rug and a big bed and a dresser." Some of her enthusiasm faded. "An' there's a picture of Cassie," she said quietly. "She drownded."

Florrie struggled to keep up with Mag and the child. "Oh, shooer?"

Jen nodded, but as they started down the ramp to the boat, she forgot about Sylvia's sister and launched instead into an account of her experience as special person for the day. In between stories, she peppered the two sisters with questions. Were the goats giving lots of milk? Did Mag find the hen that went missing the day she left? Were they having meatballs for supper? Because Sylvia never made meatballs and her porridge wasn't as good as Florrie's, because she didn't put enough sugar in it.

While Jen's stories delighted Florrie, who had as many questions to ask as Jen, the chatter gave Mag a headache. She was glad when they were finally on the water where the noise of the motor drowned both of them out.

The girl had changed, Mag decided. Her hair was fastened in a tidy braid, and she wore a new blouse and skirt and fancy town shoes. "You'll ruin them," Mag warned. "If you don't kill yerself slipping on something first." Sure enough, when she docked the boat, Jen jumped out as she usually did, but skidded on the wet dock and almost fell into the water.

"Sylvia bought them fer me," Jen said, recovering her balance. "She bought me dresses and skirts and shoes, and my own shampoo, and my own comb, and a toothbrush."

"What fer?" Mag growled, following the girl up the ramp. Florrie came behind at a slower pace, stopping every few feet to catch her breath.

"I gotta learn to be a lady," Jen said. They started along the trail to the cabin. "Sylvia says I gotta have a bath every day and wash my hair so it shines and always brush my teeth."

Mag snorted her disgust. "No place fer ladies here," she said flatly. "You want to be a lady you better stay in town."

"And not come home?" Jen asked, a horrified expression on her face. She stopped at the porch and tears filled her eyes. "I won't be a lady, Mag."

Florrie panted up beside them. "She don't mean it, Jen," she gasped. "This is yer home." She pulled the girl against her and glared at her sister. "Don't need to be mean joost 'cause she got some new t'ings."

Mag stomped off to the shed to feed the goats. Would've been best if this whole school thing had never come up, she decided. Putting wrong ideas in the girl's head. Next thing she'd be expecting Mag to haul up water from the creek every day for a bath. Then she grinned. *Girl wants a bath every day, she kin haul her own water,* she thought. It would only take about one trip to the creek and back for Jen to decide that town ideas should remain in town.

On her way back home, after taking Jen to school the following Monday, Mag stopped at Sylvia's with more goat's milk and the girl's backpack.

"Strap broke on them fancy shoes when the girl was climbing over a log," she said with some satisfaction, "but I joost punched in a hole and tied it up with some twine from the hay."

Sylvia thrust a bag of empty jars at Mag. "Of course they broke!" she retorted. "What were you thinking, letting her wear them up there?"

Mag's lips thinned. "What else was she gonna wear?"

Sylvia unzipped the main compartment of Jen's pack and removed the runners Mag and Florrie had purchased. "What was wrong with these?"

"Humph!" Mag looked at the shoes. "Little bugger never said they was in there."

"Well, in future, perhaps you or Florrie should check her bag when she gets home," Sylvia said sternly. She returned the shoes to the pack. "I can't afford to purchase new shoes for the child every week."

"No reason fer buying them anyways," Mag retorted. As far as she was concerned, entirely too much time had been spent discussing shoes. She stepped off the porch. "I'll pick the girl up on Friday," she said, and started down the trail.

A snowstorm hit Serpent Cove the first weekend in December. On Monday morning, winds from the northwest churned the inlet waters into an icy froth, preventing Mag from taking Jen to Sechelt. Instead, she and the girl refurbished the traps Mag had stashed away at the end of the last trapping season.

"Me and you kin start setting them out tomorrow," Mag told Florrie when they stopped for lunch. "Soon's I get back from town."

Florrie was eating cold porridge topped with a thick layer of brown sugar and goat's milk. She paused, with the spoon halfway to her lips. Clumps of porridge spilled over the edges. "I can't go nowheres, Mag," she said, dropping her spoon back into the bowl. She rubbed her right hip. "My leg shooer is hurting."

Mag stabbed her knife into a mound of goat cheese, breaking off a thick slab. Ever since Jen had started school in September, Florrie had been using her bad leg as an excuse to let Mag do the outside chores by herself. "It shooer didn't bother you when we was in town last week," she grumbled, ramming the slab onto her bread. "You was walking all over with it. Buying out the stores."

Jen, who was sitting between them, tightened her grip on the bread and cheese sandwich she was eating.

"I was getting what we needed to eat," Florrie argued. "I told you how the hurting comes and goes. Joost the way it was with our dad. He said it was arter-itis."

Mag snorted contemptuously. "He listened to them doctors too much," she scoffed. "It was terrible what they done to him. Put him in that hospital so those terrible mean nurses could kill him." It was a story Mag launched into every time anyone talked of being sick. Her anger increased with each telling.

"Weren't them nurses that killed him," Florrie said. "He got the ammonia and couldn't breathe. That's what killed him."

"Noo-monia don't come from nowheres, Florrie. It was them terrible nurses leaving the windows open. When I come in he was freezing cold."

Jen took her bread and cheese over to her cot. Mag knew the girl didn't like their fights, but she didn't care. *This thing's got to be settled*, she told herself. Florrie, however, lowered her voice. "I shooer don't have noo-monia," she said, stirring her porridge into a brown sludge, "It's the cold what makes it start hurting."

"It's not moving yerself, that what's making it hurt," Mag snapped. "You sit around in this shack doing nothing. That's what happened when our dad stopped working."

But Florrie's jaw was set, and Mag knew it would take nothing less than dynamite to get her sister out of the cabin now. "Shitah!" She shoved away from the table and the movement sent two days' worth of dishes and cutlery sliding toward the floor. Florrie grabbed her bowl of porridge and held it aloft.

"I'm setting the traps out," Mag snarled. "So I'll keep Jen outta school to help."

"We'll see about that," Florrie retorted, but her sister had already stepped outside. The door slammed behind her.

Jen scurried over to the table and picked up dish fragments scattered on the floor. "How come Mag's so mean?" she asked.

Florrie had resumed eating her porridge. "Aw, that's joost her way. Long as I kin remember—even before she was yer size—she was bossing me around. Her and our dad. We used to haul shingle bolts outta the bush. I remember our dad hitching Hest to a sled. Gosh, that old horse shooer was strong." She paused for a bite of porridge.

"But what did Mag do?" Jen prompted.

Florrie smiled, enjoying the memories flooding back. It was as if she was actually back in the bush with her father and sister. With an effort—because it took her slightly out of the memory—she resumed her story. "Our dad cut down the cedars. Gosh, they was big buggers some of them. He sawed them into bolts, and Mag and me hauled them to the sled. She got to lead Hest down the skid road to the beach." Florrie's smile broadened. "Sometimes I'd hitch a ride on the sled when she wasn't looking. Gosh, she'd get so mad! She'd yell and stomp her foot! After Mother died, Dad said I was to stay home and cook. She shooer didn't like that."

Jen put the dish fragments in the slop bucket. Later she would dump them down the outhouse hole. She placed the dishes that were still intact on the counter. "Didn't you want to be outside?"

"Sometimes. But gosh, not when it was raining or cold like it is now. Sometimes I still had to work outside. When our dad said someting had to be done, you had to do it."

"Even after you growed up?"

Florrie's expression grew troubled. She didn't like to think about those years after she became pregnant. "I weren't around much then," she said. She cleaned the rest of the porridge from her bowl and handed it to Jen. "You wash them t'ings up," she said, rising heavily to her feet. "I gotta feed my sourdough befer it goes off."

While Jen poured water from the kettle into the pan they used for washing dishes, Florrie went to the other end of the counter where she kept a jar of sourdough starter, grunting as she bent to retrieve the flour she needed to add to the jar.

"Mother showed us how to make the sourdough," she said, as she stirred the grey mixture in the jar, "but I fergot all about how to do it 'til Mag remembered fer me." She shook her head in wonderment. "That Mag, she shooer is good at remembering."

"Humph." Jen sloshed a plate in soapy water. "Still don't got to be mean."

In the end, it took more than a few days to set the traps, so it was almost Christmas before Mag took Jen to Sechelt again. They stopped at Sylvia's cottage to pick up some books Jen said she needed. Outside, the little house was bright with coloured lights, and inside it smelled of gingerbread and spice candy.

"I was worried," Sylvia said as Mag and Jen came into the kitchen. "I thought one of you must be sick."

Jen hung her coat in the entranceway. Mag kept hers on, but hooked her hat on the back of a chair. "Jen and me had to set traps," she said. She sat on the edge of the chair, anxious to be on her way back to the cove. "I'm gonna be checking them in the dark if I don't get back."

Sylvia brought her a cup of coffee. "You can't keep Jen out of school this long without a good reason," she protested. She poured coffee for herself and a glass of milk for Jen.

Mag's chin lifted. "How d'you t'ink I kin pay fer all those school t'ings if I don't set the traps?"

"You could get social assistance," Sylvia said. She sat at the other end of the table beside Jen. "And so could Florrie."

"I guess not," Mag said, then changed the subject. "Anyways, I brung her now."

"Now is too late, Mag. School has closed for the holidays. It won't open until after the new year."

Mag's face brightened. "Oh, shooer? So I guess we'll joost get back home. Gosh, I saw a couple of logs by Gustafson Bay."

Jen's expression clouded. Mag knew the child liked staying at the cottage. She came home every weekend, chattering about the room Sylvia had given her, how the bed clothes were always clean and smelled good, and how you should always make your bed after you got up. The girl even had Florrie washing her hands in the morning.

"You kin help me with them logs," Mag said gruffly. Her thick fingers curled around the coffee cup. "And we gotta set some more traps."

Sylvia shook her head. "No, Mag. Jen needs to stay here and get caught up in her lessons. If she doesn't, the teacher's going to start asking questions; the child could be taken away from you."

Mag choked on the coffee she was swallowing. "Who's gonna take her?" she demanded when she recovered. "She's Florrie's kid. That letter her mother wrote us says so."

"That letter is worthless," Sylvia said sternly. "If you don't send Jen to school, the principal will contact the authorities. They'll find out you aren't her legal guardians, and we'll all be in trouble. Jen will be put into a foster home."

Mag scowled. She'd heard about foster homes. Duncan's kid had come from one of them. A living hell, John Duncan had said. She hunched over her cup. It didn't seem right to her that people could take the girl away, but they could.

"Florrie wants her home on Christmas," she said finally.

"Why don't you and Florrie come here for Christmas?" Sylvia invited. "I'll get a turkey and make mince pies and candied yams.

You could come Christmas Eve and sleep on the couch—it opens into a bed."

Mag shook her head. "Animals need to be fed," she said, although it was the thought of spending a night away from the cove that bothered her more than the animals' welfare. Still, the idea of a meal cooked by someone other than Florrie was appealing. "Christmas day Florrie and me'll come fer dinner," she said.

Sylvia smiled. "I haven't had anyone for Christmas dinner for years. Not since Charlie died." Charlie had been Sylvia's husband, but she seldom mentioned him. John Duncan had once told Mag that after Charlie suffered a stroke, Sylvia had nursed him for three years before he died. She never got over him, Duncan said.

However, it wasn't Sylvia's tragedy that disturbed Mag. She wished that Jen didn't look so happy about staying. Florrie was going to be in a real temper when Mag told her she wouldn't see the girl for six days.

"Joost until Christmas," she said again.

The post office was crowded with customers waiting tiredly to mail their last Christmas packages. When Mag joined the line, the postal clerks looked at one another with dismay. Oblivious to their grimaces, Mag studied the catalogue order form she had been trying for the past two days to complete. All she had managed to put down so far was her name.

"Maybe you kin help me," she said to a woman immediately ahead of her. "They want some numbers. I shooer can't figure out what ones."

The woman, who was juggling two large parcels, shook her head. "Sorry. I'm not good at figuring those things out either." She turned her back on Mag. The man behind Mag simply shook his head and focused his attention on a sign advertising a stamp collection kit. When she finally reached the counter, Mag was no closer to solving the puzzle. She thrust the dog-eared catalogue across the counter.

"I want to order this," she told Claire Wilson, the postal clerk, and pointed to a gold locket.

Claire frowned. "This is a post office, Mag. We mail things for you. We don't fill out order forms."

"Here," Mag said, pushing the form at her. "What does it say I'm supposed to do?"

"Mag, I can't fill it out for you," Claire repeated firmly. "You'll have to get it done somewhere else. There are people waiting to do *post office* business."

"Gosh, it's gotta go today," Mag said, unperturbed. "See," she pointed to a large-print section of the order form. "It says it's gonna take five days to come back. I gotta have it by Christmas."

Claire gritted her teeth and took a deep breath. "That schedule doesn't work at Christmas time," she snapped. She slammed the catalogue closed and pushed it at Mag. "It'll take a lot longer to come back now. You better buy something at one of the stores in town."

Mag shook her head slowly. "Oh, gosh. They don't got somet'ing like this fer ten dollars. They want lots more money."

Behind her, the lineup was growing almost as fast as the annoyed expressions on the faces of the people waiting. Claire smiled apologetically at the crowd, then turned back to Mag, who had reopened the catalogue and was pointing to the necklace again.

"See . . . it says real gold," she read, her stubby finger picking out the words. "Florrie t'inks Jen is gonna really like that."

Claire's face grew red. Her voice lost some of its polite officiousness. "Mag, you will have to go. There are *real* customers waiting."

Mag looked around at the lineup. "Oh, shooer," she agreed, raising a hand to Stu Phelps who was standing near the end. She returned to the catalogue, removing the order form again. "I joost can't figure out what they want me to write," she said. Pulling a worn leather wallet from her hip pocket, she extracted a twenty-dollar bill and dropped it on the counter. Claire's face grew even redder. Finally she snatched up the order form and began writing down the numbers from the catalogue display. When she finished, she added Mag's address.

"You'll need a money order," she said. "It'll cost a dollar." She passed the money order to Mag. "You have to sign here."

Mag looked closely at the amount. "This don't say ten dollars," she protested.

"It includes tax and postage," Claire said, the edge to her voice growing more distinct.

Mag eyed the catalogue page suspiciously. "I didn't see nutting about that in there."

Claire grabbed the order form. She jabbed her finger at the shipping and tax charge line. "It's right there. See? There!"

"Oh, shooer . . ." Mag agreed slowly, then grinned. "I guess they gotta have Christmas money too," she joked as she bent over the money order and laboriously scrawled her name.

Claire snatched the order back. "Okay," she said tersely, handing Mag the change. "It will go out in today's mail. There's nothing else you need to do."

Mag counted her change carefully. Satisfied that the amount was correct, she smiled and retrieved her catalogue.

"Thanks," she said, adding as she finally left the counter, "and Merry Christmas."

Florrie was in more than a temper when Mag told her Jen would not return to the cove until after Christmas. She refused to talk to Mag for three days. When she did finally resume communication, it was only to lament the child's absence.

"We was gonna bake the *julekake* on Saturday," she complained. "Who's gonna take the porridge to the barn for the *nisse* on Christmas eve?"

"Nobody." Mag scowled at the burned potatoes on her plate. "Same as befer the girl come here. Same as when she leaves here fer good."

Mag had been working long hours, tending her trapline, searching the shoreline for more logs to salvage, looking after the animals, and bringing in wood for the stove. She was exhausted and in no mood for the revenge Florrie had been exacting. Every meal her sister had served up lately was either burned, half-cooked, or cold.

Florrie knew Mag wouldn't send Jen away, but she also knew if Mag was mad enough, she'd find a reason not to go to town on Christmas Day. "I t'ink I'll make some venison steaks fer supper," she said. Venison steak was Mag's favourite meal.

The day before Christmas, Florrie baked the *julekake* without Jen's help, and that night she ventured outside long enough to take a bowl of porridge to the barn.

"Goats'll eat it soon's yer outta there," Mag scoffed when Florrie returned.

"Don't matter," Florrie said stubbornly. "Joost so Jen knows I done it."

Mag tacked an otter pelt to the fleshing board. "She prob'ly don't even remember."

On Christmas morning Florrie was up before daylight.

"Did you shit the bed?" Mag asked, astonished at the early rising.

"I gotta pack up the *julekake*," Florrie said, "and get dressed so we kin leave soon as it's light."

Mag poured herself the remains of the previous night's coffee. Ignoring Florrie's protests, she cut a slice of cake from the loaf. It was tough and heavy and the bottom was burned, but it was also sweet. She dunked it in her coffee. "Be a while befer we go," she said. "I gotta check the trapline."

Florrie stopped stuffing wood into the firebox. She stared at her sister. "But that'll mean we won't get there 'til after lunch!" she cried, oblivious to the smoke pouring from the open stove.

"Not if you help."

"I can't," Florrie said sorrowfully, replacing the stove lid. "My leg's hurting real bad today."

Mag shrugged. "Suit yerself," she said gruffly. She gathered her coat and pack and headed out the door.

A light rain was falling. The breeze from the water had an icy edge to it, but there was no snow and for that Mag was grateful.

Once the trails turned icy, she wouldn't be able to travel the whole line alone. It was too easy to get hurt; if she was that far away, Florrie would never find her.

"Should have the girl with me," she muttered. She stepped over the rotting remains of an alder that had fallen across the trail. "She shooer isn't much help staying in town."

Mag didn't like all the fuss Florrie was making about Christmas, either. It had started the first year after the girl came. Now, every December, Florrie hauled out the old decorations their mother had collected and pestered to have a tree installed on the porch. Mag had adamantly refused to put it in the cabin.

The path she was following veered close to a small creek. Mag paused to wipe her hands on a piece of goat hide, ridding them of human scent, then crouched by the stream. Under a clump of willows was her trap and the corpse of a small martin. His head was clamped between the trap's steel jaws, causing his glazed, lifeless eyes to bulge outward. Mag pushed down on the spring long enough to release the martin. She reset the trap with a fresh piece of bacon and slipped it back under the bush. With the dead animal stowed in her pack, she continued down the trail to find her next set.

They couldn't afford Christmas, Mag reasoned. She pulled the brim of her hat lower to keep the rain off her face as she trudged along. The ingredients for Florrie's cake had cost almost twenty dollars, to say nothing of the necklace they had ordered for Jen. Mag wouldn't admit the real reason she didn't like Christmas, but she couldn't prevent the memory of the last day she celebrated it from intruding on her thoughts. She and Florrie had travelled to town in a snowstorm to visit their dad at the hospital. Florrie had baked a *julekake* for him, and for once she hadn't burned it. But when they arrived, his room was empty. The nurse at the desk told them their dad had died in the night. Pneumonia, the doctor said when Mag tracked him down. Mag didn't believe him. She'd seen the patients lining the hallways. She knew they'd let him die so they could use his bed for someone else. Figured he was too old to matter.

The wind was picking up, and Mag quickened her steps. She

wondered if they might have to miss the Christmas dinner after all. Then she thought of Florrie. It would take a full-blown gale to stop her sister from going to town.

Florrie hadn't hurt as much as Mag when their dad died. She'd already done her hard mourning over their mother's death when she was sixteen. It was soon afterward that Florrie started going to the dances and from then on there had been no peace between her and their dad.

The last trap was empty, but the bait was gone. Mag reset it in a different spot, then started for home. She walked slightly bent forward, partly from the added weight of the three dead animals and two damaged traps in her pack, and partly to keep the rain from blowing in her face. She focused her attention on the ground, picking her way over the roots and windfalls that littered the trail. In this way she could walk faster. Overhead, the trees groaned and crashed together, then suddenly an alder branch snapped above her. There was a sudden *whoosh*. Instinctively, Mag dove for cover, but she was too late. The snag struck the side of her head, and she felt herself falling. Then there was only darkness.

Florrie waited until almost two o'clock before heading out to find her sister, certain that Mag was deliberately taking her time. "She t'inks I'll joost ferget about going if she don't come back in time," she grumbled. "But I am shooer not gonna ferget! I'm going to Jen's Christmas! Even if I got to take the boat myself in the dark." She hobbled painfully along the trail, trying to remember where Mag had said she was setting her traps this year. A half-mile from home, as she rounded a turn in the trail, a fallen snag blocked her way. It took a moment for her to realize that Mag was lying beneath it, her face smeared with mud.

"Mag?" Florrie whispered uncertainly. "You okay, Mag?"

She forced herself to step closer, then pulled at the snag. It wouldn't move. She moved the limbs aside until she saw that a broken branch was caught in Mag's pack. When it was free, she tugged on the snag once more. It gave way abruptly and she fell backward, landing on her bad hip. Grunting with pain, she crawled to her knees. "Mag?"

A thin trickle of blood oozed from a gash on Mag's temple. Florrie touched it gingerly. Mag's forehead was warm, but the blood was congealed. Encouraged, Florrie put her moist fingers to Mag's lips. Her breath felt cool. With renewed hope, Florrie gently rolled Mag onto her back and propped her against the pack.

"You okay, Mag?" Her sister's eyes remained closed and her skin had a greyish colour. Florrie looked around helplessly. Finally, she took off her coat and wrapped it around Mag's chest. "I'll come back," she promised. "I'll come back real quick."

At the house she collected another coat, the wheelbarrow, and some rope. It was next to impossible to push the wheelbarrow over the uneven trail. Twice she stopped to haul broken trees out of her way. Fortunately, they were small enough for her to move without having to cut them. By the time she returned to Mag, Florrie was gasping for breath. Her leg was throbbing, but she couldn't let herself think about it. She grabbed Mag under the arms and half-pulled, half-lifted until her sister was in the wheelbarrow. Then she began the slow, tedious journey back to the cove.

It was dark when Florrie reached their clearing. Her breath was coming in short gasps, and she was dizzy with hunger and exhaustion, but at least the rain had stopped. Mag seemed no worse than she'd been on the trail, so Florrie left her at the top of the wharf while she made a fast trip to the house. She grabbed the package of cake, and blankets from her bed, then hurried back to Mag.

"I'll joost take these t'ings down," she said as she squeezed past the wheelbarrow. The ramp connecting the dock to the shore was slick with algae, but she tried to stay on the sheets of old duroid roofing that Mag had nailed to it for traction. The duroid was torn in a dozen places and it would be easy to trip on those tears, but by shuffling one foot before the other Florrie made it safely to the boat. There she fashioned a bed for Mag with some lifejackets and blankets, before returning to the head of the wharf to collect her sister.

Manoeuvring the wheelbarrow onto the dock was more difficult because the extra weight caused the ramp to wobble up and down. Though Mag hauled things over it all the time, Florrie didn't have the same strength in her arms. Still, she had no choice. As she progressed down the ramp, the wheelbarrow picked up speed and she couldn't hold it back. She lost her footing when it bounced over the break between the plank and the dock. The wheelbarrow tipped onto the dock, dumping Mag, then landing on top of her. Florrie pitched forward on top of the wheelbarrow. She heard a sickening crunch.

"Shitah!" Florrie exploded. She struggled to her feet and shoved the wheelbarrow aside. Mag's leg was twisted at an odd angle and, for the first time since she'd found her, Florrie was glad her sister was unconscious. She grabbed Mag under the arms, dragged her to the boat, hoisted her over the side, and dumped her onto the bed she'd made. She straightened the leg as best she could, then covered Mag with the blankets.

Although it had been years since Florrie had operated the motor, it only took a few minutes for her to figure out how to start it. By the time she headed into the choppy waters of the main inlet, the motor was running smoothly.

Long past midnight, Florrie made her way up the hill to Sylvia's house. The building was dark and still. She pounded on the back door for several minutes before a light came on. Sylvia opened the door cautiously.

"Florrie! What on earth's happened?" She reached out and helped Florrie inside.

"Mag got hurt," Florrie said when she'd caught her breath. "They joost come and got her in the ambulance."

"Came where?"

"I brung her to town in the boat. She's hurt terrible bad. The doctor at the hospital says she's all shocked up. Gosh, she's broke her leg and smashed her head. It's joost terrible."

While Sylvia hurried around the kitchen fixing tea and sandwiches, Florrie told her what had happened. She described how she managed to get Mag to the boat, but left out the part about dumping her out of the wheelbarrow.

"Got them people living on top of the coffee shop to call the ambulance," she said. "Gosh, she's all chained up now and she's got needles sticking in her arm. . . ." She sniffed noisily and wiped at her eyes with the back of her hand. "Mag, she come to fer a minute after it was all done. She was real mad."

"She's lucky to be alive," Sylvia said, setting a large turkey sandwich in front of Florrie.

"She t'inks they busted her leg at the hospital," Florrie said sadly. "I told her it was broke when I brung her in, but she says that snag hit her on the head not her leg."

"A snag hits her and she doesn't think it did any damage?"

Florrie took a large bite of the sandwich. "She don't t'ink it was that big," she mumbled, chewing around her words. "She never saw it coming." Florrie's hands were shaking. She was having trouble breathing and eating at the same time. "Mag's real mad at me for bringing her there," she said glumly. "I joost didn't know what else to do."

"You did the best you could," Sylvia said soothingly. "And Mag's going to be fine. She's a tough lady."

When she finished her sandwich, Florrie looked around the kitchen as if seeing it for the first time. "You shooer made t'ings pretty," she said. She glanced at the hallway leading to Jen's room. "Was she terrible fussed?"

Sylvia nodded. "She thought you forgot it was Christmas. Sat by the window most of the afternoon waiting. And yesterday she kept worrying about feeding the *nisse*. I was almost ready to hire Billy Thom to take her home, but I decided it would be foolish since you were coming out today."

"Mag and me got her a present," Florrie said. "It's at the post office." She gazed sorrowfully at the tea Sylvia had poured for her. "I don't know what we're gonna do with Mag laid up. I can't run that boat by myself. If somet'ing happens with the motor, I can't figure out what's wrong like Mag does."

Sylvia reached over and patted Florrie's shoulder. "We'll arrange something. Right now you need to rest. I'll get some blankets, and you can sleep on the couch."

In the half-lit hospital room, Mag stared at the cast surrounding her right leg. The limb was throbbing worse than a tooth that had gone bad. But it wasn't that, or the hammering headache, that disturbed her. It was the feeling of being trapped, trussed up with wires and pulleys so she couldn't move. She felt like the martin she'd caught that morning and almost envied his ability to die so quickly.

A noise sounded in the hallway and, as her door opened, Mag feigned sleep.

"Mag?" The nurse touched her shoulder gently. "Wake up, Mag."

Reluctantly, Mag opened her eyes.

"I have to check your vital signs." The nurse took hold of Mag's wrist. She studied her watch for several seconds, then let the wrist go and picked up a silver instrument from the bedside stand. "This will just take a minute." A light shone into Mag's eyes. When it clicked off, the nurse held up three fingers. "How many do you see?"

"Lots," Mag said sullenly, tired of the counting game that had been going on all evening.

"Pouting won't help you, Mag," the nurse said sternly. "Now tell me how many you see."

Mag held up three fingers of her own.

"All right. And what day is it today?"

"It's not day."

"Well, if it was day, what day would it be?"

"How should I know if it's not day yet?"

"Mag, you aren't helping."

There was no response. The nurse sighed dramatically, then abandoned the questions. She took Mag's temperature, inspecting the intravenous line while she waited. When she finished, she patted her patient's shoulder. "I'll check on you again in an hour," she said. "You go back to sleep."

Mag turned her head away to stare out the window. The darkness was beginning to grey. It would be morning soon. The goats would need milking, and the chickens and rabbits needed to be fed.

"I gotta get out've here!" She tried to sit but the action jiggled her leg. Pain surged through her body. She wasn't going anywhere for a long time, and suddenly she knew it. With a low moan she closed her eyes.

CHAPTER FIVE

"Nurse!" Mag jabbed at the call button near her pillow. She ignored the annoyed expressions on the faces of the patients in beds numbered '2' and '3', just as she had ignored the nurse's scolding about using the call button too often. Trussed up, as she had been for the past eleven days, she had learned it was the only way to get her needs met. When they took the button away from her as punishment, she simply shouted. Then, having found that method considerably more satisfying, she had continued to shout even after their hasty return of the call button. Now she bellowed, "Nurse!" again, and a young, harried-looking aide appeared at the door.

"Mag! You're disturbing the other patients," she scolded.

"I joost gotta go," Mag said, unrepentant. "Florrie's coming today. I don't want to be wasting her time peeing."

The aide moved the call button beyond Mag's reach. "Look, Mag, I'm just bathing Mrs. Wentworth. I'll give you the pan now and as soon as I'm finished with her, I'll take it away." She pulled the curtains around the bed and helped Mag position herself on the bedpan. "No more shouting, okay?" she pleaded. "And don't try to get off by yourself again. Last time I had to remake the whole bed, remember?"

Mag merely grunted. She finished peeing moments after the aide left and began waiting impatiently for her return. Soon the pan's metal rim became uncomfortable against her skin, and she knew from past experience that her leg would begin jabbing with pins and needles. She tried wriggling her butt from side to side. When that didn't help, she supported herself with one arm while she removed the pan with the other, but her arm gave out before the job was complete and she collapsed on the edge of the pan.

"Damn," she muttered as a warm wetness spread around the leg that wasn't in the sling. "Nurse!"

When Florrie and Jen arrived, Mag's bed had been moved to the visitor's lounge. The doors to the rest of the ward were closed and there were no call buttons within her reach.

"They're joost trying to kill me," she complained. "Putting me in here with all them windows open. Like they done with our dad." She insisted that Florrie close each window. The smell of the salt air drifting in from the blue waters of the Strait of Georgia, which Mag could see from the windows, was making her homesick.

"It stinks in here now," Jen complained, making a show of coughing. "I can't hardly breathe!"

Although Mag hated the inescapable stench of soap and disinfectant that pervaded the hospital, there was something about the child that was even more disturbing. Mag looked at her sharply. It wasn't the chocolate smeared on her face or the tangled condition of her hair.

"I don't like this place," Jen whined.

Suddenly, Mag realized that it was the pout on the girl's face that was different. "Yer spoiling her," she accused Florrie.

"She's joost tired," Florrie said. "We was up befer light, feeding and milking." She didn't add that the girl had done all of the chores herself because her own hip was hurting worse than usual.

"She's always up befer light," Mag snorted. "Yer spoiling her joost like you spoiled Dog." Florrie had always made excuses for the dog they used to own, letting him come into the shack and feeding him from the table. Mag had warned her that the animal would come to no good that way, but Florrie wouldn't listen. Nor would she believe it when Mag told her that Dog was stealing chickens, until the day Mag caught him with a hen in his mouth. It was Mag who had to shoot him. She hadn't allowed a dog on the place since then.

"I t'ink the girl better stay in town," Mag announced. "Sylvia says school's starting again."

"I guess not!" Florrie exclaimed. "Who's gonna look after the goats and chickens and bring in firewood fer me?"

Mag smiled maliciously. "You will."

Jen's chin tilted stubbornly. "Nope. I gotta stay and look after Mr. T."

"That billy kin look after himself," Mag retorted. She was always annoyed when Jen named the male goats. They were for butchering. Naming them just made it harder to do. "I t'ought you liked staying in town."

Jen's belligerent expression melted into uncertainty. "I do . . . sometimes. But Sylvia doesn't have no goats or rabbits. And she makes me do school stuff all day and don't let me go into the bush or nothing."

"Well, that's where yer staying," Mag said with finality.

"I shooer can't do all them chores by myself," Florrie protested.

"You done it befer," Mag said. "Anyways, it was you that started her going to school." Tiring of the argument, she demanded, "You cleaning out Nanny's shed? Them goats gotta have fresh hay or they'll get terrible sick."

Florrie sat heavily on one of the visitor's chairs and wiped her brow with her sleeve.

"Jen cleaned it out yesterday. But it's hard, Mag. We can't haul them big bales like you do, and the hay's almost gone."

"Get Billy to haul some fer you," Mag said. "There's money under my mattress you kin pay him with. Joost make shooer he tells you how much it's gonna cost first, and don't pay him nutting more!"

A gloom had settled over the room. While Florrie struggled to think of a new argument for keeping Jen at home, the girl frowned angrily at the floor.

"Humph." Mag couldn't understand why her visitors were so despondent when she was the one stuck in bed. Suddenly she remembered the package Florrie had brought with the mail. She pulled it out of the pile on her bed and thrust it at Jen. "This is fer you," she said gruffly. Jen stared at the box, her mouth open with surprise. "Well, you gonna take it?" Mag demanded. The girl stepped closer and her fingers wrapped around the package. Florrie beamed with anticipation. The child peeled off the layers of brown paper, extracted a slender cardboard case, and removed the lid. She gasped when she saw the tiny gold locket inside. She looked uncertainly at Mag. "For me? For keeps?"

"It's yer Christmas present," Florrie said happily.

71

Mag glared at the locket. "It don't look like it did in the catalogue," she grumbled. "It was bigger in the picture."

"You think it's real gold, Mag?" Jen held the locket as if it might disappear at any moment. "Like you and me was looking fer in the creek?"

"Looks like real gold to me," Florrie said. "Here, I'll put it on fer you."

Reluctantly, Jen passed the locket to her. It looked even smaller in Florrie's huge hand, but the child didn't seem to notice. When it was fastened around her neck, she touched it reverently. "It's beautiful," she breathed.

Mag stared out the window. The afternoon sun was getting low on the horizon. "You better be heading back," she told Florrie. "You gotta stop and see Billy on yer way."

Florrie's expression grew troubled again. "I t'ink I should stay with Sylvia tonight," she said. "Then I kin see Billy in the morning."

"No! You go back tonight, Florrie."

"Gosh, I don't t'ink so Mag. There's somet'ing wrong with the motor. It keeps stopping on me." She looked pleadingly at her sister. "And my leg hurts terrible bad."

"You gotta go back!" Mag said fiercely. "You need to check fer logs or somebody else is gonna get them. And you shooer gotta feed them animals. They're all gonna die if you don't." She glared at the traction holding her leg aloft. "Shitah. I can't do nutting with this t'ing holding me down!"

Florrie grew hopeful. "You t'ink they'll take it off soon, Mag?"

Mag's face was grim, but she didn't speak.

The next morning the young doctor burdened with Mag's care stopped briefly at her bed. "And how is Mag doing this morning?" he asked cheerfully without looking up from the chart he was reading.

Mag pointed at the traction. "You kin take this t'ing off now," she snarled. "I got too many t'ings to do to be stuck in here."

He looked up from the chart and smiled. "Even if I take it off, you won't be able to walk, Mag. The bones haven't set."

"They wasn't broke in the first place," she growled, "'til you broke 'em. So you kin joost take this t'ing off so I kin go back home."

His eyes narrowed slightly. "Tell you what, Mag," he said, as he released the wires that held her leg in the air and gently lowered it to the bed. "You show me you can move that leg on your own, and I'll take the cast off and discharge you this afternoon."

Although Mag was already sweating from the discomfort that lowering her leg had caused, she was determined to show him she meant business. But when she tried to move the leg herself, she was engulfed with pain and nausea. She gasped and choked back a yelp of anguish.

"Well?" he asked.

It was a minute before Mag could answer. "How kin I move it with that damn cast on it?" she demanded defiantly, but she didn't resist as the doctor reconnected the sling, and the pain slowly eased.

"In another three weeks we'll change the cast and take an x-ray. If everything's fine, we'll ship you over to the rehab centre in North Vancouver. They'll have you walking by spring."

Mag stared at him aghast. "Vancouver? I don't t'ink so."

"You don't have any choice, Mag. Your quadriceps were damaged when you fractured your femur."

"Gosh, Florrie won't never get to Vancouver," Mag worried. "She kin hardly get here."

"I'm sure your sister will do just fine," he said calmly. "She can phone the rehab centre whenever she wants."

"No," Mag said. "You'll joost have to fix me up here."

"Let's see what you say in three weeks," he said. Retrieving her file from the table, he continued on his rounds, leaving Mag smouldering on the bed. She wanted to lash out like the bear cub that once got caught in the tangle of barbed wire she had stored behind the goat shed. His misery had ended when Mag fired a .22 bullet into his brain. She wasn't going to be so lucky. Fuming, she grabbed the call button.

"Nurse!" she shouted. "Nurse!"

Jen and Sylvia came to see Mag after school on Monday to report that Florrie had gone back up the inlet the evening before, and Billy was delivering hay that day. Jen's hair was combed and neatly braided, and her face was clean, but her right eye was swollen shut and bruised purple. The gold locket and chain was in her hands.

"What happened to yer face?" Mag demanded.

Jen glowered silently.

"Apparently she was in a fight at school," Sylvia said, her tone disapproving.

"They broke my locket!" Jen shouted fiercely. "They was all laughing and pushing me and stupid Sandy Cooper pulled it right off me!"

Mag had never heard her speak so loudly or forcefully before. She studied her curiously. "And joost how did you get a black eye?"

"I punched her," Jen said sullenly, "and Cal Saari pushed me down. So I got up an' kicked him in his pecker."

Mag stared at her then started to laugh. She laughed until her guts began to hurt and she started choking. Sylvia held a glass of water to her lips.

"I don't find it amusing," Sylvia said sternly. "The child behaved like a savage."

"Oh shooer, she's gotta stand up fer herself," Mag said, recovering.

Jen looked down at the chain in her hand. Her lips quivered. "It's all broke," she said sadly. Sylvia took it from her and examined the chain.

"It's only a link that's broken, Jen. I can fix that."

The child's eyes brightened. "You kin?"

Mag leaned back against her pillow and closed her eyes, remembering her first fight. She'd been older than Jen, more like fourteen. She and Florrie had gone into town with their dad. Florrie was so pretty she always drew a lot of attention, but Mag thought the deserted school playground would be a safe place to wait for him. Florrie loved to swing, and Mag was pushing her when three older boys came by. They shoved Mag out of the way and started pushing Florrie so high she got scared and jumped, landing face first in the dirt. Before any of them could touch her, Mag was on them. By the time she dragged Florrie from the playground the boys were rolling on the ground nursing splattered noses and painful testicles. None of them ever bothered Florrie again—at least, not when Mag was around to catch them.

"We'd better go," Sylvia said softly to Jen. Mag didn't hear her. She was snoring and dreaming of walking her trapline.

The x-rays showed Mag's fracture was mending well, but the damaged quadriceps would need extensive physiotherapy if she was ever going to walk normally again. Although she continued to protest, plans were made for her to be taken to Vancouver. Florrie hadn't returned to town, but Billy Thom had stopped by the hospital to report that he'd been up the inlet and things looked just fine, although there weren't any more logs in Mag's holding pond. The day before her transfer, Sylvia came to the hospital alone. She was wearing denim slacks and a cotton T-shirt instead of her usual skirt and blouse, and she seemed flustered and excited.

"This came in the mail today," she told Mag, waving a white envelope at her. "I've been granted permission to visit an archaeological dig in Turkey!"

Mag was in a wheelchair, her right leg stretched out on a support in front of her. She stared blankly at Sylvia.

"It's near the place where Adam and Eve were banished from Eden," Sylvia explained. "The professor in charge of the dig is *the* world expert on ancient glass."

Had she been talking in a foreign language, her words would have made more sense to Mag. The only turkey she knew was served at Christmas. She'd never heard of any Adam or Eve.

"I'll be gone for six months. . . ." Sylvia left the words hanging in the air between them.

Mag was silent while the significance of the announcement sank in. "Florrie's gonna be real mad at you fer taking Jen away," she said finally.

Some of Sylvia's excitement faded. She shook her head. "You don't take children on an archaeological expedition, Mag."

"Why is that, you t'ink?"

"Well, for one thing it is not a holiday. I'm going there to work. Besides, I could never get Jen a passport, not without the authorities finding out that Florrie isn't her legal guardian."

Mag fingered the blanket on her lap. "There's no way Florrie kin bring her to town every day."

"That shouldn't be a problem," Sylvia said. "I won't be leaving until May, and the doctor says you should be home by then." She frowned down at the envelope. "I'll be back before the end of October, and can see what my future plans are at that point."

"Humph."

Sylvia's voice became defensive. "I did warn you about my travels, Mag. I did tell you it wasn't going to work for me to have Jen."

Mag met her gaze. "Oh, shooer, but now she t'inks she needs you." She reached over to the bedside table and selected a toffee from a bag Florrie had brought her. Slowly she removed the cellophane wrapping. "There's gonna be lots to do when I get home. Florrie joost don't look after t'ings good." She put the candy in her mouth. "I'll need Jen to help me fix t'ings up."

Sylvia looked down at her letter and ran her fingers carefully along the edge. "I'm not going to miss this opportunity, Mag."

Mag stared out the window and chewed the toffee, grinding it into a paste.

CHAPTER SIX

For a long time Jen watched the chickens through the small opening near the floor of the shed. There were no windows and the shed smelled sour and musty, a mixture of manure, alfalfa, and dust. A few hens huddled in the nest boxes nailed to the far wall, while four others balanced on the three alder pole roosts.

How would it feel, Jen wondered, *just sittin' there, all covered in feathers, cluckin' away?* She decided to find out. Dropping to her knees, she crawled through the opening and, imitating the chickens' walk as best she could, climbed to the middle roost. The alder pole, not intended for a seven-year-old girl, sagged under her weight. She made a few clucking noises and raised her arms, bending them at the elbows, flapping mythical wings. She lifted one leg and balanced on the other as she'd seen the hens do. Slowly, so slowly she couldn't tell exactly when it began to happen, she felt herself changing. Her chest puffed up and her mouth puckered into a pointy beak. She could feel the softness of her feathers as she arched her neck back and forth.

"Bahwha-a-a-ck, bahwah-a-a-ck," she clucked.

Suddenly, the darkness was shattered as the shed's main door was wrenched open. Sunlight splashed around a menacing figure in the doorway.

"JEN!"

Jen teetered on the roost, lost her balance, and sprawled face first on the chicken house floor.

"Joost what the hell you doing in here?" Mag demanded. "You was supposed to clean the goat shed!" She leaned heavily against the door and waved her cane at the girl.

"I was just checking the hens," Jen said meekly, scrambling to her feet. "Seeing if they laid any eggs."

"I don't t'ink yer gonna find any nests on a roost," Mag said tartly. "What was you doing there, anyways?"

"I was just seeing how strong it was." Brushing straw and chicken dung from her pants, Jen dodged the cane that Mag had been threatening all summer to land against her backside, and ducked out the door.

"You get that goat shed cleaned," Mag snorted, "or you'll be slipping yer way to the Welfare." She hobbled back to the house. Although she was relieved to be back at the cove where the air smelled natural, and she wasn't forced to bathe every time an aide had nothing better to do, Mag was frustrated by the mountain of work awaiting her and by the fact that she was already dipping into the "joost in case" money she kept for emergencies. "If I could joost get around good enough to pick some salal," she told herself, "or maybe even sell some of them logs, it wouldn't be so bad." But Gus Stevenson had shut his logging camp down for the summer, and there were no other buyers up the inlet.

She thumped her cane against the porch step, angry with the girl and angry with her own inability to do the work she'd always done. It wasn't her way to depend on others, especially not a snip of a girl who could scarcely lift a pitchfork.

"Yer always yelling at her," Florrie admonished when Mag complained that Jen was playing instead of doing her chores. Florrie was sitting at the table, one foot resting on the floor, the other cradled on a pillow on Jen's chair.

"If you was any help at all, I wouldn't need the girl," Mag snapped. She had planned to have a cup of coffee and rest, but she was too furious to sit still. "I'll joost go see if she's still talking to them chickens," she muttered, slamming back out the door.

But Jen was in the corral where the three nannies and a small, year-old billy were nibbling leaves from salmonberry bushes. Although Mag simply referred to the goats as Nanny and Billy, without differentiating between the individuals, Jen had made up names for each one. The nanny with the broken right horn was Cob, the one with white markings on its legs was White Foot, and the oldest nanny was Granny. The billy goat, Mr. T., was Jen's favourite, mostly because he was the youngest and would run up and down the pen with her. Sometimes she would put her forehead against his and they would push at each other.

Mag leaned against the fence rail and watched them. She used to do the same thing with her father's goats, and now she didn't even dare go into the pen. The billy was especially frisky today, and toppled Jen over when they butted heads. She lay on her back laughing up at him.

"That billy's too old for that kinda playing," Mag warned. "His horns are terrible sharp. He gets mad enough he kin put a hole right through you."

Jen's arms encircled the billy's neck. "Mr. T. won't hurt me," she said smugly. "He's my best friend."

Mag had wanted to butcher the goat a month earlier but had held off because of Jen. Now she regretted her weakness. The girl's attachment to him was growing stronger every day. With a dismissive grunt, she went into the shed. "You didn't get any water," she complained. "You better get it quick, and stop farting around with that damned billy!" She limped to the gate where Jen was letting herself out, and shook her cane at the girl. "I told yer—"

It might have been the cane she raised, or it might have been that he saw a brief chance for freedom. Whatever the cause, as soon as the gate opened, Mr. T. crossed the pen at a full gallop.

"Watch out!" Mag yelled. She pushed the girl aside, but the movement put Mag's back to the billy. Mr. T. didn't break stride. He ducked his head and rammed Mag's butt, knocking her down into the dust.

Jen screamed. Mag swore. Mr. T. headed for the creek.

"Goddamned billy joost about broke my leg again!" Mag shouted. She used the gate to pull herself up. "Gimme my cane, girl, and quit yer damned screaming!"

Jen scrambled for Mag's cane, handed it to her, then tore down the path after the billy. "Mr. T.! Mr. T.!"

Mag stared at their retreating backs. She was filled with a mixture of fury and regret. "Shitah!"

Jen found the goat by the winter watering hole, but he was in no mood to be coaxed back to the pen. Each time Jen approached him, he jumped away, keeping just beyond her reach.

"Mr. T., you have to come," Jen pleaded. "Mag'll get you if you don't."

The goat surveyed her with his dark, solemn eyes. He didn't understand what she was saying any more than he understood the meaning of the rifle slung over Mag's shoulder as she approached the creek.

"Outta the way, girl," Mag ordered.

Jen turned as Mag raised the gun.

"No! Mag, no!"

The rifle exploded and Mr. T. crumpled to the ground. Jen stared at Mag, then ran to the billy, kneeling on the ground to cradle his head in her arms. "Mr. T.! Oh no, Mr. T.!" she cried, her hand caressing his neck. "I'm sorry, Mr. T.! I should've shut the gate quicker!" She buried her head against his warm neck and sobbed.

"That billy needed butchering anyways," Mag said gruffly. The girl didn't usually cry, and it made Mag uncomfortable to see her crying now. "That's joost how come I told you not to give him no name."

Jen lifted her head. Her eyes blazed with anger. "He was my friend!" she shouted. "You're a stupid ol' witch, and I hate you! I hate you!" She collapsed into tears again, her chest heaving.

Florrie limped down the path to the creek. "What's going on?" she asked. "Did somet'ing get billy?"

Mag's mouth thinned. "I got billy. Befer he got me. Again."

Jen scrambled to her feet. "He wouldn'ta got you at all," she said furiously, "'cept he figured you were hurting me with that cane!" She ran to Florrie and buried her face in the soft, familiar bosom. "Why'd she do it, Florrie?" she sobbed. "Why'd she have to kill my friend?"

Florrie patted her gently, but she couldn't find any words to answer the question. She glared at Mag. "You didn't have to kill him with her watching," she reproved.

Mag was tired of the commotion being made over a goat that was always meant to be butchered. She leaned her rifle against a tree and unfastened the hunting knife she wore on her belt. "She has to learn sometime." Grimacing with pain, she knelt beside the goat. She searched its rear legs for the scent glands that had to be removed before the animal could be dressed out properly. "Joost can't have billies butting us. Not with me all bunged up and you not helping."

Florrie decided against taking the argument into areas that might jeopardize her daily routine. Instead, she started to lead Jen away.

"I'm gonna need yer help dressing him," Mag said tersely.

"But my leg—" Florrie began.

"It's you or the girl. I shooer can't do it alone."

Florrie hesitated, then pushed Jen gently toward the trail home. "You go back to the house, girl. You kin have some cookies from that box by my bed."

Jen wiped her eyes with the back of her hand as she trudged back to the house. Ignoring the box of cookies, she lay down on her cot near the window and pulled the pillow over her head.

Mag let Mr. T.'s body hang in the shed for the night before she butchered him. Florrie worked all the next day canning the meat that Mag cut from the bones. As soon as her chores were done, Jen escaped into the woods. That evening, when Florrie served up a platter of fresh steaks, the girl refused to eat.

"If you don't eat what's on the table, you kin go hungry," Mag said. She shoved a large forkful of meat into her mouth and chewed it with gusto. The meat was at its prime.

Florrie looked kindly at Jen. "Not eatin' won't help Mr. T.," she said gently. "I fried yer steak real good, joost the way you like it."

But Jen shook her head. She nibbled at the pile of potatoes Florrie scooped onto her plate and drank a glass of milk.

"I t'ink I should go to town tomorrow," Mag said when Jen began clearing away the plates. "I t'ink maybe you should come with me." When Jen didn't respond, Mag added, "I got all them beer cans we picked up on the beach last week. There joost might be enough money fer some ice cream."

"I won't go nowheres with you," Jen snapped.

"Oh? Is that so?" Mag grinned, enjoying the girl's show of spirit. "Well, I can't carry everyt'ing myself." Her expression sobered and she turned to Florrie. "If the girl's not gonna help, I can't get them t'ings you wanted. Unless," she added slyly, "you come too."

Florrie was planning to bake bread the next day, but she knew Mag wouldn't be able to haul groceries to the boat by herself. It would be hard enough for her to handle the gas cans. "I guess I could do that," she said slowly.

Jen's shoulders slumped. "I'll go," she said sullenly. She carried the rest of the dishes to the counter.

"Hate going to town," she muttered, but Mag was too busy studying the Sears catalogue to hear her. Jen knew it would not have changed things if she had heard. Mag didn't care if folks stared at them when they walked up the street carrying their packs and gas cans and wearing their bush clothes. When Jen's schoolmates laughed at them, Mag thought they were just happy and having fun. Sometimes she even laughed with them.

Jen used to laugh too, until she started staying in town with Sylvia. Nobody made fun of her then. Sylvia bought her dresses and pant sets that fit. She showed Jen how to shampoo her hair with sweet-smelling soap and brush it 'til it shone. Some of the children had even asked her to play with them. After Sylvia went away, Jen went to school from Serpent Cove, where clothes were washed only when Florrie got around to it. Often Jen wore the same soiled outfit all week.

"You smell funny," Sandy Cooper said loudly one day. To avoid further ridicule, Jen started keeping to herself at school, hiding in the library at recess and lunch hour.

Mag should have shot Sandy Cooper, instead of Mr. T., Jen thought forlornly. But Mag didn't care about Sandy Cooper any more than she cared about Jen's objections to the trip to town.

Bobby Tigard and Calvin Saari were on the dock fishing when Jen and Mag pulled up to the government wharf. Jen saw Bobby nudge Cal in the ribs.

"Hey, Cal," he said so loudly that everyone on the wharf could hear, "you smell somethin' godawful?"

Cal grinned and pinched his nose with his fingers. "Smells like goat shit and dead fish," he twanged, just as loud. "Must be Smelly Jenny and Mag the Hag."

Jen's cheeks burned as she tied the mooring ropes.

"Them yer friends?" Mag asked, lifting the gas can onto the wharf.

"They're assholes," Jen said shortly. She picked up the can and started walking toward the ramp. Mag caught up with her a few moments later.

"I'm going to the post office first," she said, breathing heavily. "I t'ink maybe there'll be some money from them sweepstakes. That's what it said in the letter."

There were no cheques in Mag's mailbox, but there was a postcard from Sylvia. It showed a brown building with a domed roof and two thin steeples that Jen thought looked like giant needles. Mag pocketed the card and took Jen to the Village Restaurant, just down the street from the post office.

"You got apple pie?" Mag asked the waitress. The woman nodded. "It fresh?"

"Just baked this morning, Mag."

"Oh, shooer? We'll have some then." Mag beamed magnanimously at Jen. "With ice cream."

Jen didn't smile, but Mag knew the girl's favourite treat was ice cream.

While the waitress went to fill their order, Mag studied the card. Sylvia had printed a message on the back and Mag read it aloud slowly, leaving out the words she didn't understand. "'Dear Jen, Mag and Florrie, this is . . . close to my house. I am happy here. Today we found a glass . . . Oldest glass I ever saw. You'd like it here, Jen. Love, Sylvia.'"

When she finished reading, Mag turned the postcard over and studied the picture. She scratched her head. "Funny house," she observed. "I wonder what all them pointy t'ings are fer?"

Jen studied the card for a long time. She was fascinated by the strangeness of the building. Her curiosity mellowed her hostility toward Mag. "Maybe it's some kind've church. My teacher showed me a picture of a church and it had those skinny things on top. Only they didn't look like needles."

"She should'a stayed here," Mag said dourly. "We got lots of old bottles buried in back of our place. She could'a come and dug 'em up. Like Billy Thom's cousin, Louis. He's always digging fer old Indian stuff."

Jen traced the building with her finger. "Must be cool seeing all them people and the castles she told me about!" When the waitress brought their pie and ice cream, Jen set the postcard reluctantly aside. "One day I'm going there," she promised.

"Humph!" Mag dipped her fork into her pie. "Nutting there that you don't have here, girl."

Jen's chin tilted up. "Is too," she said. "And I'm going."

When August arrived, it was Mag's idea to attend the Pacific National Exhibition in Vancouver. She saw it advertised in the newspaper she was about to use to light the morning fire. "We ain't gone to the fair since the girl come." She walked to the table with the paper. Her limp was almost gone and she hadn't used her cane for weeks, but she'd already been outside checking the boat and the animal pens, and now she was glad for a chance to sit down. She spread the paper out on the table and pointed to the roller coaster pictured on the ad.

Florrie rolled out of bed and joined Jen, who was peering at the picture over Mag's shoulder.

"Someone fell off a roller coaster once," Jen said knowingly. "Sandra Cooper says people fall off all the time."

"I guess they could," Florrie agreed, but Mag was dubious.

"That's somet'ing I haven't heard about," she said. "They got a bar holding yer in anyways."

Florrie's brow furrowed for a moment. "I guess they do," she agreed. "And they go so fast yer pushed way back against the seat."

Jen shivered. "Sandra says it goes as high as the trees."

"Higher'n that," Florrie said. She limped to the counter where she poured oatmeal and water into a pot.

Mag went back to lighting the fire. "We'll go right after chores tomorrow. Catch the bus to Vancouver."

The next morning, when Mag went out to look after the animals, she found that Jen had already milked two of the three nannies.

"You feed the chickens and rabbits. I'll finish up here," Mag told her, pleased to see some spirit back in the child.

In the house Florrie had the porridge made and a lunch packed. Jen changed into a clean pair of denim shorts and a T-shirt that used to be white.

"My runners got holes," she worried.

"Makes yer feet stay cooler," Florrie soothed. She had put on a clean print dress, but she kept on her work boots. Mag didn't change at all.

Jen had never ridden in a bus before, and she was speechless as she took her place on the cushioned seat beside the window so high above the ground. Florrie sat next to her, while Mag sat in front of them, glowering at the bus driver who had refused to allow Jen to travel free.

"She takes up a seat same as an adult," he said. For one heart-stopping moment, Jen thought Mag was going to refuse to board the bus. She almost did, but Florrie had nudged her, and one look at her sister's face convinced Mag that this time it might be best not to argue. Muttering about "terrible thieving bus drivers," she pulled the extra bills from her wallet to cover Jen's fare.

A few miles out of Sechelt, Jen found her voice, and from there to the Langdale ferry terminal she peppered Florrie with questions. "How come we keep stopping, Florrie? Are these people goin' to the PNE, too? Is it far now?" She had even more questions when the bus drove onto the ferry that would carry them across Howe Sound to Horseshoe Bay, and the highway to Vancouver. Mag was glad she'd found a seat closer to the front where she could keep an eye on the bus driver and make sure he was paying attention to the road.

When they finally climbed off the bus at the fairgrounds, Jen was overwhelmed by the size of the buildings, the cacophony of noise—people shouting, music blaring, horns honking, brakes screeching—and the smell of diesel exhaust and hot dogs and hamburgers. She grabbed Florrie's hand and held it tight as they walked across the street and through the exhibition gates. In a cloudless sky, the August sun burned down onto the tarmac without mercy. Florrie was already sweating heavily.

"Animal sheds is over there," Mag said. She headed out across the midway while Jen stared at the food and game booths, the rides, and the endless strings of coloured lights. Within seconds, Mag was swallowed by the crowd. Jen tugged at Florrie's hand, willing her to walk faster.

"Hold on, Jen!" Florrie puffed. "I'm joost going as fast as I kin!"

"But Mag's goin' faster!" Jen cried. "I can't even see her now, Florrie! How're we gonna know where to go?"

Florrie stopped to get her breath, oblivious to the stream of people that ebbed around them. "It isn't like I never been here befer, Jen," she said. "I kin find the animal sheds as well as Mag kin." She turned around slowly, then suddenly smiled. "There!" she said. She pulled Jen toward a white booth.

Jen looked back at the crowd into which Mag had disappeared. "But what if you forget, Florrie?" she fretted. Florrie handed a five-dollar bill to a lady in the booth and received two tickets.

"We'll get to them sheds faster'n Mag," she said smugly. She led Jen to a gate where a man and woman were sitting on a small seat attached to a white pole. The pole was connected to a cable above their heads, and Jen stared as the seat moved away, lifting the couple high off the ground. Suddenly Florrie pulled her forward. She handed the attendant their tickets and settled heavily on the seat, pulling Jen down beside her. A moment later they were floating over the crowd.

"We're flyin', Florrie!" Jen shrieked. "We're flyin' just like the birds!"

Florrie chuckled as she studied the people below them. "There's Mag!" she shouted.

After a moment Jen, too, saw the battered felt hat bobbing beneath them as Mag marched across the fairground.

"Mag!" Jen screamed. "Up here, Mag!" But the noise of the fair drowned out her words and, as the sky chair moved forward, Mag was once again lost in the crowd.

"There's the animal sheds," Florrie pointed out, as the chair stopped on a platform. Jen hopped off and helped Florrie to hoist herself up, and together they walked toward the building that housed the agricultural displays.

It was quieter inside because there were fewer people than on the midway, but not much cooler, although they were sheltered from the direct sun. Here the noises were ones Jen understood—animal noises. She breathed deeply. Animal smells, too. She let go of Florrie's hand and waited near the door for Mag to join them. Florrie found some bales of hay stacked in a corner and had just settled on one when Mag entered the barn.

"Mag!" Jen danced over to her. "We rode in the sky on a chair! An' we saw you below us! Didn't you hear me callin'?"

Mag pulled a soiled handkerchief from her pocket and mopped her brow. She felt worn out from the trek across the tarmac. "Gosh, I should'a brought my cane," she muttered. She waved her hand irritably at Jen. "Stop jumping around like a chicken without his head! Yer gonna be tired out befer the day's half through."

It was mid-afternoon when Mag took Jen to the roller coaster, while Florrie rested in the shade. Jen had seen the ride in the distance all day and heard the screams of riders as they rounded the curves and swooped down the hills, but not until she stood beneath the immense frame did she realize how huge it really was. Suddenly she wasn't so sure she wanted to ride it after all. Especially not alone.

"I'm too small, Mag." She stood beside the measuring line. The top of her head was a fraction of an inch higher than the required forty-eight inches.

"I don't t'ink so," Mag said. She joined the lineup of people waiting to go on the ride.

"Maybe I'll just watch," Jen hedged. The lineup moved forward, bringing her closer to the gate.

Mag frowned. "Yer not scared, are you?"

Jen shook her head. "I just don't feel so good."

"You was feeling fine when I bought the ticket," Mag countered.

Jen watched the train of cars careen around one of the bends. "I might fly out, Mag, like Sandra Cooper said." She added hopefully, "Then who'd help you with the milking?"

"I milked befer you come along, girl. Yer joost scared."

Jen's chin came out. "Am not! I just want to look."

"Life don't give much to folks who only want to look," Mag said. "Joost might's well curl up in a hole and die if that's all yer gonna do."

The line moved closer to the entrance. The knot tightened in Jen's stomach. She'd die anyway if she went on that ride.

"You come with me," she said suddenly. "Then you won't just be lookin' neither."

"I guess not," Mag snorted. "I could hurt my leg terrible on that t'ing. Anyways," she added scornfully, "I've rode on it lots of times."

Jen was trapped. With growing horror she watched the train come to a halt, the people leave, and the attendant open the gate.

"Go on!" Mag nudged her forward. "He's waiting fer you."

The attendant had lifted the bar. He held it away from the seat so Jen could climb in. Reluctantly, she stepped forward. Her legs shook so badly she thought she'd fall. Instead, they carried her into the car. She sat on the hard metal seat, and the man slammed the bar in place. It was as if he had slammed the door on her life.

Mag had thought the girl would enjoy the ride, as she always had when she was young, but this child who clutched the bar so hard her knuckles showed white and stared straight ahead was enjoying nothing.

"Next!" the attendant said. He moved toward the next car.

Suddenly Mag stepped forward, blocking his way. "Changed my mind," she told him. "I'm going with the girl."

"You got a ticket, bud?"

Shoving a dollar into his hand, Mag bent down and lifted the bar in front of Jen.

"You can't do that!" he protested. "You gotta get a ticket!"

Mag sat down. "I paid." She pulled the bar toward her.

Jen eyed the attendant curiously, her fear suddenly forgotten. Mag caught her eye and they grinned at each other. The attendant glared at both of them, then muttered an oath. He shoved the dollar in his pocket and motioned the next person into the car behind them.

The car jerked forward. Jen fixed her gaze on the track as they slowly climbed the first hill. Suddenly the track disappeared and she was plunging face down toward the city. She shrieked and grabbed onto Mag's arm

"I'm gonna die! I'm falling out!"

Beside her, Mag laughed, but she too was having a hard time staying in place with the girl hanging onto her arm. Her injured leg was too weak to act as much of a brace. She saw the girl's eyes squeeze shut, then fly open as the car inched its way up another hill.

"No worse'n a squall on the inlet," Mag shouted to her. But as they crested the hill and jerked around a tight corner, Jen knew this was far worse than any squall. They swooped at lightning speed down another hill. She shrieked again and clung even tighter to Mag, refusing to let go even after they had plunged, jerked, and bumped their way to a halt.

On the safety of the pavement once more, Mag pried her arm loose. "Gosh, I told you it was worth doing, didn't I?"

Jen swallowed hard, thankful to be back on the ground but terrified that Mag might consider taking a second turn on the ride. "It was like nothin' I ever dreamed," she agreed faintly. Mag gave a satisfied nod. "I t'ink maybe we'll take some ice cream to Florrie," she said.

It was long past dark when Mag eased the boat alongside their dock at Serpent Cove. Jen was sound asleep on the floorboards.

"Might's well joost leave her here," Mag said when she'd tied the mooring ropes. "She won't be waking up now."

Florrie shook her head. "I don't t'ink so, Mag. It's too cold fer sleeping in the boat."

Mag rubbed her leg. All of the walking she'd done on the tarmac had made it throb. "Guess maybe it is." She stepped into the boat, knelt down, and hoisted Jen's limp body over her shoulder. "Gosh, she don't weigh as much as a sack of feed," Mag grunted. She limped slowly along the path to the house. Jen didn't stir.

CHAPTER SEVEN

Kneeling on the seat, Jen held tightly onto the steering wheel as a light breeze teased the boat toward the shore. She had to concentrate to keep the bow turned to port. Behind her, Mag was leaning over the starboard gunwale hammering a rusty dog into the hemlock log they'd found drifting near Steelhead Point. A frayed nylon line was attached to the eye of the spike, and Mag secured it to a towline, pushed the log away from the boat, and went forward. As Jen scrambled to her own seat, Mag took the wheel and shifted the motor into forward gear. The boat surged ahead until the slack in the towline disappeared and it was slowed by the drag from the log.

"We gonna get more?" Jen loved working on the water. She felt important when Mag occasionally entrusted her with the wheel.

Mag shook her head. "We're hauling as much as we can." The boat inched out of the bay and into the main inlet. "Should get home joost about supper time."

Jen went to the stern to watch the log plow through the water like a long, dark serpent following the boat. The bow of the boat was riding high, putting the stern closer to the water than Mag liked to see it. "Best come forward," she cautioned Jen. When the girl did as she was told, and the bow still didn't level, Mag contemplated setting the log free. It was a risk. A licensed beachcomber could easily pick it up before she returned. She peered through the gathering dusk. Smoke rose from the chimney of the cabin across the inlet. "Might's well keep going," she muttered. "Almost there anyways."

Suddenly the motor cut out, fired, then cut out again. Mag pressed the starter, pushed the throttle forward, and revved the engine. The misfiring continued and, within seconds, the engine began to sputter and lose power. Finally it died completely.

"Shitah," Mag said. Now she wished she hadn't brought the girl. It was the fourth time in as many weeks that the motor had quit working. At first she thought it was caused by water in the gas, so she had switched to a higher grade of fuel. After a few trips to town, however, the sputtering had returned. Adjusting the gap on the spark plugs only helped for a while.

Jen followed her to the stern. "Is it broke?"

Mag didn't answer. She placed the engine cover on the deck. In the gathering dusk she could see black oil splattered over the plugs. "Shitah," she said again, and began the lengthy process of removing the spark plugs, cleaning them, and narrowing the gap between the igniter and the plug. "You keep the wheel turned to home," she told Jen, mostly to stop the child from pestering her with questions. An incoming tide was nudging the boat and its tow toward Serpent Cove, but Mag knew a change of tide was less than an hour away. If she didn't get the motor running soon, they would be in trouble. She would have to cut the log free and try to paddle against the current, a task she wasn't sure she was up to.

When she finished adjusting the plugs, Mag told Jen to start the engine. It sputtered, caught, sputtered, then started. Mag let out her breath. She was replacing the cover when the sputtering began again. Once more the motor quit. The girl lapsed into silence. She watched Mag remove the cover and painstakingly repeat the process with the spark plugs.

Dusk settled over the inlet, stealing the light Mag needed. The log, pushed against the boat by the incoming tide, began to drift away as the current shifted.

"There's the moon," Jen announced. Silently she watched it crest the hills that cradled the inlet.

Mag replaced the last spark plug, then tackled the carburetor.

"Fetch that light fer me, girl." Jen retrieved the flashlight from the plastic bucket of ropes and tools stored under the bow. Back at the stern, she shone the feeble light on Mag's hands. "Higher," Mag said tersely. "Now lower. Not there! Shitah! I told you, shine it here!" While Jen struggled to hold the light steady, Mag took the carburetor apart, cleaned the filter, and reassembled the mechanism. By the time she finished, it was completely dark and the flashlight was all but dead. They had drifted almost to Gustafson Bay, almost three kilometres south of Serpent Cove.

"Go on up and try 'er," she told Jen. The girl stumbled as she felt her way forward in the dark. A moment later she pressed the ignition. The starter whined laboriously. Mag squeezed the ball on the fuel line, forcing gas into the carburetor. Finally the engine caught, sputtered, then roared. "Back her down joost a bit," Mag yelled. Quickly she replaced the cover and went forward. With the motor running fast, she shifted into gear, and turned the bow toward the cove. The outgoing tide slowed their progress, but the boat plowed steadily through the water. As Mag gripped the throttle, ready to pump it at the first sign of a sputter, she stared hard at the dim outline of Serpent Point, far up the inlet.

Jen sat silently beside her. Mag could feel the child's fear.

"We'll be home soon," Mag said gruffly. Jen didn't respond.

The boat inched around the point leading to the cove, a faint light from the cabin beckoning them forward.

When Mag finally idled the boat alongside the boom she'd rigged to corral her logs, the moon was high in the sky. She shifted into neutral, grabbed a pike pole, and positioned herself amidships at the starboard gunwale. With the pointed end of the pole, she released the chain from one end of the log she used as a gate. As that end drifted away, she manoeuvred the new log inside, nudged the gate log back in position, and replaced the chain.

"I'm starving!" Jen said as Mag motored over to the dock.

"It's been a long time since breakfast," Mag agreed wearily. She secured the boat and trudged up the path to the cabin while Jen ran ahead, leaping and cavorting like a billy in heat, shouting for all the world to hear that they were home. A yellow glow from the kerosene lamp illuminated the open cabin doorway. As the savory smell of coffee and fried potatoes drifted out to them, Mag realized that she, too, was hungry.

When Mag and Jen hadn't appeared by dark, Florrie had begun to imagine all the disasters that might have befallen them. Even reminding herself that Mag could handle anything, hadn't helped.

Finally, to distract herself, she had started mashing the potatoes she'd boiled for supper, adding enough flour, goat's milk, and bacon drippings to make a pastry, then rolling it into thin, plate-sized pancakes, which she fried in an ungreased skillet. She heard the motor just as she rolled out the last cake, and as she was placing it in the pan Jen burst into the cabin.

"*Lefse!*" she shouted.

By the time Mag entered, the girl was already at the table slathering blackberry jam over one of the big Norwegian pancakes. She rolled it into a tube, catching the extra jam with her tongue before it dripped onto the floor. Mag hung up her hat, poured coffee into a cup, and sat down.

"Jen says you broke down," Florrie said, adding the last *lefse* to the pile on the warming oven, and bringing the whole platter to the table. "Did you get her fixed?"

"We're here, aren't we?" Mag forked a pancake onto her plate, then reached for the butter.

Florrie helped herself to a double serving. "I t'ink school's gonna start next week."

Mag downed a cake and reached for another. Jen took one more for herself but, sensing an argument brewing, carried it to the doorstep.

"I guess when it does we gotta start taking Jen to town," Florrie persisted. "Gosh, she's gonna need new books and pencils, all that kinda stuff."

"Books cost money." Mag washed down her second helping with a long swallow of coffee. "I gotta buy parts fer the motor." She frowned at her plate. "There joost might be somet'ing wrong with the head gasket."

Florrie said no more, and Jen hoped that would be the end of it. The next day, she scampered up and down the trail to the dock fetching tools for Mag, who by late afternoon had cleaned out the carburetor once more and replaced the head gasket with an old one she had in the shed.

"It'll do fer a while," she said as she gathered up her tools. "Joost can't use her when the weather's acting up."

Jen tossed a wrench into the tool bucket. "Not fer going to school neither, right?"

"Humph," Mag snorted. "Never said that, did I?"

"But you wouldn't care, right?"

Mag shrugged, more interested in returning to the cabin than in listening to the girl's chatter. She shoved the tool bucket under the bow, then climbed out of the boat with Jen close on her heels.

"How come, Mag?" Jen asked as they climbed up the ramp.

"How come what?"

"How come you don't care if I go to school an' Florrie does?"

Normally Jen's questions bounced off Mag like hail on a tin roof, but this was one she'd never considered. They reached the trail before she answered. "The Welfare took Florrie's kids away. She don't want to give them a reason fer taking you away too."

"Do you?"

A sudden squawking in the chicken yard saved Mag from answering. While Jen ran off to see why the hens were making such a commotion, Mag went into the cabin.

Florrie was eating the leftover *lefse*. "Are you all done?"

"I patched her up." Mag poured them both cups of coffee. "Enough to last a few trips, anyways."

Florrie slowly spooned sugar into her coffee. "Gosh, I wonder what we're gonna say when the policemen come," she said casually.

Mag paused in the middle of dunking a pancake into her coffee. "And joost what would the police be coming here fer?"

"Fer not sending Jen to school."

Mag chewed the pancake, her expression thoughtful. She didn't really believe the police would come all the way to the cove just over a kid, but she wasn't keen on taking the chance.

"I t'ink we should get a new motor," Florrie said.

Mag laughed derisively. "And how to you t'ink we kin pay fer it? You didn't set the traps, remember? And you didn't get no salal."

"You kin sell them logs you been gathering," Florrie said.

"Who am I gonna sell 'em to with Stevenson's camp still closed down?"

"You kin get a licence like everyone else does and sell 'em yerself," Florrie retorted.

"Oh, shooer!" Mag snorted. "Then everybody knows how many logs we get up here. I guess not." The sisters had battled over this issue many times before. Mag knew she could get much more for her logs if she had a beachcomber's licence, but the paperwork involved in the process was beyond her. It was much easier to sell them to Gus Stevenson, even though he only gave her a fraction of their value. "No," she said firmly, "that log money's fer winter."

"We kin use mushroom money fer winter. Billy Thom says it's gonna be a good year fer pines."

"Oh, I don't t'ink so, Florrie. It's been too dry."

"You could'a had that money from the Welfare," Florrie said reproachfully. "Sylvia was gonna take you there."

"I guess not!" Mag's voice hardened. "Our dad told us never take nothing we didn't sweat fer." By her standards, scavenging for logs and other salvageable material up and down the inlet, or getting the best in a financial transaction, may have been exhausting work, but it was infinitely better than taking money from the Welfare people.

"We kin use some of that 'joost in case' money you got stashed under yer bed," Florrie persisted.

Mag shook her head. "That money's fer hard times."

"I t'ink this is hard times, Mag."

"Hard times," Mag said adamantly, "was when my leg was broke. And when our dad couldn't get work. I guess that's somet'ing you can't remember, that time when all we had to eat was fish and salal berries. You were joost a baby that time. And there was that time I remember, when the goats all got sick because we couldn't buy them no feed—"

She stopped as Jen skipped into the cabin.

"It was just an eagle. He was sitting on that snag behind the pen." The girl's shorts and top were wet and streaked with mud. "I threw rocks at him," she said, adding proudly, "almost hit him, too." She sat at the table and took the last piece of *lefse*.

"Mag and I was talking about how we kin get you to school," Florrie said.

Jen shook her head. "I don't need to go to school, Florrie. Nobody'd even care if I wasn't there."

"That principal would," Florrie said firmly, her chin set. "And he'll tell the police."

Mag eyed Jen reflectively. "I t'ought you liked going to school."

"School's stupid, Mag. Those kids are real mean."

"Lots of people are mean, girl. Animals, too. Like that billy we butchered." When Jen winced, and Florrie glowered at her sister, Mag insisted, "He *was* mean."

"I can't go to school because the kids laugh at me!" Jen fought back tears. "They call me Stinky Jenny 'cause I got goat smell on me."

Mag pushed her chair back. "They must be pretty stupid to laugh about goats." She stomped over to the tall cupboard where she retrieved a battered coffee can from the top shelf. The plastic lid cracked when she pried it off. She tossed it aside and upended the tin, scattering bills and coins over the table.

"Shitah!" Jen exploded. She'd never seen so much money at one time. "How much is it, Mag?"

"Not enough, that's fer shooer," Mag muttered. In her bedroom she found a crushed shoebox beneath a pile of broken ceramic floor tiles that she had scrounged from a dumpster. From under her mattress she extracted a manila envelope. She added the contents of both to the pile on the table.

"More money!" Jen exclaimed.

"She has it hid all over," Florrie said.

While Jen sorted through the coins, Mag separated the bills into stacks of denominations from one to twenty. With the help of a stubby pencil and a sheet of paper, she laboriously added the amounts in each stack.

"A thousand and forty-four dollars!" Jen breathed when Mag finished. She had never heard of an amount that big.

"Might be enough fer a second hand motor," Mag said. "I t'ink Billy Thom's got one fer sale."

Florrie shook her head. "You should get a new one, Mag. A big Merc like we saw in that marine shop."

Mag put the money back into the can. "Gosh, I can't never remember our dad ever getting somet'ing new," she said.

It rained the next day, so Mag decided that was as good a time as any for a trip to town. She left early with instructions for Jen to clean out the goat shed and to stack the firewood she'd cut the day before.

"You think she'll buy a new motor?" Jen asked Florrie as they watched Mag's boat disappear around Serpent Point.

Florrie shrugged. "You never know which way Mag's gonna go, Jen. It joost has to be her way."

With mixed feelings, Jen went out to tackle the goat shed. She was excited about the prospect of a new motor, but apprehensive at the thought of going back to school.

It was almost dark when she heard the sound of a motor. It was smoother than the one Mag took to town.

"She got it, Florrie!" Jen shrieked as she tore past the cabin. She was at the dock when Mag pulled alongside, and Florrie came puffing down to join them. A new grey Evinrude gleamed proudly at the stern of the old Sangstercraft.

While Jen fastened the bow rope, Mag tied the stern to the bull rail. She tilted the motor so they could see the leg and propeller. "Forty horsepower," she gloated. Mag had bested herself in this deal: she'd bartered with the dealer to take her old motor in trade, include a new gas can, and reduce the new motor's price by four hundred dollars. Although he balked when she asked him to haul the motor down to the wharf, she had caused such a commotion in the shop, blocking the counter so no one else could do any business, that in the end he gave in.

"He was shooer swearing when he come fer the old motor," she told Florrie. "Took the skin right off his knuckles getting them bolts loose."

"How'd you pay fer it?" Florrie asked wonderingly.

"Ran into Gus Stevenson. He's starting up his camp next week and he give me an advance on my logs."

Jen was inspecting the motor from every angle. "Kin we go for a ride?"

Feeling magnanimous, Mag took Florrie and Jen for a spin across the inlet to Anchor Bay.

"Shooer runs quiet," Florrie observed.

"Let me try!" Jen pleaded until Mag pulled her onto her lap and allowed her to handle the controls. Jen shoved the throttle full ahead, sending Florrie toppling off her seat.

"Slow down, girl!" Mag shouted. "You want to burn her out before she gets broke in?"

Reluctantly, Jen eased back on the throttle, but not by much. The wind whipped her long hair into Mag's face, and she brushed it aside, then clamped her hat tight against her head. She knew the joy of the power the girl was feeling, and they laughed together as the boat sped across the bay.

A week later as Jen walked toward the schoolyard, she spotted Calvin Saari lounging near the totem pole with two of his buddies. She ducked behind a tall girl from grade six, hoping she wouldn't be noticed

"Watch out!" Cal shouted. "Stinky Jenny's back!"

Some of the younger children playing nearby shrieked and pretended to run away from her. "Stinky Jenny! Stinky Jenny!" they chanted.

Jen marched toward the main building as if she had far more important things on her mind than silly children. In the office, a stressed out secretary directed her to the grade two classroom. She squared her shoulders as she approached the door.

A blond lady with blue eyes and a kind smile stood near the blackboard. She wore a crisp white blouse and a flowery skirt and Jen thought she had to be the most beautiful person in the world. "You must be Jen Larson," she said when Jen hesitated in the doorway. "I'm your teacher, Miss Beck." Jen drew closer, clutching the straps of her pack. "They tell me you travel to school by boat."

Jen nodded silently, slipped off her pack and turned toward the desks. Most held a sweater or a cap or a notebook to show that they were already claimed. A few were occupied by students colouring pictures.

"Why don't you sit up here by my desk?" Miss Beck suggested. She showed Jen where to put her supplies, on a shelf under the windows. With some reluctance, Jen pulled a pile of used notebooks from her pack and placed them beside the stack of shiny new ones belonging to the other children.

"Mag says there's still lots of good pages left in these," she said defensively.

Miss Beck smiled. "She's right, Jen. But it's nice to have new ones to start the year, isn't it?"

Jen nodded.

"Well, I have an idea how we can make those old books into new ones," said her teacher. "You come see me at lunchtime and we'll work on it together. In the meantime, while we're waiting for the bell to ring, how would you like to colour this picture of Benny Bear's first day at school?"

True to her word, at lunchtime Miss Beck brought out a stapler, scissors, and a stack of stiff paper with flowered patterns. "I got these wallpaper samples from the hardware store," she said, as she removed the used pages from Jen's notebooks, wrapped the remaining sheets with the flowered paper, and stapled them in place. "Now you've got the prettiest notebooks in class."

Overwhelmed, Jen took one of the books in her hand. "I'll take good care of 'em," she promised.

"I know you will, Jen. And we'll fill them with all sorts of wonderful things this year. Just you wait."

It didn't take long for Jen to discover that Miss Beck's classroom was a safe place to be, and back at Serpent Cove, she raved about the new teacher. "She's pretty, Florrie! An' she smells just like roses. An' she has lots of nice things. She's even got a glass castle on her desk!"

"What fer?" Florrie asked dourly. The way the girl talked, it seemed as though Florrie and Mag didn't matter anymore. She was also fed up with washing Jen's school outfits every other day.

"Sandra Cooper told Cal Miss Beck has a boyfriend. That's what her mom says. He's the one who gave her the castle. Miss Beck says no one is to touch it." Jen shook her finger. "Look, but don't touch!" she mimicked sternly.

Even Mag was annoyed with Jen. In her eagerness to leave each morning, the girl was rushing through her chores. "We gotta milk befer we kin go," she said one morning when Jen pressed her to leave earlier than usual.

Jen followed her outside. "Maybe Florrie could milk this one time, Mag. Miss Beck says it's my turn to read first this morning, before anybody else!"

"Florrie don't milk 'em dry," Mag said. When they reached the goat shed, she handed Jen the second bucket. Four goats stood patiently inside, knowing that as soon as they were milked they'd be allowed to go out. Mag positioned her container under the nanny furthest from the door. "An' this time don't run off befer yer done," she grumbled. "Them nannies you milked was still half full when I got back yesterday. They get terrible mean when I have to milk them all over again."

Resigned, Jen knelt beside Cob, grabbed her teats, and squeezed the warm milk into her bucket.

"I don't know why anybody thinks goats stink, Cob," she mused, breathing in the honey-sweet aroma from nanny's hide. "You smell just wonderful."

When she finished with Cob, Jen took her bucket over to White Foot. She was glad Mag was milking Granny, who was older and cranky and sometimes liked to kick.

"Mind yer manners," Mag growled when the goat lifted her leg, "or you'll find yerself in the stewpot."

Jen sent a silent plea to Granny not to kick.

The inlet was rough when they headed out, and Mag was still breaking in the new motor, so they took longer than usual to reach town. As soon as they reached the dock, the girl jumped out and ran toward the ramp, forgetting to help secure the ropes. "See you!" she called over her shoulder. Mag shook her head. "Girl don't know her own mind," she muttered, grabbing the edge of the wharf as the boat started to drift away. "First she don't want to go to school, then she do." She fastened the mooring lines and lifted her gas cans onto the wharf. She had planned to get Jen to help her carry them to the gas station. "She's getting more like Florrie every day."

The last bell had already rung when Jen arrived at school. She went to the office for her late slip and meekly entered the classroom. Miss Beck frowned. "Is everything all right, Jen?"

"We just had to milk the goats, an' it was real rough coming in," she said, then hurried to her desk.

The other children tittered. Cal, who was seated in the desk across from her, sniffed loudly.

"That's enough," Miss Beck told them sharply. "We're working on our printing books this morning, Jen."

Jen stared at her. "But you said . . ."

"We'll be reading this afternoon," Miss Beck said crisply.

Swallowing her disappointment, Jen collected her printing book and opened it to the page she'd been working on the previous day. As she bent over the white sheet of paper, her head itched. When she reached up to scratch it, a bug fell onto the page. She covered it with her hand, but not before Cal had seen.

"Jen's got bugs!" he shouted.

Jen's cheeks burned. Sandra Cooper, who sat directly behind her, jumped from her seat.

"Sit down, Sandra," Miss Beck commanded. "And Calvin, quit shouting."

"Jen's got bugs!" Sandra shrieked. She refused to go back to her chair. The other children gathered around, peering at Jen's hand but keeping a safe distance from her.

Miss Beck gingerly touched Jen's shoulder. "Let me see, Jen."

Slowly, Jen lifted her hand to reveal a small brown louse. She heard Miss Beck's quick intake of breath. "It's from the goats," Jen said. "It won't hurt nothin'."

Miss Beck swallowed hard. "Maybe not, Jen, but we'd better check it out." She tore a small piece of paper from a stack on her desk and wrapped it around the louse, crushing it with her fingers.

"The public health nurse is here today. You take this to the office and tell them I asked you to show it to her. All right?"

Jen nodded and slowly got out of her seat. She didn't look at any of her classmates as she walked to the door.

When Mag returned to the boat just before noon, the tide was out, steepening the ramp to the wharf. She had to concentrate hard to keep her balance as she carried the two full gas cans down the incline, so it wasn't until she'd almost reached the boat that she saw Jen sitting disconsolately in the passenger seat. The girl didn't look up or offer to help—just stared straight ahead. Mag hoisted the cans into the boat.

"How come yer not in school?"

"I'm quitting," Jen said defiantly. "I'm never going back, and you and Florrie can't make me!"

Mag took off her hat and scratched her head. "Yer was shooer wanting to go this morning."

Jen scowled, still refusing to look at her.

Mag shrugged and busied herself untying the mooring lines. As she steered away from the dock, she said offhandedly, "Yer gonna make Florrie terrible mad."

Jen stuck her chin out. "I'm not goin' back."

Nothing Florrie said would move Jen. The next morning she refused to get out of bed. "I'm sick," she mumbled. "I got a bellyache in my stomach."

Florrie nursed her for two days and coaxed her for a third. On Friday, she decided Jen might as well wait to go back to school until Monday. When the new week started and Jen still refused to leave the cove, Florrie got mad. "There's nutting wrong with you, Jen! You get outta that bed and get ready fer school. Mag's already done yer milking."

Jen turned her face to the wall.

Florrie rounded furiously on Mag. "Do somet'ing, Mag! She can't joost stay home!"

Mag shrugged indifferently. "Girl's decided she's gonna be a scaredy-britches. I don't t'ink she's gonna change her mind about that." She thought about the jobs she had planned for the day, and her eyes brightened. "I kin use her help picking mushrooms."

Jen rolled over. "I ain't no scaredy-chicken."

Mag ignored the child. "Gosh, up 'til now I always t'ought she had more guts than a cougar-cat."

Jen clenched her fists and sat up. "What do you know about it?" she yelled. "You're so stupid you don't even know they call you Mag the Hag!" As soon as the words were out, Jen wished she could suck them back into her mouth.

Mag gazed at her silently, then picked up her hat and headed for the door. She paused before stepping outside. "I know," she said coldly. "I joost don't let it scare me off."

When the door closed behind her, the kitchen was silent except for the crackle of wood burning in the stove. Florrie turned to the counter and busied herself with the morning dishes.

"It's Miss Beck," Jen said finally in a small voice. "She doesn't like me no more. She saw I had a bug in my hair. The nurse said it was just from the goats an' it wouldn't hurt nothing, but Miss Beck was scared."

Florrie studied the bowl she was washing. She had wanted to see Miss Beck toppled from the pedestal Jen had created for her, but she didn't like to see the girl hurting. "If she liked you fer shooer," she said finally, "I don't t'ink a goat bug's gonna make her stop."

"But what if she starts letting the kids call me names again, Florrie? Like last year?"

"Then you shut yer ears so you don't hear 'em, Jen. Like me and Mag done."

Jen lay back against her pillow and closed her eyes. "I ain't a scaredy-chicken," she muttered, turning on her side.

"Joost one way yer gonna make Mag believe that," Florrie said calmly.

Jen stared at the ceiling. Slowly she got out of bed and pulled on her school clothes. Florrie handed her a sandwich wrapped in waxed paper. "I'll make some cookies today," she promised.

Jen nodded. When she got to the dock, Mag was waiting in the boat.

At first it seemed as though nothing had changed at school. When Jen walked into the classroom Miss Beck smiled at her.

"We've missed you, Jen," she said, ignoring the snickering from the other children. "I hope you've recovered from your illness." She called the class to order and, after checking the attendance, opened the day's lessons with a sharing of experiences from the weekend. When show-and-tell was over, she announced read-aloud time. Jen's heart quickened as she collected her reader from her box of supplies. Miss Beck smiled benevolently at her charges. "This morning Sandra is going to start our reading, class. She has been practicing all weekend on her chapter."

Jen stared unbelieving at her teacher whose whole attention was focused on Sandra Cooper. "But Miss Beck . . ."

"Shhh!" Miss Beck said sternly, frowning at Jen. "It's Sandra's turn."

Sandra's dry, monotonous reading was followed by equally monotonous Robert, and finally by LeAnn Joe, who spoke so quietly Jen could barely hear her. Then the recess bell rang. While the rest of the class rushed out to the playground, Jen lingered at her desk.

"Would you like me to clean the brushes, Miss Beck?"

Her teacher looked up from the papers she was marking. She seemed surprised that Jen was there. "That's the monitor's job, Jen," she said crisply, even though she had frequently asked Jen to perform the chore in the past. "Besides, I have a meeting in three minutes. You'll have to go outside with the other children today." She hesitated a moment, then added, "I think it would probably be a good idea for you to spend all of your recesses and lunchtime with the other children, Jen. It's not healthy to be alone so much. You need to get out and make friends." She pushed her papers aside and got to her feet.

Jen looked at her solemnly. There had been no friendliness in

Miss Beck's voice, no evidence of special concern. "Can I still go to the library?"

"That's up to Miss Paul. But you should think about what I said." She went to the door and held it open. As Jen walked past her, Miss Beck stepped aside hastily. "Hiding in the library isn't going to help you make friends."

Outside, Jen stood in a corner where she could watch the other children without being too visible. Matt Duncan ran past, dribbling a basketball.

"Hey, Jen," he called over his shoulder.

"Hey, Matt," she returned, feeling suddenly better. *Maybe Miss Beck was right*, she thought. Emboldened, she walked over to the swings. There was one empty and she was just about to sit down when Cal darted toward her. He had a large black beetle in his hand.

"Want some more bugs, Stinky Jenny?" he taunted. The children around her laughed and began searching the ground for more bugs.

"Shit," Jen muttered, turning away from the swings and running for the library, chased by a group of children pretending to have bugs in their hands. "Shit, shit, shitah!"

Mag returned to town late that afternoon with two buckets of mushrooms. Reluctantly, Jen went with her to sell them. Mag was always in a bad mood after dealing with Pete Saari. Today was no exception.

"He's a terrible man, always stealing t'ings from people," she raged as she stomped down the ramp to her boat. "Some day I'm gonna call the cops on him." She was in the boat, ready to go, before she realized Jen wasn't with her. The girl was standing beside Pete Saari's speedboat. It was dented and scratched, the canvas top torn and ragged, but it was the faded blue paint on the forward deck that had caught Jen's attention.

"Yer planning to stand there all day?" Mag demanded.

"That's where we threw them eggs!" Jen exclaimed, pointing to the stain. For the first time that day she smiled.

The next morning, Miss Beck addressed the grade two class. Her expression was severe.

"Children," she said coldly, "someone has borrowed the crystal castle without my permission." She surveyed each child in the room before continuing. "I would like that person to return it to me before the end of this lesson. If so, there will be no punishment, but we will talk about the importance of asking before we take things." She paused to give the perpetrator a chance to come forward. When no one did, she went on to outline the arithmetic lesson she had prepared. The children worked quietly. Every once in a while they glanced nervously at each other, but no one stood or went to the teacher's desk. When the bell rang for recess, Miss Beck tried a different tactic.

"Today, before going for our break, we are going to do some housekeeping." She ignored the indignant grumbles from the most vocal students. "We'll start by having everyone empty their desks."

Jen clenched her right hand around a wad of tissue paper as she stacked her notebooks and pencil box on the desk. Miss Beck watched her closely, then knelt and looked inside the compartment. It was empty. She straightened. "Let me see your pencil box, Jen," she said sternly, but before Jen could hand it over, several students called out, "Look, Miss Beck! Cal's got your castle!"

"An' it's broken."

The teacher turned. Cal glowered at the shattered crystal he'd pulled from his desk. "I never stole it!" he said hotly. "And I sure's hell never broke it!"

"That's enough, Cal," Miss Beck said coldly. "We'll talk about it in a moment. The rest of you children can put your things back neatly now and go outside."

"But I never took it!" Cal shouted. He was still shouting when Jen left the classroom.

Outside, away from prying eyes, Jen opened her fist, relieved to find the cut on her palm was no longer bleeding. *Now we're even.*

On the second Monday in October, as the Sangstercraft sped down Porpoise Bay, Mag pointed toward Sylvia's cottage. A thin line of smoke was curling from the chimney. "Renters left a while back," she observed. "Must be Sylvia's come home." She grinned. Sylvia would be buying eggs and goat's milk again. More importantly, Mag wouldn't have to be making the trip to town every day.

Jen bounced excitedly on her seat. "Let's go see her!" she cried, but Mag kept the boat headed toward the government wharf. "Please, Mag! Can't we go see her?"

"She'll be there after school."

"But what if she's not? What if she's forgot about me?"

"Oh, I don't t'ink so. She sent you that picture, didn't she?" Mag guided the Sangster to the edge of the float, grabbed the bull rail, but didn't moor the boat. "I gotta haul that wood that washed up on Anchor Beach before Billy Thom grabs it," she said. "So I joost might be late coming fer you."

Jen climbed out of the boat. She knew there was no stopping Mag when she was on the trail of something free.

The cottage living room was cluttered with boxes and suitcases. Jen stood breathlessly in the doorway, having run all the way up the hill.

"You've grown," Sylvia said approvingly. When Mag arrived a moment later, she led the way to the table where tea was set out.

"I haven't even had time to unpack," Sylvia said. She poured Jen a glass of milk and motioned to a plate of graham wafers. "The renters left the place absolutely filthy. I've spent the whole day scrubbing."

Mag surveyed the kitchen. Dishes were stacked on the counters and the floor was littered with used cupboard liners. "Looks okay to me," she observed.

"The cupboards are a mess, and I still have to defrost the fridge." She looked at Jen. "Did you get my postcard with the picture of the donkey?"

Jen nodded, overcome with shyness. Sylvia wasn't at all like the woman who had left for Turkey last May. Outwardly, except for her newly tanned and weathered arms and face, she seemed the same, her dark brown hair hanging straight to her shoulders, her shirt and slacks stylish but practical. But an excitement surrounded her, as if she had just discovered some great secret.

Sylvia smiled. "There's a box for you on the coffee table," she said. Jen stared at her, then ran into the living room.

"Yer shouldn't spoil her," Mag admonished. She helped herself to a handful of cookies. "Makes her start wanting t'ings she can't have."

Sylvia was unperturbed. "How is she making out at school this term?"

Mag laughed. "She was doing joost fine 'til last week. Come home and said she'd had enough of school. Even Florrie couldn't make her go."

Jen ran into the kitchen with the box. She set it on the table in front of Sylvia. "Is this the one?"

But Sylvia was staring at her. "Why wouldn't you go to school, Jen?"

The girl's face burned. She tried desperately to think of a better reason than the goat louse.

"Ah, she got a goat bug in her hair," Mag said, unaware of the mortification on Jen's face. "I guess it come out at school an' the kids laughed about it."

Jen's embarrassment changed to fury. "You didn't have to blab it all over!" she yelled. "I hate you!" Before Mag could stop her, Jen had run out of the house.

Mag stared at the door Jen had slammed on her way out. "What the hell's got into her?"

"She seems to have become very sensitive. I hope you haven't been working her too hard. . . ."

Mag's eyes narrowed. "Girl does chores, same as me and Florrie done," she said coldly.

She pushed away from the table, wincing as the movement sent pain shooting into her hip.

"Oh, goodness, I forgot about your leg," Sylvia said. "How is it doing?"

"Getting better." Mag grabbed her pack from the floor, then

hesitated. If she left the girl with Sylvia, Florrie would be unbearable. "I'll joost have to go find her," she muttered.

"Maybe she took the trail into the bush," Sylvia suggested. "She did that last winter whenever she was upset." Mag limped outside. From the walkway, Sylvia pointed out the trail. "I'd go with you, but I've got to get this place back together."

Mag had to pick her way carefully. She was not as sure-footed as she had been before the accident, and salmonberry bushes and fallen branches littered the pathway. Once, she stumbled and almost fell. She swore loudly when a branch whipped back across her cheek, and by the time she discovered Jen she was in a foul mood. The girl was lying under a cedar tree, her face next to the dead leaves that littered the ground. She sat up at Mag's approach.

"What you bugger off fer?" Mag demanded.

Tears streaked the dirt on Jen's cheeks. She swiped at her eyes and nose with her shirt sleeve. "You told her about the bug!"

Mag took off her hat and wiped her brow with her sleeve. "That don't mean you had to take off. I could've broke my leg again chasing after you." Relieved that the girl wasn't hurt, she started back to the cottage. She stopped when she realized Jen wasn't following her. "You coming?"

Jen's shoulders slumped. She stared unhappily at her lap. "She won't let me stay no more."

Mag's expression grew perplexed. The girl looked like she was going to start crying once more, and Mag hated crying. She scratched the hat line on her forehead, then wiped her brow again. Finally she said, "She wants you to come tomorrow."

Jen eyed her suspiciously.

"After school. Joost like befer."

"When did she say it?"

"After you run off," Mag said irritably. "What the hell does it matter, anyways?"

"You sure she said it after?"

"After what?"

"After you told her about the bug!"

"Already said that, didn't I?" Mag waved her hand disgustedly. "Shitah." She started along the trail again. Jen scrambled to her feet and hurried after her.

"She really wants me to come tomorrow?"

Mag didn't bother answering. She was already thinking about the work she could get done, now that she didn't have to go to town every morning. Sylvia came out on the porch as they trooped past the cottage. "See you tomorrow, Jen," she said.

Jen stopped and looked closely at Sylvia's expression before she shouted back, "See you tomorrow." With a wave, she ran after Mag. It wasn't until she reached the dock that Jen remembered the present.

"You kin get it tomorrow," Mag said. She started the motor, leaving Jen no choice but to release the mooring lines and jump into the boat.

The next morning, Jen milked her two goats, fed the rabbits and chickens, and was ready to leave for school long before Mag finished milking Granny. "You'll be needing these," Florrie said gloomily, handing her a black plastic bag filled with clothes. The two sisters had argued long into the night about Jen's return to Sylvia's, but Mag was adamant. "You want her to stay here, you kin take her to school every day," she had said finally. Knowing she was trapped, Florrie fell silent.

Mag set her milk bucket on the kitchen table. "We gotta go," she said.

Florrie sniffed loudly. "Gosh, I shooer don't see why you can't run her to school when the weather's being so good."

Jen wrapped her arms around Florrie's waist. "I'll be back every weekend, Florrie. An' I'll bring lots of new books from the library."

For a moment Florrie's face brightened, but as she watched Jen scamper down the path to the wharf, her eyes filled with fresh tears.

Order had been restored in the cottage by the time Jen arrived after school. The usual plate of cookies and glass of milk waited on the table, but there was no evidence of the present. Sylvia seemed to have forgotten it. She asked about school and gave a nod of approval when Jen told her she had received an A on her spelling test. The child squirmed with impatience, but it wasn't until Jen had eaten the last cookie that Sylvia changed the subject.

"Now," she said, when Jen had eaten the last cookie, "how about sorting through that bag of clothes Mag dropped off?" Jen felt a warm sense of belonging as she went to her room. It was just as she'd left it. The soft-blue papered walls made it seem like she was surrounded by sky. The hardwood floor gleamed with polish, and the Berber rug near her bed looked as inviting as ever. A yellow night table rested beside it, and a matching yellow dresser with a large mirror stood against the opposite wall. The bed was covered with a bright green and yellow flowered spread, on which rested a long, rectangular box.

Sylvia stood in the doorway while Jen untied the string and slowly lifted the lid.

"Shitah!" she gasped. A porcelain doll nestled in a bed of tissue paper. She had dark skin and long-lashed brown eyes, and she wore a costume of brightly coloured cotton, intricately woven in a mixture of geometric designs. Gingerly, Jen touched the face and the costume, then carefully lifted the doll from the box. "She's beautiful!" she breathed.

A relieved smile touched Sylvia's lips. "She's dressed in the traditional costume of a Turkish peasant woman. I've brought you a book that tells all about her." Her voice held the air of excitement Jen had noticed before. "When I go back next year, I'll bring you another one."

Jen's stomach tightened. "Go back?"

"Yes. Paul . . . Doctor Simmons . . . said I was so helpful he wants me to come back and work with him again next summer."

Jen returned the doll to the box, suddenly hating it. "I gotta put these things away." She turned her back on the gift and began pulling clothes out of the black plastic bag.

That night after supper, Sylvia showed Jen the mountain of photographs she'd taken, most of them pictures of glass and pottery.

She described how they had found the fragments under layers of soil and pieced them together like a puzzle to form a vase or a perfume flask. But everything Sylvia said seemed to include Doctor Simmons' name.

"This is my favourite." She pointed to a broken vase. "Paul and I found it in a section that wasn't actually part of our dig. It dates back to pre-Roman times."

Jen studied the dusty-looking fragments in the picture. "Humph," she sniffed, the way Mag did when she didn't think much of something. "Looks like it come from the dump."

Sylvia laughed. "Well, maybe it was their dump, but it's thousands of years old, Jen, and that makes it very valuable. These artifacts help us to understand how people used to live and how we came to be the way we are."

"Are you gonna marry him?" Jen asked irritably.

Sylvia looked startled. "Who?"

"That doctor guy."

"Paul?"

Jen nodded and Sylvia laughed, but there was an edge to her amusement. A fleeting sadness crossed her face. "Of course not," she said briskly. "Doctor Simmons is already married." She gathered the remaining photographs and put them in a pile. "Time for bed, my dear."

While Jen got into her pyjamas, Sylvia turned down the covers of her bed. It wasn't something she usually did.

"I'm going to write a book, Jen," she said suddenly.

"A story?" Jen asked.

Sylvia laughed. "Well, sort of. It's a story about glass, but first Dr. Simmons thinks I should take some archaeology courses." She tucked the quilt around Jen. "So I'll be going to Vancouver for classes this winter. . . ."

Jen frowned.

"But Agnes Greystone said she'll take care of you after school 'til I get home."

"I hate her!" Jen protested. A retired schoolteacher and a widow,

Agnes lived in the cedar panabode next door. She had no patience with children, and she had been upset when Sylvia took Jen in. Coming upon them in the kitchen one afternoon, Jen had heard Agnes scolding Sylvia. "Those two old biddies will rob you blind," she had predicted. "And the girl is just like them. Cut your throat in the night, she will."

"I've never known either Mag or Florrie to steal," Sylvia had responded tartly. "I'd say they're a lot more honest than certain people who slip their garbage into their neighbour's bins."

Agnes's cheeks had grown very red and a moment later she had found an excuse to leave. Jen hadn't seen the old woman again until shortly after the new year when Sylvia had to spend a day in the city and arranged for Jen to stay with her until she got home. Although Agnes gave Jen cookies and milk, just as Sylvia did, Jen could feel the old lady watching her the whole time she was there, waiting for her to take something.

Sylvia smiled reassuringly. "Agnes is just a very lonely person." She straightened up. "When spring comes and I go away again, you'll go back to Mag and Florrie like you did this year."

"Mag's mean," Jen said crossly.

"She took you in," Sylvia reminded her, "and she's looked after you better than most people would have done."

"She kilt Mr. T."

"Who is Mr. T.?"

"Our billy. He was my friend an' Mag shot him."

"Oh." Sylvia patted Jen's hand. "It probably looked as if Mag was being mean, Jen, but she generally has a good reason for what she does. Now you go to sleep so you can get up early and do your homework. We forgot about that tonight."

Sylvia switched off the light and left the room, closing the door behind her. For a long time Jen lay in the dark feeling alone and strangely sad. She had been so excited about coming back. Now she wished she was at the cove where she could climb into bed with Florrie.

CHAPTER EIGHT

One Friday morning on their way to Sechelt, the spring that Jen turned twelve, she and Mag saw the *Squawk Box* headed up the inlet, passing close enough so they could see Billy Thom at the wheel, and his cousin Louis John on the deck sharpening a hatchet. ·

Mag scowled. "Them buggers are going to get shitty bark."

"It's *cascara* bark," Jen corrected primly.

Mag turned to stare at her. Although still thin, she was showing early signs of womanhood. She had taken to having her hair cut in a short, wedged fashion and wearing the kind of lacy blouses Sylvia wore. To Mag's chagrin, she had also taken to using Sylvia's opinion as a yardstick to measure everything else, including cascara.

"Sylvia says it's used as a laxative."

"Oh, shooer," Mag agreed, remembering the day Jen had eaten cascara berries. "That's why they call it shitty bark."

Jen rolled her eyes and turned her attention back to the fish packer. Its decks were piled haphazardly with a collection of scrap metal, outboard motor skeletons, crab and prawn traps, and anything else Billy had salvaged on his trips up and down the inlets. "What makes you think they're looking for cascara?"

"Only two t'ings bring Louis out. One t'ing is that Indian stuff he's always hunting fer, and the other t'ing is shitty bark, and there's shooer no Indian stuff around here." Mag didn't like to be gone from the cove when Louis was around. He knew the location of every cascara tree on the inlet and he wasn't averse to taking bark from areas that Mag considered her territory. Especially if she wasn't there. "Shitah," she swore and started to turn the boat.

"What are you doing?" Jen demanded.

"Going back."

"You can't!" Jen cried. "I have a test today! I've got to be in school by nine o'clock."

"You kin do that next week," Mag reasoned. She gripped the

wheel to steady herself as they bounced over the Sangstercraft's own wake.

"I can't take it Monday, Mag! I gotta take it today! I've studied and everything." When Mag showed no sign of relenting, Jen grew desperate. "If I don't go, I won't be able to mend Mr. Duncan's crab trap nets and I won't get the twenty bucks he was gonna pay me."

Mag slowed the motor. She weighed the twenty bucks against the amount she figured to make from the cascara bark. "You kin fix 'em another day," she decided, pushing the throttle forward again. Moments later, they passed the *Squawk Box*. Billy Thom waved from the wheelhouse, but Mag didn't acknowledge him.

"Florrie's gonna be pissed," Jen warned sullenly. Mag merely grunted. Keeping Louis John away from her cascara was more important than Florrie's mood. When they reached the dock, Mag instructed the girl to watch for Billy's boat while she collected some lunch and tools.

Florrie was at the table pummelling bread dough. She looked up in surprise when Mag entered. "You break down?"

Mag rummaged through the shelves by the door. "That Louis John is out looking fer shitty bark." She extracted a broken chisel from a box of outboard motor parts. One end of the tool was wrapped with grimy adhesive tape, the other had been sharpened into a blade. She collected her whetstone from the counter, poured a cup full of coffee, and sat down at the table. Her cup trembled as Florrie pounded the bread dough.

"And joost how is Jen gonna get to school?"

"Girl's having a day off, I guess." Mag concentrated on the chisel blade she was sharpening against the whetstone.

Florrie wiped her forehead with the back of her hand, leaving a white streak of flour behind. "I t'ink she had a test or somet'ing. It was real important." When Mag didn't respond, Florrie pounded the dough with renewed vigour. "You should take her to town."

Mag held the chisel up to the light. Satisfied that the blade was sharp enough, she put the whetstone away. "That's a pretty good idea. I kin take her to town and you kin help me with the shitty bark."

Florrie glared at her. "You know I gotta watch this bread."

"Is that so?" Mag met her gaze. "Then I guess you shouldn't pester me about the girl."

"Yer the one said I should make bread!" Florrie dropped the mound of dough into the bowl. "Yer the one won't eat store-bought stuff."

"Humph." Mag stuffed the chisel into her pack. "Guess you kin make us a lunch."

After a trip to the shed, to find the sacks she would need to hold the bark, Mag grabbed the bag of sandwiches Florrie had made. She called to Jen before starting along the trail past the creek. The girl caught up to her a few minutes later.

"Billy went right on by," Jen said, her voice hostile. She had stopped long enough at the cabin to change into an old pair of jeans and a work shirt. "Probably wasn't even looking for cascara."

"Oh, he's looking," Mag said. "Billy's got that truck at Sechelt Creek. He'll be coming in the back way." The roads from an abandoned logging camp at Sechelt Creek, three miles northeast of Serpent Cove, extended almost to the far end of Mag's trapline. From there it wouldn't be much of a hike for Billy and Louis to reach her cascara grove. "They'll come in right by them shitty bark trees we cut last year." Mag smiled triumphantly. "By the time they get to the new ones, we'll have 'em stripped."

Mag and Jen followed the trapline route until they came to a less worn secondary trail that wound into a small canyon. A clump of cascara trees grew along the lower side of the ravine. Many years earlier, Mag had chopped down the main tree and harvested the bark, but shoots had grown around the stump, and every few years the new growth reached a size that she could harvest. After waiting for this particular crop to mature for three years, she was damned if Louis John or anyone else was going to steal it from her.

Storing her pack under a gnarled fir tree, she used the chisel to cut into the bark. She pried out strips that were roughly twelve inches long and two to three inches wide, but left a narrow strip of bark running up the tree to keep it alive. As the strips fell away,

Jen stowed them into one of the gunny sacks. She worked silently, answering Mag in monosyllables, still angry about missing school. When Mag grew tired, they switched jobs. She watched approvingly as the girl cut into the bark with swift, sure strokes. By early afternoon they had almost worked their way out of the canyon, and the first gunny sack was bulging with bark. Only then did Mag allow a lunch break, settling herself on the moss beneath a large cedar.

"Gosh, I'm so hungry even Florrie's bread tastes good," she said, chewing one of the goat cheese sandwiches her sister had made. Jen wasn't particularly fond of the bread, which was always heavy and often burned on the bottom, but she was in no mood to agree with Mag.

"It's better than the bread you make," she snapped, biting into the crust that she usually discarded. She washed it down with water from the quart sealer Mag had packed.

Mag grinned. "Shooer is hard to swallow."

"I'm just thirsty." To prove her point, Jen took several more bites and didn't touch the water. On the last mouthful she began to hiccup.

Mag chewed contentedly on her own sandwich. "Florrie's bread'll do that."

After they had rested, Jen hoisted the sack of bark onto her shoulder while Mag carried the chisel and extra bags. They hiked up the canyon and back along the trapline trail until they reached a stretch of bottomland and another clump of cascara. By the time they quit for the day, they had filled both sacks. Jen was exhausted when they returned to the cabin, but Mag was feeling too victorious to be tired.

"Got two sacks full," she gloated as she spread the bark out to dry on the cabin floor. "Should get another one tomorrow from them clumps above the beach."

Although she hadn't forgiven Mag for keeping her from school, Jen was in high spirits Saturday morning as she led the way along the beach, skirting the mud flats, then crossing a gravelly stretch of shoreline. The sun was shining, and the light breeze drifting in from the water was scented with an intoxicating mixture of salt, seaweed, and warm earth.

Mag hadn't slept well, kept awake by cramps in her hands that no amount of liniment would ease. This morning her fists and fingers were swollen and uncooperative. "You don't have to run," she snapped.

Jen paused at the foot of a trail overgrown with brush that snaked from the shore up a steep hillside. "I thought you wanted to beat Billy and Louis to your patch."

Mag adjusted her pack, wincing from the pain the movement caused in her fingers. "Joost so long as he sees me working it, he won't go there."

Jen plunged into the brush, breaking branches as she went, to clear a bit of a path for Mag. Fortunately, it didn't take as long to reach this cascara grove as it had the day before, but the bark here was more difficult to harvest. The trees were anchored on a steep bank, which meant Jen had to brace herself with one leg on the hill and one on the sapling she was cutting. Her bracing leg was soon aching, but when Mag offered to take a turn at cutting, Jen shook her head. "It's fun," she lied. For once, Mag didn't argue.

By midday, they had cleaned out the patch and were on their way back to the beach.

"I guess it's time to start digging the garden," Mag observed as they walked in the sun along the gravel shore.

Jen was looking out at the water. "Isn't that the *Squawk Box*?"

Mag paused to inspect the boat which was just rounding Thornhill Point to their right. As it edged past the cove, the boat slowed. Billy came out on deck, lifted his hand and waved, then disappeared back into the wheelhouse. As the boat picked up speed they saw a stouter figure near the stern. He was leaning over several large sacks which he seemed to be securing to the cover of the hold. Mag's eyes narrowed. "That bugger found another patch," she grumbled.

"We got lots," Jen said, slightly bent under the weight of the bark she carried on her back. "Way more than last year."

119

"Oh, shooer. Joost remember that when yer wanting school stuff that there's no money fer."

They reached the mud flats and, from habit, Mag surveyed the beach for logs. She often found one there after the tide retreated. Today there were none, but Jen pointed to a bright red object, half-hidden by a snowberry bush. "What's that?" she asked.

"Plastic stuff them hippies tossed overboard," Mag said. "We kin take the boat and check it out when the tide comes in."

"No way. I'm checkin' it out now!" Jen dropped her sack of bark on the shore. While Mag continued along the upland trail, the girl picked her way across the mud, carefully avoiding the swampy spots where she could end up knee-deep in thick black mire.

"It's a canoe, Mag!" she called excitedly. Although one side of the wooden craft had been gouged by a rock or a log, it seemed sturdy enough to be worth fixing.

"I'm going back for it when the tide comes in," she said when she rejoined Mag on the path to the cabin.

"What good is a boat with a hole bashed in the side?"

"We can patch it," Jen said. "I seen you do it lots of times."

"I guess not. I got enough to do without fixing up a useless boat."

When the tide came in that afternoon, Jen motored over to the canoe in Mag's Sangster. With much twisting and turning and a lot more swearing, she managed to wrestle it free from the mud and towed it over to the dock where she turned it upside down. Curiosity brought Mag and Florrie down to inspect her prize.

"Guess it kin be fixed," Mag allowed, examining the hole. "I t'ink I got some cold cure up in the shed."

Jen grinned. "I could paddle all over the inlet with this!"

Florrie fingered the wood around the hole. "Yer not old enough to be out on yer own."

"We was younger than her when we got a canoe," Mag said. "Remember? That Indian guy traded it to us fer them shake blocks we stole from our dad."

"It was you and me cut them shakes, anyways," Florrie retorted.

Mag chuckled. "Our dad t'ought Erik Saari took 'em."

The next morning, Mag and Jen searched through the shed until they found some fibreglass and cold cure epoxy left over from patching the power boat. Mag showed Jen how to sand the old finish from around the hole on the inside of the canoe, then soak the fibreglass in resin and lay it over the hole. On the outside they used more epoxy to glue the bits of wood back into place, like pieces of a jigsaw puzzle. "Take a day to dry," Mag said. "After that we kin sand 'er down and do another coat."

On Monday it was Jen who wanted to miss school to work on her boat. Only after Florrie threatened to take a hatchet to the canoe did she consent to go. Mag spent the day in town. In the morning, she collected a buck rabbit that was advertised for free in the paper. Since it had been there for the last three editions, she figured it was somebody's pet and they were probably desperate to find a new home for it.

"It's my son's rabbit," said the carefully coifed lady who answered the door. "He's gone off to university and I can't look after Felix because I travel a lot with my work." She led the way to the hutch that held a large black buck. "I promised my son I'd find him a good home."

"Oh, shooer," Mag said. "My old buck's getting terrible mean, but this guy don't look mean."

The lady looked at her sharply. "You wouldn't eat him, would you?"

"I guess not!" Mag chuckled. "My rabbits can't make no babies if I eat their bucks."

She still looked doubtful. "And you have a proper hutch for him?"

"Oh, shooer," Mag said then added slyly, "but maybe you could give me this one so he wouldn't have to get used to a new place."

"That's a good idea!" the lady said. She added proudly, "My Jesse built it himself."

"Only t'ing is, I'll need some way of getting it down to my boat."

The woman smiled. "That's no problem. I'll drive you."

Mag eyed her station wagon. Even with the rabbit hutch in it, the car would be big enough to hold a bale of hay and a bag of feed for the chickens.

By the time school was out, Mag was back at the dock with the hay, the feed, and the rabbit hutch ensconced safely on board the Sangstercraft. She felt smug as she readied her boat for the trip home. An hour later her smugness had turned to irritation. By the time Jen finally made it to the wharf, Mag was in a sour mood. "I got better t'ings to do than wait two hours fer you," she grumbled when Jen climbed aboard.

"It's your own fault," Jen retorted. She knelt down to inspect the rabbit. "I had to write the test I missed."

"Humph," Mag snorted, but she said no more as she thrust the throttle forward and headed for home.

After they had set up the new hutch, and cared for the rest of the rabbits and the goats and chickens, there was no time for Jen to do anything but eat and complete her homework. It was Saturday before she had another opportunity to finish repairing the canoe. On Sunday she tried it for the first time. Florrie refused to take part in the event.

"You want to kill yerself, you kin do it without me watching!" With a bowl of bread pudding laced with raisins and sugar, she settled into her rocking chair.

Mag had fashioned a paddle for the boat from a slab of cedar. She knelt on the wharf and held the canoe while Jen climbed inside, then gave the stern a shove that sent the craft skimming across the water.

"Joost stay close to the dock 'til you get used to it," Mag suggested.

"I'm used to it already," Jen shouted as she paddled out into the cove.

"Is that so?"

The girl hadn't looked toward the other side of the bay where a tug was hauling a barge from the logging camp at Clowhom. When its wake caught the canoe broadside, she fell sideways, causing the gunwale to dip beneath the surface. As water poured in, the canoe tilted even more, and Jen toppled into the bay. Mag laughed as the girl swam back, towing the boat. Sputtering and swearing, she climbed onto the dock.

"It's no damned good!" she sputtered.

"Take her out again," Mag said.

"But I'm cold . . ." Then she caught Mag's expression. Scowling, she climbed back into the canoe. This time she kept the craft upright as she paddled from one end of the cove to the other, then back to the dock. "Piece a' cake!" she gloated. She pulled the canoe onto the dock and turned it upside down.

Thereafter, every time Mag wanted Jen to do a chore, she would discover that the girl had disappeared in the canoe. "I never should'a fixed that t'ing," she grumbled.

Florrie was unsympathetic, but not wanting Mag to take her frustration out on the girl, she added, "You were shooer happy when she found that boomstick washed up in Misery Bay."

Mag thought about the forty dollars Gus Stevenson had paid her for hauling the boomstick back to his camp. *Florrie was right,* she decided. Still, as she forked soiled hay out of the goat's shed—a chore that Jen was supposed to take care of—she wondered if the money was worth it. What she didn't like to admit was that she missed the girl's company more than her help.

Surprisingly, the canoe made a positive difference in Florrie's life. She was already used to the girl being away from the house, either helping Mag or wandering through the bush. But now, to make up for the time she spent away in the canoe, Jen spent her evenings reading to Florrie from library books. Sometimes she made up her own stories, or repeated those that Sylvia had told of her travels. One tale was about a donkey ride Sylvia had taken along a mountain trail in Greece.

"She was so scared," Jen said, dramatizing the event much more than Sylvia had. "She was riding on the edge of this drop-off. Nothin' but air and rocks as far as she could see down. Then the donkey slipped, and Sylvia thought she was going over the side."

Florrie leaned forward. "Did she fall?"

Jen shook her head. "Nah. She said that donkey knew what it was doing."

"I had a donkey once," Mag said. She was sitting near the stove splicing loops onto the ends of a new mooring rope. "Gosh, he wouldn't do nothing I wanted. I t'ink he cost more to feed than all my goats." She paused to force the rope end between two braids. "Didn't taste so good neither."

One night, while doing the supper dishes, Jen told the sisters about some of the strange customs associated with living in town, such as the way Sylvia set the table for a formal dinner, using a snowy white table cloth and napkins, and five pieces of cutlery at every place.

"What's she want all them t'ings fer?" Mag asked.

Jen thought for a moment. "I'm not sure, but you have to have 'em."

"And you have to wash them?" Florrie asked, astonished. Jen hated doing dishes.

"Well, we don't eat like that always." Jen immersed a stack of plates in the dishpan. "And a lot of the stuff goes in the dishwasher." She swished a rag over one of the plates, lifted it out, and dried it with a towel Florrie had made from an old sheet. "But not the china cups or teapot. Sylvia says they're special."

"Our mother had a pot fer tea like Sylvia's got," Florrie said reminiscently. She ran her finger around the chipped rim of her coffee mug. "Our dad didn't want nutting to do with tea, so she didn't use it when he was home."

Mag looked up from the crab trap frame that she was covering with new netting. "I never seen Mother drink nutting but coffee."

"I guess not," Florrie retorted. "She knew you was joost like our dad."

Jen put the dish she'd dried onto a shelf beneath the counter. "What happened to the teapot?"

"Mag sold it after I was gone." Florrie said resentfully. "Like she did with all of Mother's nice t'ings."

"I shooer didn't want to," Mag said. "I liked them pretty t'ings too. But gosh, I couldn't work and I couldn't hunt because our dad was so sick. Only t'ing I could do was trade them t'ings to Billy Thom. That sack of feed he give me kept our goats from starving that time. And then he give me some of that big buck he shot up in Narrows."

Jen put the last plate on the shelf and dumped the soiled cutlery into the pan. "Sylvia says her mother never used nothing but the finest china. She always had to stop playing and dress up so they could have tea and some kind of cake or something. She says you an' Mag are lucky 'cause you don't have rules makin' you do things you don't like."

"I shooer liked that tea our mother made," Florrie said sadly.

Jen finished washing the last of the cutlery and emptied the dirty water into a slop bucket by the stove. "Maybe we can get some music tonight." She turned on the battery-powered radio Sylvia had given them one Christmas. Since Mag kept using the batteries for her flashlight, the radio often didn't work and, even when it did, the reception at the cove was inconsistent. Tonight, static filled the room until Jen found a station playing classical music. "Sylvia's got this on her tape machine," Jen said, but her companions weren't enthused.

"It don't have no words," Florrie complained.

"Find somet'ing that isn't so terrible noisy," Mag added. Jen twisted the dial until she found a country and western station that met with both sisters' approval.

In grade seven, Jen made friends with a girl whose family moved into a house down the street from Sylvia's cottage. Marlene Greaves was short and thin, with limp, straw-coloured hair and a nervousness that made her movements jerky.

"Girl acts like she's got a hornet in her britches," Mag said one day as she and Jen were carrying groceries down to the boat. They had come upon Marlene and her mother in the supermarket. The mother was in an advanced stage of pregnancy, and Marlene was carrying a year-old infant on her hip, while at the same time trying to keep track of a three-year-old who kept darting away from her.

"She's real scared of her dad," Jen explained, as she piled the groceries in the stern. "He won't let her do anything that's fun. Except read." They had met when they both signed up for library duty, and their love of reading had made them immediate friends.

"Marlene and I are going to be archaeologists like Sylvia," Jen told Florrie one night, "but we're gonna do our dig right here in Sechelt."

Mag looked up from the saw chain she was sharpening. "I got some fence post holes need digging. You kin help me with them."

"Not that kind of digging, Mag," Jen said hastily. "We're gonna dig for artifacts. Look . . ." She pulled a book from her backpack and laid it out in front of Florrie. "See these things?" She pointed to a picture of cobble core tools found near the Gulf of Georgia. "Sylvia says they're just like ones the Sechelt people used. There's lots and lots of 'em buried all over the place."

Florrie peered at the picture. "They look joost like rocks," she said doubtfully.

"If they're buried all over," Mag said slyly, "there's gotta be some where them fence posts is gonna go."

"And look at this." Jen turned the page to reveal a stone image of a crouched human form clutching something to its bosom. "It was found right in Sechelt. Sylvia says there used to be thousands and thousands of Indians here once."

Florrie turned the page and studied an array of stone points. "Mag, I t'ink you found one of these t'ings." She held up the book so that her sister could see.

Mag frowned. "I guess not."

"You give it to Billy Thom, anyways."

Mag was about to argue further, but she still had postholes on her mind. She nodded. "Oh, shooer. I found it out back when I was building the goat pen."

Jen eyed her suspiciously. "You found one of these out back? For sure?"

Mag shrugged. "Ask Billy. Or Louis John. He's the one that's got it now."

Florrie's expression had grown puzzled. "I t'ought you said yer found that rock up—" She caught Mag's look of warning and fell silent.

"How come you never said nothing before?" Jen challenged.

"Don't want nobody to come snooping around looking fer more," Mag said. "Billy says they'll tear yer whole place apart if you find any of them t'ings."

Jen went back to studying her book, but Mag could tell from the frown wrinkling her forehead that the girl was torn between curiosity and her reluctance to dig.

It wasn't until the next morning, however, that Mag discovered which had won the battle. She was pacing off the dimensions for the new goat pen, marking the spots for holes with pink survey tape from a roll she'd found last fall at Gus Stevenson's logging camp. Although it was early in the day, the mid-April sun had already reached the clearing, creating a mist as the moisture from the cool ground evaporated. Jen appeared through the fog like an apparition, dressed in a grey sweat shirt and pants, bent slightly from the weight of the pick and shovel she had hoisted on one shoulder.

"Where do you want the holes dug?" she asked.

Mag suppressed the grin tugging at the corners of her mouth. "Joost where I put them ribbons," she said. "When I'm done here, I'll give you a hand."

Jen eyed the half dozen ribbons Mag had already tied. "All those?"

"Oh, shooer. And about three more," Mag said cheerfully. "It'll take them goats a long time to eat their way outta this patch." Although unschooled in agricultural practices, Mag had adapted a primitive system of crop rotation by periodically building new pens for the goats and chickens, allowing their old pens to go back to wilderness. Unfortunately, by the time she got around to the next rotation, the old fence lines had disintegrated, obliging her to dig new holes and rescue the wire fencing from years of accumulated weed growth.

Jen attacked the first site with the pick, breaking up the salal and salmonberry roots and pulling them free. As the dirt was exposed, she knelt down with a stick to sift through the mixture of sand and rock. Except for a few stones that had been split by weather and erosion, nothing she saw looked anything like the pictures in her book or the artifacts Sylvia had shown her at the museum in the neighbouring town of Gibsons. Carefully, she sank the shovel into the soil, but it only went partway in before it was blocked by another stone. She knelt again.

Mag dropped a fence post beside the girl. "Be winter before you get them holes dug that way."

"I gotta look!" Jen insisted.

One by one, Mag distributed the remaining posts around the perimeter she'd marked out. When she finished, she was pleased to note that Jen had completed the first hole. While Mag positioned the post, Jen shovelled dirt around it, alternately stomping the surface down and adding more dirt until the pole could not be moved. "You really think there's Indian tools here?" she asked, pausing to catch her breath.

Mag removed her hat while she wiped her brow with her sleeve. "T'ought Sylvia told you they was all over?"

"Well, yeah . . . but maybe they're not all over right *here*."

"Hmmm." Mag thought for a moment, then replaced her hat. She nodded toward the head of the inlet. "What about them rock paintings up there?"

Jen followed her glance. She'd often stopped to stare at the rock paintings when she was out in her canoe. Little stick figures and a double-headed snake. "But they're not right *here*," she said.

"Well, you won't know fer shooer 'less you dig down and find out."

Jen sighed, shouldered the pick and trudged to the next site. *Maybe she could just write a book about archaeology*, she thought. Like Sylvia was doing. Somehow she couldn't imagine Sylvia all sweaty and grubby as she dug through layers of dirt.

It was the following weekend before they finished the fence, and that's when Jen found her artifact. Not in the post holes as she expected, but beneath a rotted alder stump that she had to move to extract the old fence wire. It was raining that day. As she tugged at the wire, which seemed to have welded itself to the stump, she wished she was inside by the fire with Florrie, reading one of the books she'd brought home. Suddenly, part of the wire pulled free, toppling her backward amid a spray of rotten wood and leaves. She brushed herself off and knelt beside the sodden stump to free the remaining strand. The ground beneath her knees felt uncomfortably hard. To see what was hurting her, she pushed moss aside and uncovered a hard grey stone, shaped like one of the ancient hand mauls she'd seen in her book. Her hands trembled as she scraped the dirt away. The rock was smooth, as if it had been polished. Reverently, she picked it up, then leapt to her feet.

"Mag! I found one! I found one!"

Mag was hammering a staple into a fence post, and distracted by Jen's cry, she hammered her thumb instead of the staple. She winced as pain shot through her arthritic joint and up her arm. "Shitah!"

"Look, Mag! It's a hammer or something!" She shoved the rock at Mag, almost knocking her backward.

"Watch what yer doing!" Mag pushed the rock aside with a force that sent it flying into the bushes. While she regained her balance, Jen plunged into the brush after it. A moment later she emerged with the stone back in her hand.

"See, Mag! It's an artifact!"

Mag surveyed the stone. "Shitah," she muttered again. She hadn't really thought the girl would find anything. "Looks joost like a rock to me," she said dismissively, but Jen wasn't fooled.

"It's a tool," she said firmly. "I saw one just like it at the museum. I'm gonna show it to Florrie!"

Mag watched her run down the trail to the house. There was no sense calling her back. The girl wouldn't hear anyway. When she eventually lost interest in the artifact, Mag would slip it away so the girl didn't take it to town. Louis Paul would love an excuse to search the farm at Serpent Cove.

By the time Mag remembered to confiscate the artifact, however, it was nowhere to be seen. Fearing that Mag would toss it into the cove, or worse, Jen had hidden the maul in the burned out hollow of an old-growth cedar stump that stood near the creek.

CHAPTER NINE

Early one afternoon in March, Sylvia began filling out the forms to renew her passport in anticipation of her seventh expedition with Doctor Simmons. She had changed in the past few years. The lines on her face were more pronounced, and her hair, worn tied at her neck, was now dyed rather than natural brown.

"This trip is going to be different," she said glumly. "Paul is taking us to join a group exploring a Roman shipwreck in the Mediterranean." She hesitated, then added almost inaudibly, "We'll be working from a research boat, the *Neptune*. It's a floating laboratory."

Jen looked up from her homework. "But you hate the water," she said. "I can't even get you into the Sangster to come to the cove." Jen knew the story of Cassie's drowning, how as small children she and Sylvia had been riding in their grandfather's power boat when it hit a submerged log and the boat overturned. As a result, Sylvia had developed a love–hate relationship with the water, wanting to be near the sea but refusing to travel on it in anything smaller than a ferry.

"I know," she agreed morosely, "but I promised Paul I'd be there."

The intimate way she said the professor's name sparked Jen's old jealously of the mystery man who lured Sylvia away each spring. "I wish you'd finish your book for that stupid man."

Sylvia frowned. "It's not respectful, Jen, to refer to anyone as 'stupid'—especially not someone as brilliant as Dr. Simmons. And the book is not for him . . ."

"But everything goes smoother when you're here," Jen argued. "I always get to school on time and I hardly miss any days at all." At fifteen, Jen was as tall as Mag. She had let her auburn hair grow long again, and now wore it tied back from her face as Sylvia did.

"If you miss any time this year, it will be your own fault," Sylvia said tartly. She signed the last of the forms and placed them in an envelope.

"Yeah, right. Like anyone can move Mag when she decides we

have to go beachcombing, or looking for cascara."

"You won't need to wait for Mag," Sylvia said mysteriously. "Not this year." She wrote her name and address on the envelope, then set it aside and got to her feet. "Come."

Puzzled, Jen followed her through the kitchen, out onto the porch, and down the hill to the wharf. Her eyes widened as she stared at the aluminum Princecraft moored alongside. It was fourteen feet long, dented in several places, and its blue and grey paint was peeling, but a gleaming ten-horsepower Honda outboard was fastened to the stern.

"It's yours, my dear," Sylvia said.

"Mine?"

"You worked hard for me this winter, Jen, cataloguing my pictures and putting my notes into the computer. This is a bonus for a job well done."

The old dock swayed as Jen jumped into the boat, and Sylvia had to fight to keep her balance. Jen scrambled to the stern, lifted the gas tank, and found it full. "Can I start it?"

"You have a better way of trying it out?"

Jen grinned. She yanked on the starter cord. On the second pull, the motor purred to life. "Oh, man, she's right on, Sylvia!" As she pumped the throttle, the motor roared. "You coming?"

Automatically, Sylvia shook her head. "No. You go ahead."

"Please?"

The older woman studied the flat-calm water, her face etched with fear. Finally, she took a deep breath and slowly let it out. "I suppose I must." She climbed cautiously into the boat and took a seat near the bow, her hands gripping the gunwales on each side.

"I'll go slow," Jen promised. But as she eased the boat away from the wharf and headed across Porpoise Bay, her delight with the motor made her forget Sylvia's anxiety. She circled Poise Island, meeting the wake of an incoming barge on the other side, and marvelled at the way the Princecraft handled the waves.

"Where'd you get her?" she shouted over the sound of the motor.

Sylvia didn't answer. Her knuckles were almost as white as her face. Her lips were compressed into a tight line.

"Sorry," Jen said contritely. Releasing her pressure on the throttle, she slowed the boat and guided it back to the dock.

Sylvia didn't relax until after Jen had secured the mooring ropes and helped her onto the wharf. "Surely the *Neptune* won't be as bad as that," she said. Jen suppressed an urge to suggest it could be a lot worse. Instead, she repeated her earlier question.

"Billy Thom sold me the boat," Sylvia said. "The motor came from John Duncan. He bought it for trolling, but it wasn't big enough. I got it for half price."

Jen felt an unfamiliar urge to hug her benefactor, but Sylvia had never been the kind of person who invited or gave hugs. "Thanks," Jen said instead.

"Just keep going to school," Sylvia said. She walked unsteadily up the ramp. "Mag's wrong when she says you've had enough education. Learning is a lifetime project."

Jen grinned as she followed her. "It'll take a really awesome storm to stop me now," she promised.

Sylvia stopped and turned to her. "This is not a boat for storms, Jen."

"Are you kidding? The way it handled that barge's wake?"

"All the same, I don't want you travelling in bad weather. And it wasn't storms that kept you back last fall. It was Mag." Sylvia resumed walking. "The Bakers won't be using the house until July, and they're leaving at the end of August, so you can stay here if it gets stormy. Or whenever you want to, for that matter."

"Alone?"

"You're old enough," Sylvia said simply. "And I trust you."

When Mag got back to the cove, she discovered that one of the nannies had cut her leg on the traps she had left piled outside the goat shed. It had been raining the day she closed down her trapline for the season, and she had left them out so they would dry when the weather turned warmer. She tended to the animal's wound, then flung the traps into the storage shed.

"Guess I won't be using them t'ings again, anyways," she said when she went back into the cabin for a cup of coffee. "Hardly got any pelts at all this winter."

Florrie was straining the whey from a pan of goat cheese. She put the bucket of whey aside and brought the rounded mound of goat cheese to the table. "Guess all that logging up back of us has scared the critters away," she said.

Mag sandwiched a thick hunk of cheese between two crackers. "Price shooer don't make it worth doing," she grumbled. "Not with all them hippies bellyaching about killing them poor little critters." She stuffed the whole thing in her mouth and chewed noisily.

Florrie lathered her own cracker with butter before adding the cheese. "Gosh, Mag, yer getting too old to go out on that trapline, anyways."

"I guess not," Mag snorted angrily. She refused to admit that sixty-nine was old. "I joost can't be out there setting them traps and in here looking after you at the same time!"

"I can't help getting sick," Florrie retorted. "Especially when yer always leaving the door open so I get them miserable chills."

It had been a bad winter for Florrie. She had spent days in bed, coughing and gasping for air. Mag almost stopped Jen from coming home on weekends, believing that the girl was bringing sicknesses with her from school, but she knew keeping Jen away would only make Florrie worse. Deep down she also knew it wasn't Florrie's illness or the falling price of fur that was behind her decision to stop trapping. In the past few years the arthritis that had settled into her hands had grown worse, making the job of setting the traps too dangerous. She could almost bear the pain that coursed through her fingers as she secured the bait and set the trigger, but the stiffening of her joints was making her movements awkward and clumsy. Twice that winter she had accidentally tripped the trigger and had just managed to pull her fingers away before the steel jaws snapped together.

She pushed her cup away. "I want to put in that new joe poke befer I head to town fer Jen," she said sourly. "Or you t'ink I'm too old fer that, too?" Without waiting for her sister's answer, she stomped out of the cabin, slamming the door behind her.

On the dock, Mag used a pike pole to position a log between the float and the shore. When it was in place she would secure one end to the float, then fasten the other end to a tree, thus creating a brace, known locally as a joe poke—that would keep the wharf from grounding on the mud flats at low tide. As she worked, she saw Billy Thom's scow rounding Serpent Point. He was coming in fast and his wake, as he approached the dock, jolted the log out of position. "Shitah!" She glowered at Jen, who was waving to her from the deck of Billy's boat.

"What you do that fer?" Mag shouted, brandishing the pike pole at Billy.

Unconcerned, he handed her his mooring line, then untied the Princecraft from the stern of the *Squawk Box*, and jumped down to the dock. He tied the new boat loosely to a log staple that Mag had hammered into the side of the float. "I come in easy as I could, Mag" he said. Although he spoke in the slow, soft voice of the Sechelt Native people, remnants of his father's Acadian dialect were also present. He nodded toward Jen as he added, "I saved your girl from driftin' down the chuck."

Mag looked at him suspiciously. "I didn't hire you."

Billy grinned. "Dis one's on the house. For the girl." He winked at Jen, but she didn't respond. Mag was in one of her moods, and Jen elected to stay safely on board the *Squawk Box*, while Billy told of how he'd found her drifting in the Princecraft near Nine Mile Point.

Mag glared at the Princecraft. "Where'd this t'ing come from?"

Reluctantly, Jen collected her bag from the wheelhouse, then climbed down to the dock. "Sylvia gave it to me. She bought it from Billy."

"But she got the motor from Duncan, you know," Billy said quickly. He retrieved his line from Mag and boarded his boat. Within minutes he had backed her away from the dock and, with a brief wave, had headed back down the inlet.

Jen secured the Princecraft's stern as Mag jabbed the point of the pike pole into the wharf beside the old canoe.

"So how come Sylvia give you a boat when you already got one."

"I can't take the canoe to town," Jen said. "Sylvia thought if I had this, I wouldn't miss as much school."

"Humph." Mag scowled at the aluminum boat. "She wasn't very smart to let you take it out in this kind of weather." She stepped into the boat and tilted the motor so the leg came out of the water. "So what was it doing when it quit?"

Jen knelt on the edge of the wharf. "Sort of sputtered," she said. "Then it wouldn't start again."

Mag found no scratches or other signs of abuse on the outside of the motor. When she gripped the housing and twisted, it didn't move. "Solid," she admitted grudgingly. She unfastened the catches, removed the cover, and inspected the power head. "Clean." She replaced the cover. The boat itself was sturdy, she decided. It would handle well in choppy water.

Jen searched her face for signs of approval. "So?" she asked uncertainly.

"Guess she'll be okay." Mag climbed out of the boat and stomped up the ramp. Near the pathway was a pile of boards she had rescued that winter from an abandoned camp at Sechelt Creek. She sorted through them, then indicated that Jen should come and help, and together they carried two long planks and a two-by-four into the house.

Florrie was at the stove cooking sausages for supper.

"What's that fer?" she demanded as they set the lumber on the floor. Mag cleared a spool of wire and a stack of newspapers from the end of one of the shelves between the door and her room. Then she went back outside, returning with a sawhorse she'd made the summer before out of cedar saplings.

"Need a work bench," she said. She nailed one end of the boards to the shelf and propped the other ends on the sawhorse.

Jen tossed her suitcase on the cot. "I'll help you with supper, Florrie," she said, but Mag stopped her. "Get the wheelbarrow," she ordered, "and bring yer motor up here."

Jen and Florrie both stared at her.

"Why?" Jen demanded at the same time as Florrie asked, "What motor?"

"Joost do it," Mag said. While Jen went back to the wharf, Mag told Florrie about Sylvia's gift.

Florrie shook her head. "Don't she know Jen's already got a boat?" She forked the sausages onto a dish and dumped a mound of mashed potatoes into the frying pan, where the grease hissed and spat in protest.

"That Sylvia, she's got more money than brains," Mag snorted. She nailed a long two-by-four to the shelf and the sawhorse, creating a four-inch ledge along the plank. "That should hold 'er." She wriggled the structure and found it firm.

Florrie was setting plates of sausage and potatoes on the table when the door burst open. Jen stepped into the room, breathless from lugging the motor up the hill.

"Joost clip it over that two-by-four," Mag said.

The girl did as she was told, then went to the basin on the counter to wash the grease off her hands. "You think you can fix it?" she asked, as she joined Mag and Florrie at the table.

"No," Mag said. "But you kin."

Jen stared at her. "Me?"

"Oh, shooer. You start by taking everyt'ing apart." Mag shovelled a fork full of sausage and potato into her mouth.

"But why should I take the motor apart? Billy says it's just the fuel line."

"Oh, is that so?" Mag filled her fork again. "Well, I guess you'll find that out when you put it back together."

"But I need it on Monday!" Jen wailed.

Florrie hadn't touched her own plate of food. She wished Mag would just tell Jen to give the boat back to Sylvia. "Jen's too young to be going into town alone," she said suddenly.

Mag guffawed. "We rowed to town lots of times when we was her age, Florrie. That's how come you—"

"Oh, shooer, but that was different," Florrie said quickly. "There

137

was two of us." She looked sadly at Jen. "Guess you won't be wanting to come home at all anymore."

"I won't have any choice," Jen said bitterly. "Not with my motor in pieces."

John Duncan had sent a repair manual with the Honda, but Mag dismissed it with a wave of her hand. "I been fixing motors all my life and I didn't have no book telling me how I gotta do it," she growled.

Under her watchful eye, Jen detached the motor cover and, with trembling fingers, slowly unfastened every movable piece in the case. As she extracted each part, Mag explained what it was for.

"Them plugs are what starts yer motor," she said. "They make a spark and the gas inside them holes explodes, sending that rod flying up. That's what turns them gears and that other rod so the prop spins."

When it came to the electronics, however, Mag was stumped.

"I never seen this stuff befer," she muttered. "Joost take them apart and we'll figure it out when yer putting the t'ings back together."

Jen worked until almost midnight, then fell into bed and dreamed of parts falling off the bench and between the cracks in the floor, never to be seen again. When she awoke just past dawn she felt exhausted, but she made herself get up. Mag was already down at the dock. Having secured the joe poke that Billy Thom's wake had knocked askew, she was readying the Sangster for a trip to town.

"Where you going?" Jen asked anxiously. Without Mag's help she would never get the motor back together.

"I have to get feed and deliver some milk to Sylvia," Mag said. "Should'a done it yesterday."

When she climbed the hill to Sylvia's cottage two hours later, Mag's face was grim. She handed Sylvia the bag of milk, but refused her invitation to tea.

"How come you give Jen that boat?" she demanded crossly as she waited by the door for Sylvia to gather her empty jars.

"She needs to get to school regularly," Sylvia answered levelly.

She placed the jars she had collected into a plastic bag and handed it to Mag.

"You t'ink I don't know that? Gosh, I'm spending all my money on gas joost so I can bring her to school."

"You bring her when it's convenient for you, Mag. When you're hunting or trapping or gathering cascara, you stay home. Jen's in grade eleven now. She can't afford to miss any classes."

"Girl don't need all that schooling," Mag retorted. "She kin read and write. She even adds numbers pretty good."

Sylvia shook her head. "That's not enough. Not for a girl as bright as Jen. She has a chance to go much further. . . ."

Mag's eyes narrowed. "She's fine where she is."

"No, Mag, she is not. She needs to get away from this small town. Go someplace where she can experience the full flavour of life. . . ."

Mags voice was bitter. "Like all them places you been to?"

"That would be a start," the other woman agreed.

"Hasn't done you no good."

There was a pause while Mag's jab dug in and Sylvia's eyes grew steely. Then she said very calmly, "Jen needs an education, Mag, and I'm going to see she gets it."

"Humph." Mag stepped out onto the porch. "Joost don't send her out in no more storms. She could'a drowned out there if Billy Thom hadn't showed up."

As she started down the trail, Sylvia called after her, "I didn't even know she was thinking of taking the boat up the inlet! She said she was taking it over to the dock so you could tow it to the cove."

Mag didn't respond. She was too busy wondering what would happen if Jen did leave the cove for good. "Shooer would be a terrible t'ing fer Florrie," she muttered.

Jen had the motor disassembled when Mag returned to the cove.

"Now you kin put it back together," she said, ignoring Jen's moans. She picked up a circular piece that looked like a tiny pot. "What did I tell you this was from?"

Who the hell knows? Jen thought grumpily, but she studied the part carefully. "The gas thing?"

"And what's it fer?"

Jen wracked her brain for the answer. "Mixes gas and air? So it explodes when it goes into the holes?"

Mag picked up another part. "What about this t'ing?"

"Distributor," Jen said promptly.

By midmorning on Sunday Jen had most of the motor back together. All that remained were the electrical connections. Mag scratched her head and frowned at the pile of wires.

"Gosh, I shooer can't figure those t'ings out," she murmured, before deciding she needed to clean out the goat shed.

"But I've got to have it running by tomorrow morning!" Jen wailed as Mag disappeared out the door.

"She's gone now," Florrie said, happy with the reprieve. Without a motor, Jen wouldn't be using the new boat. "You'll joost have to go to Sechelt in Mag's boat, like always."

Jen scowled at the wires then remembered the manual. "Like hell I will," she said. For the next two hours she pored over the book. The names they gave to the motor parts were vastly different from those Mag had used, but after a while, with the help of pictures, she was able to translate them. It took her much longer to decipher the wiring diagrams and longer still to make the connections on her own motor. When she had everything in place, she carried it back to the boat.

By then it was early afternoon. The sky overhead was blue, and the sun so warm that steam rose from the wharf. Jen fastened the motor to the Princecraft's stern, connected the gas hoses and pulled on the starter cord. Nothing happened. She pulled again and again, but still nothing happened.

"Shitah." She returned to the house, collected the manual and her tools, and brought them back down to the boat.

Mag stayed away from the dock even after she finished cleaning the goat shed. Instead, she started to work on the woodpile. She had no doubt the girl would fix the motor. Sylvia was right about her being smart. Which probably meant she was also right about the need for her to go. Mag swung the axe hard, crashing it down upon the block she was chopping, burying it midway into a knot. She wrenched the blade free and swung again. This time the blow ruptured the knot and split the block in two. Normally Mag liked the sound of the splitting and the feel of the wood giving way. Today she didn't even notice. "Girl wants to go, she kin go," she muttered.

Inside the cabin, Florrie heard the motor start, followed by a loud whoop. She stared disconsolately at the venison soup she was making for supper. "I guess she won't be needing us anymore," she said when Mag came in with an armload of wood.

"Didn't need us in the first place," Mag said. She dumped her load onto a pile by the stove. "Should'a took her to the Welfare like I said."

The door swung open and Jen stormed into the room. She flung the tools and manuals she was carrying onto the workbench. "It works," she said sullenly, glaring at Mag. "No thanks to you."

Mag was unperturbed. "Now you know what to do when it breaks down again."

Sylvia left for the Mediterranean in early April. As she had hoped, the Princecraft saved Jen from missing any school and the girl's marks were so high that she didn't have to write final exams. In mid-June Jen packed her bags, then gave the cottage a thorough cleaning so it would be ready for the Bakers. Marlene Greaves came over to help her.

"It'll be totally boring this summer with you gone," Marlene complained as she handed Jen a stack of plates from the cupboards they were cleaning out.

Jen set the plates on the table and returned for the cups Marlene was holding out. "Why don't you come and stay with me at the cove?"

"I have to look after the little kids," Marlene grumbled.

"Just for a day? I could pick you up and bring you back."

Marlene's expression grew hopeful. "Cool!" But as quickly as it had come, the hope died. "My dad would never let me go," she said bitterly. "He says it's my duty to stay and help Mom."

Jen shrugged. She'd met Marlene's dad just once. He'd asked her what church she went to. When she said she didn't believe in that stuff, he gave her a long lecture on the virtues of godliness. After that, whenever she knew Marlene's dad was around, Jen refused to go anywhere near the Greaves' home.

Marlene had left when Mag arrived later that afternoon. She was hot and sweaty, but there was a gleam in her eye. "You kin bring yer boat over to the Sechelt wharf," she announced. "I got extra feed and two more bales of hay so we don't have to come back to town fer a while."

Jen folded the last towel from a pile she'd taken from the dryer. She had planned to collect some oysters on the way home as a treat for Florrie. "It won't hold all that stuff. It'll sink."

"We'll joost tow it behind mine."

Mag couldn't understand why the girl wasn't happy about doubling their benefits from this trip to town. She collected a box of spoilables Jen had gathered from the fridge. "We should get going befer the wind gets worse."

Jen locked the door and picked up her suitcase. As they started down the path to the wharf, she glanced at the house next door. On the verandah, Agnes Greystone stood watching them. *Probably figures we're stealing all the silverware,* Jen thought. Mag held the box with one hand and waved at the woman. "I guess she's sad to see you go." Jen looked at her sharply. Sometimes she couldn't tell if Mag was being sarcastic or sincere.

That evening, while Florrie fried the steaks that Jen had brought from Sylvia's freezer, Jen carried in a fresh bucket of water and placed it at the end of the counter. Beads of moisture stood out on Florrie's forehead, the combined result of the hot June day and the heat of the cookstove. Mag sat near the table, cleaning her rifle.

"One more week of bear hunting left," she remarked, pulling a cleaning rod out of the barrel. From the end of the rod, she removed a small, oily rag blackened with old powder.

"Where you going?" Jen asked

Mag changed the rag for one only slightly less black and poked it down the barrel. "I t'ink I'll try and get that big bear Billy Thom says is up Narrows." She described the logging road she planned to follow up the mountain to find her bear.

Florrie's eyes sparkled with mischief. "You gonna give yer bear to Lenny Laval again, Mag?"

Her sister grimaced. "He stole it, the bugger."

Florrie laughed out loud, but the laugh changed to coughing, and it was several minutes before she could retell the story of the bear Mag had shot the previous year. Jen had heard the tale many times over the winter, but she couldn't deny Florrie the pleasure she got from telling it again.

"She goes all up that mountain," Florrie wheezed, turning the steaks, "and after she walks all day without seeing a t'ing, not even any shit, she starts t'inking maybe there's no bears up there. That's when this big bear comes walking down the road, swinging his head like he owns everyt'ing around him." Florrie swung her own head, imitating the bear. "So Mag shoots him. Joost one shot. Bang! Right t'rough his ears. He falls right down in the dust. Don't move even a hair, not even when she pokes him. So she starts gutting and skinning him and wondering how she's gonna pack such a big bear down by herself."

Mag's lips thinned as she worked the cleaning rod. It was easy for Florrie to enjoy the story. She wasn't the one who climbed the damned mountain.

"So she gets the skin all stored away in her bag," Florrie went on. "And puts the meat she's gonna keep in another bag, then makes herself a skid to haul it all down the mountain."

Jen had seen the skids Mag made. They were shaped very much like a travois—thin alder trees lashed together with twine, tight at the top and spread out at the bottom.

"It's almost dark befer she gets everyt'ing done," Florrie continued.

"She's tired and cold, but she starts down the mountain. And that's when Lenny Laval comes along. He's wearing his game warden clothes, but he don't act like nutting's wrong. Walks all the way to the beach with Mag. She's hauling that heavy load all by herself and he walks along, talking about everyting. But he don't say nutting about bears or hunting."

Some of the mirth left Florrie as she told this part, but returned when she described Mag and Lenny's arrival on the beach—how Lenny pulled out his ticket book and told Mag that she was one day late in hunting her bear. While Florrie roared with laughter, Mag glared at Jen as if she were Lenny. "I shooer don't care that he give me a ticket," she growled. "But that bugger took my meat after I hauled it out!"

She pushed the cleaning rod aside and pointed the lower portion of the rifle at the lamp so she could see down the barrel. Then she snapped it shut. "This year I got my licence," she said grimly, "and a whole week of hunting befer the season closes."

Still laughing, Florrie returned to the steaks while Jen set the table. Suddenly the frying pan crashed to the floor and Florrie fell toward the stove. As she slammed her hand down on the hot lid, Jen grabbed the back of her shirt and tried to pull her away. Mag's gun clattered onto the table. Springing forward, she grasped her sister's arm. With Jen supporting the other arm, they helped Florrie to a chair. Mag grabbed the water bucket and plunged Florrie's burned hand into it.

"Run to the crik and get more!" she ordered. Jen was out the door with the milk bucket before she finished speaking. As soon as she came back with fresh cold water, Mag transferred Florrie's hand to the new bucket and sent Jen for more.

"Everyt'ing went black," Florrie muttered weakly. "I couldn't see nutting. I was joost lifting the pan off so it wouldn't burn."

It took an hour before the pain in Florrie's hand subsided and Mag permitted her to take it out of the water. Jen was breathless from running back and forth to the creek.

"I need some egg white," Mag said, gesturing toward the bowl on the table, and Jen grabbed an egg, broke it, and removed the yoke. Mag plastered the albumen over Florrie's hand, which now showed only a light redness.

"Gosh, it don't hurt anymore," Florrie marvelled, but her face was unusually grey, and her hand trembled as she took the shot of whisky Mag handed her.

"We should take her to the doctor," Jen said.

Mag shook her head. "She don't need no doctor. She joost got too hot." She looked sternly at her sister. "I told you to use the camp stove!"

"It joost doesn't cook t'ings the same as wood," Florrie complained, but Mag was adamant. "I'm not bringing no more wood in," she said, "and Jen won't neither. You cook on the camp stove from now on."

Jen knew better than to argue with Mag about Florrie going to a doctor, but she was determined that Florrie should see one.

"What'll it hurt?" she coaxed Florrie the next morning after Mag had left for her hunting trip. "We could go into town, see the doctor and be back here before your nap time."

"In yer boat?" Florrie asked anxiously. "Gosh, I don't t'ink so."

Jen had a moment's hesitation. Florrie's bulk made the Princecraft seem a lot smaller than it was. She looked out at the water. "It's a calm day," she decided, "and I'll be careful."

The girl seemed so eager that Florrie didn't have the heart to refuse a second time. But her misgivings increased when she saw how little freeboard there was after she climbed aboard.

"Go slow," she warned. "And stay real close to shore."

Florrie hadn't been in the doctor's office since Mag's leg had healed, and she stood in the doorway wrinkling her nose at the antiseptic smell. It always made her remember her mother's death. "Gosh, I'm shooer feeling lots better," she said. "Guess I don't need to see any doctor."

The receptionist looked up as Jen tried to persuade Florrie not to leave. "Can I help you?"

Hoping to enlist her aid, Jen said quickly, "Florrie fell yesterday. Against the stove."

The receptionist focused her attention on Florrie.

"She's okay," Jen added. "We fixed the burn up, but I thought she should see a doctor."

"I think Dr. Mayle can see you right away." The woman disappeared down the hall.

Jen helped Florrie inside and she sat heavily on the bench that stood against one wall of the clinic. "Shooer is hot," she muttered, fanning herself with a magazine. "Should be back home where it's cool." But she was too tired to protest further.

"This won't take long, Florrie," Jen said. She was relieved when the receptionist reappeared. She insisted that Florrie should stand on the scale before she led them to a tiny office that shrank even smaller when Florrie entered.

Dr. Mayle was a thin, greyish man with a brow forced into a perpetual frown. "You fell?"

Florrie nodded. She wiped at the moisture forming on her forehead. "Shooer is hot in here."

"How?"

Florrie looked confused. "What?"

His lips thinned. "How did you fall?"

"Oh! I joost went over. Almost wrecked the steaks. They was all over the floor, but Mag and Jen cleaned 'em up."

"You didn't trip over anything? You just went down without warning?" The coldness of his voice made Jen wince. Florrie nodded.

"Have you had attacks like this before?"

Florrie looked at Jen and rolled her eyes. "I never got attacked by nutting. I told you, I joost keeled over."

"I mean," he said, enunciating each word, "have you fallen like that before? Without warning?"

"Mag says Florrie just got too hot," Jen put in quickly. "She did the same thing last summer when she was cooking. Only then she just sat down and Mag and me finished making supper."

With a sigh, the doctor got up and squeezed past Florrie to his examining table. "You'll have to get undressed—to the waist," he said, pulling some light blue paper from a drawer. "Put this on, opening at back, and climb up on the table." He handed the paper to Jen and left the room.

"You have to take your shirt off, Florrie," Jen said.

"What fer?" Florrie asked, horrified. "I'm not having no baby!"

"So he can examine you," Jen explained patiently. "So he can check everything out."

Florrie grumbled but took off her shirt. She was red from exertion, and her massive breasts spilled out of her ancient bra. Jen was afraid of what would happen if she removed the bra, so she left it in place while they both tried to decide which way to put on the paper shirt the doctor had given them. Jen was certain that Florrie had it on backward and was about to remove it, when the doctor knocked and re-entered the room. He motioned to the examining table and Jen helped Florrie sit on it.

Putting on a pair of plastic gloves, the doctor placed the cold metal end of his stethoscope against Florrie's chest. She gasped, but he made no apology. "Deep breaths," he said tersely as he transferred the scope to her back. He measured her blood pressure and took her pulse and temperature. "You need to lose a lot of weight," he said sternly, removing his gloves and tossing them in the wastebasket.

Jen felt her stomach tighten. She wished the doctor would talk nicer to Florrie. She seemed so defenseless sitting on the examining table, her upper body only partially covered by the ill-fitting paper shirt that was now darkening with her sweat.

The doctor returned to his desk and scribbled something on a piece of paper. He handed it to Jen. "We need an electrocardiogram. You'll have to get her up to the hospital. I'll call ahead and they'll do it right away."

Florrie's jaw set hard. "I guess not!"

He stared at her with some surprise. "The tests can't be performed here."

"I'm not going to no hospital," she said again. She didn't care how upset it made Jen, she wasn't going to get stuck in that place like Mag did.

"Then you'll probably die," he said coldly. "You're overweight, your blood pressure is excessively high, and I can't make a definitive diagnosis without the ECG."

"It's just a test, right?" Jen asked quickly. "She doesn't have to stay in or anything?"

"Depends on what the ECG shows."

Jen turned to Florrie. "You could just go for the test, Florrie. So he can tell what's wrong."

"It's too far up there, Jen. I joost can't walk that far."

Dr. Mayle said severely, "You shouldn't be walking at all, Mrs. Larson."

Florrie ignored him and turned to Jen. "Come on, girl, we gotta be getting back home."

Jen felt close to tears. "But, Florrie, he says you need to have the test!"

"Humph!" Florrie ripped off the paper shirt, crumpled it into a ball and tossed it on the floor. She slid off the examining table and grabbed her own shirt.

"I've got fifteen bucks and that money in my savings account," Jen said desperately, helping her fasten the buttons. "We could use some of that for a taxi."

"That money's fer yer schooling," Florrie said. "Anyways, Mag and me don't need no doctors telling us we got someting wrong when we don't."

"You're mistaken about that, Mrs. Larson. I am quite certain that you have a serious heart disorder. You need to go on a strict diet and get your blood pressure regulated." The doctor seemed genuinely perplexed by Florrie's sudden change of mood. For a moment his manner softened. "If you won't have the test, at least let me give you a prescription that might bring your blood pressure down."

He scribbled something on a prescription pad and held it out to Florrie. She brushed past him on her way to the door. Jen took the prescription, but nothing would induce Florrie to go to the pharmacy. "I'm joost tired, Jen. I want to go home."

Jen helped her down the street, past the dress shop, the pet store, and the Seawind Café. Here Florrie paused for breath. As she leaned against the building, the tantalizing aromas of sweet chocolate and freshly baked cinnamon buns made her mouth water.

"How about having a snack before we head out?" Jen suggested. Florrie peered inside the restaurant. "They have chocolate pie," Jen coaxed.

Florrie licked her lips. "Guess we could stop fer one piece," she said.

Once Florrie was seated inside, with a plate of chocolate pie and a cup of coffee in front of her, Jen decided they needed potatoes.

"I can run over to the grocery store and be back before you're finished," she said. When Florrie started to protest, she added ominously, "Mag'll sure be mad if she comes back with a bear and we don't have spuds for stew."

"We got spuds," Florrie mumbled around a mouthful of pie. "Mag got some a couple 'a weeks ago."

"Yeah, and we ate them, remember? I peeled the last of them yesterday."

Before Florrie could protest further, Jen hurried out of the café. But instead of going straight to the grocery store, she slipped into the neighbouring pharmacy.

"She's to take these with her breakfast and supper," the pharmacist said. He handed Jen a bottle of white pills. "That'll be $9.05." Jen swore softly. All she had after paying for Florrie's pie was a ten-dollar bill. She slid it across the counter. At the grocery store she had just enough left for a small bag of potatoes.

Florrie was waiting on the sidewalk. She was grey around the mouth and wheezed heavily as they trudged down to the boat. "It's shooer getting rough out there," she said, looking anxiously at the whitecaps out in the bay. She wished again that she hadn't let the girl talk her into the trip. It was going to be a rough ride home.

Jen helped her into the boat, then untied the Princecraft's mooring ropes. Away from Porpoise Bay, she stayed close to shore, making the trip twice as long but not as bumpy as her usual route down the middle of the inlet. Though Florrie fought to stay awake, whenever they reached a relatively calm spot she would doze, her head falling forward so her chin rested on her chest. At the cove, it took all of Jen's strength to help her out of the boat and up the trail to the cabin.

"How about peanut butter sandwiches for supper, Florrie?"

Florrie nodded tiredly from the bed, but she felt too sleepy to even care about food. She lay back against the pillow and closed her eyes. Jen lathered peanut butter and honey on two slabs of bread, then quietly crushed one of the tablets with a spoon and sprinkled it over the filling. By the time she had put the sandwich together, Florrie was snoring softly. Jen set it on a chair by her bed and went outside to look after the animals.

Cob Junior had escaped from her pen again, and it took almost an hour for Jen to coax her back inside. When she finally returned to the cabin, the lamp was lit, and the sandwich was gone. Florrie smiled at her from the bed. "How about reading me the story about that bear that likes honey?"

Jen pulled the table and lamp closer to Florrie's bed, settled herself in a chair and began to read. "Edward Bear, known to his friends as Winnie-the-Pooh . . ."

CHAPTER TEN

Oblivious to the sweat trickling down her forehead, Mag revved the motor of her ancient power saw and set the blade against the alder log. White sawdust sprayed into the air as the chain cut through the wood. A few yards away, Jen was splitting the blocks Mag had already cut. Sweat had plastered her T-shirt to her flesh, and deer flies were tormenting her face.

During a storm the previous evening, the huge old alder had fallen across the goat pen, pulling the fence down with it. Cob Junior and Granny-Two glared at them from temporary quarters in the chicken yard, while the other two goats, tethered near the tool shed, grazed contentedly on salmonberry leaves. Jen wondered how content they'd be if they realized the significance of Mag's rifle leaning against the stump of the alder. She needed it, she'd said, because a cougar had been hanging around, but Jen didn't like to see it so close to the goats.

The block Mag was cutting fell away from the log. She moved a step forward, revved the motor, and started a new cut. Neither she nor Jen heard the shouts from the dock. Jen was too intent on positioning a new block for splitting. Holding the block with one hand, she raised her axe with the other. Suddenly, a dark shape loomed before her. With a startled yelp, she dropped the block but held onto her axe as she surveyed the burly, dark-haired man gesturing toward the house.

"The old lady in the shack said to come out here," he shouted.

As Mag completed her cut, she let up on the throttle. The motor sputtered and died. "Shitah," she grumbled, kicking the cut block out of her way. She lowered the saw to the ground and turned toward Jen. "Go get me the damned tool bag," she said. Then she saw the man. Her eyes narrowed, and in one swift movement she stepped back and retrieved her rifle. "What you doing here, Saari?"

For just a moment the man appeared uncomfortable, but his voice boomed across the clearing. "We were up checking on some real estate," he said, "and the boy run the boat into your crab trap. Rope got snarled in the prop and bust the shear pin."

Mag looked toward the water and, for the first time, saw the boat. A young man was walking up the trail from the wharf. Unlike his father, Cal Saari was tall and wiry with dark wavy hair, but she remembered that Pete had looked like that long ago. *Probably meaner than his old man*, Mag thought. She didn't trust either one of them. "Last time you was here you killed my goat," she snapped, aiming the rifle barrel at Pete Saari's chest.

Pete held out his hands fan-like, palms up. "Hell, Mag, that was an accident. I said I was sorry, didn't I? Jeez, that damned goat looked like a whitetail, sure's hell."

"She was in my yard," Mag said flatly. "You had no business being in my yard, and you shooer got no business being here today."

Cal gave Jen a nod of recognition, then smiled obsequiously at Mag. "We could sure use a tow, ma'am. Into Sechelt, maybe?"

Jen felt like gagging. She'd never heard Cal refer to Mag as anything but "Mag the Hag."

"I got wood to cut," Mag said, but she lowered the rifle and set it back against the stump. Steadying the saw motor with her left foot, she yanked on the starter cord. The flywheel spun noisily, but the motor didn't start. She knelt down, fingered the throttle lever, and made a slight adjustment to the carburetor. Another yank to the cord caused the engine to sputter. "Shitah!" She tried again. This time the saw came to life, roaring crankily as she pumped the throttle.

"Tell you what, Mag, the boy here'll do your wood for you," Cal's father shouted, "while you give me a tow in."

Mag let the motor die. She studied the two men. "Does he know how to run a saw?"

Cal nodded. "I use one at home sometimes."

Mag set the saw on the ground. She turned to Pete. "Okay, then. Your boy kin cut the wood, and I'll go look fer a shear pin. Fer fifty bucks."

Pete choked. "Fifty bucks? For a two-dollar pin?"

"Oh, shooer. Twenty fer looking. T'irty fer the trap you joost wrecked."

"Bullshit! You didn't have the goddamn thing marked proper. I should be chargin' you fifty bucks and reporting you to boot."

"Is that so?" Mag said indifferently. Since she didn't mark her traps there was no way anyone could prove it was hers. She pulled on the starter cord again.

"Fuck you!" Pete swung on his heel as if to leave, walked a few steps then swung back. He scowled at his son. "See if you can cut this stuff without screwin' up for once." He turned to Mag. "I'll pay—when I get the pin."

Mag shook her head. "I guess not. You'll pay befer I start looking."

They were still arguing when they left the clearing. As they vanished around the house on their way to the wharf, Cal picked up the saw and yanked the starter cord. The machine roared to life, but as soon as he started his first cut the motor began to labour. A moment later it stopped.

"Damn," Cal muttered.

"You're cutting crooked," Jen observed. "The wood pinched the chain."

"I know that." He yanked the saw free of the log, started it again, and went back to the cut. This time he held the saw straight. When the block fell away, he stared at it in pleased surprise. Jen grinned and went back to splitting blocks. When Cal had almost reached the end of the tree, he stopped the motor. He set the saw on the ground and wiped his brow. "You got any water here?"

Jen brushed a fly from her face. "In the jug." She nodded toward a bottle of water lying by a tree stump. "Or the creek."

Cal eyed the bottle dubiously. "Where's the creek?"

Jen split the block she'd set up, buried her axe in a new one, then walked along the trail to the stream. She knelt down and splashed cold water over her face and T-shirt. Putting her lips to the surface, she sucked in a mouthful of water. Cal watched then walked upstream, dropped to his knees, and put his face in the stream. When he'd finished drinking, he dunked his head.

"You got any place to swim here?" he asked as he smoothed his hair back with his hands.

Jen hesitated. "There's a place I go," she said quietly.

He waited expectantly. "Well?" he prompted, flashing a smile. "Are you going to show me?"

Jen took a deep breath then nodded. She led the way along another trail that went up a small rise and came down on a sandy beach sheltered from the cove by Serpent Point. She slipped off her runners and stepped into the water. Cal kicked off his own sneakers. "Beat you in!" he challenged, splashing past her. Jen raced after him. "Not a chance!"

In the shed beside the cabin, Mag finally located a damp paper bag that held a half-dozen shear pins. The wad of bills rested snugly in her pocket, and she smiled as she selected the rustiest pin in the bag, then tucked the rest into a coffee tin.

"Jesus!" Pete stared at the tiny pin she placed in his hand. "This sure ain't worth fifty bucks."

Mag shrugged. "It is to me." She started walking toward the goat pen. "I'll send yer kid back."

She hadn't heard the chainsaw running for a long while, so she wasn't surprised that the butt of the tree was still uncut. There was no sign of either Jen or the boy. Mag's stomach tightened. She had been aware of the way Jen had looked at Pete's kid. It was just like Florrie had looked at the boys when they went to dances, and Mag knew no good ever came from such looks.

"Shitah." Grabbing her rifle, she stomped up the trail to the creek. Jen and the boy were not there. As she stood wondering where they might be, she heard Jen cry out. The shout came from the beach where Jen liked to swim, and it took Mag only moments to limp up the slope that overlooked the bay. Below her, the boy's shorts lay in a heap on the sand. Nearby Jen struggled against him. With one knee pressed into her chest, he was fighting her swinging fists and trying to remove her shorts at the same time.

"No!" Jen slammed her fist against his thigh. "Fuck off, damn it!" The flimsy cotton material of her shorts gave way with a ripping sound. Hysterically, she writhed beneath him, trying to free her arms from his grasp. "You fuckin' asshole!" she shrieked, tears streaming down her face. "Let me go!"

Suddenly he did release her and scrambled to his feet.

"Oh, Jesus!" he gasped. He grabbed his shorts and ran toward the water.

As she pulled together the remnants of her own shorts, Jen stared at the rifle. "No, Mag!" She jumped up, started to run, then stumbled. Mag's face was set in the same expression it had worn when she shot Mr. T. a thousand years before. The gun's safety latch clicked as Mag took aim on Cal's bare ass.

"No!" Jen screamed again. Recovering her balance, she ran between the gun muzzle and Cal. He dove beneath the surface and Mag lowered the rifle. "Aw," she said, disgusted, "he's not even worth the bullet." She looked the girl over. "You okay?"

Jen scowled. "I could've handled him."

"Oh, shooer, I can see that." Mag pointed the rifle at the pair of sneakers resting in the sand. Jen's hands flew to her ears as the gun went off. One shoe flipped over, its sole torn apart. Mag fired again and the same thing happened to the other shoe. The sound of the shots echoed across the bay then died away. In the silence, she turned back to Jen. "I t'ink you should talk to Florrie. She knows about this stuff." She hoisted the rifle onto her shoulder and limped up the hill.

Florrie was snoring when Jen entered the cabin. She went quietly to her own cot and dug out clean clothes. The cabin was cool and dark, and she shivered as she pulled on her T-shirt.

The bed creaked. Florrie yawned loudly. She had meant to rest for just a few minutes after sending Peter Saari up to see Mag. Instead she had fallen into a deep sleep. "It shooer is hot today," she said. "Makes me sleepy."

Jen didn't respond. Florrie shifted into a sitting position. "Did Saari find Mag?"

"Yeah, he found her."

"Guess she was pretty mad about them wrecking her crab trap."

Jen shrugged. She didn't want to talk about the visitors. "You want a sandwich?"

Florrie squinted at the counter. The remains of their breakfast porridge sat heaped in a bowl beside a jug of milk. "Oh, I don't t'ink so. But maybe you kin put some raisins in that porridge. Then it tastes joost like pudding."

Taking advantage of the dim light in the cabin, Jen crushed one of the pills the doctor had prescribed. She mixed it into the porridge, then added some vanilla, brown sugar and milk. By the time she was finished, Florrie was at the table. Jen set the bowl in front of her.

"What happened to your babies, Florrie?"

The older woman paused in the act of reaching for her spoon and laughed uncertainly. "What you want to know that fer?"

Jen shrugged. "Mag said the Welfare took them away from you."

"Oh, shooer," Florrie said glumly. She took up the spoon and slowly stirred the porridge into a sludge.

"How come?"

"Gosh. That was a long time ago," she said evasively. She didn't like the feelings Jen's questions were awakening. But there was something desolate in the girl's expression, a sadness that prompted Florrie to continue. "Our dad took the first one away." There was a harshness to her voice that Jen had never heard before. "He said he didn't have no room here fer bastards."

"You weren't married?"

Florrie didn't answer. She was too busy reliving the moment that the nurse took her baby from her arms.

"So how many babies did you have?"

The question brought Florrie out of her reverie. "T'ree. All boys. First one I didn't get to name, but the next one I called Ben. Last one was Jack." Saying the names created a painful lump in Florrie's throat. She shoved a spoonful of porridge into her mouth. As she chewed, the lump slowly subsided.

"What happened to Ben and Jack?" Jen prompted.

Florrie swallowed. "Mag took 'em to the Welfare. It was joost gonna be fer a while, but that Welfare lady wouldn't give 'em back. She said they was whisky babies." She fell silent, concentrating on her meal. Jen waited patiently while Florrie emptied the bowl.

"What did she mean—whisky babies?"

"It was Schwabby done it."

"Schwabby?"

"We was fishing together, him and me." Florrie glanced at the door. She wished her sister would return. "Mag says I shouldn't talk about it," she said, hoping to forestall any further questions. "She says talking will bring us more trouble."

Jen shifted impatiently. "She won't care if you tell *me*, Florrie." She remembered what Mag had said on the beach and added, "She told me to ask you about babies and stuff."

"Oh, shooer?"

"So what did Schwabby do?"

Florrie wiped a few drops of milk from her chin. "He didn't like my babies."

Jen shook her head, thoroughly perplexed. "Wasn't he their dad?"

"I guess not!" Florrie snorted. "Svend Jedson was their dad. Gosh, him and I lived together almost t'ree years, but he got killed by that tree falling on him. That's when I went with Schwabby. Ben, he was joost starting to crawl, and baby Jack was still in my belly. Mag was looking after our dad, and he shooer wasn't gonna let me come home with them babies."

"So you married this Schwabby?"

Florrie laughed harshly. "No, I never done nutting like that. I was a deckhand on Schwabby's fish boat. Nobody else'd go with him, he drank so much." She looked earnestly at Jen. "I never seen anybody drink like Schwabby," she marvelled. "In joost one night he drunk down a whole gallon of wine. I didn't know anybody could do that!"

"But what about the babies?" Jen prompted.

Florrie sighed. "That Schwabby never liked drinking alone. That bugger wanted me to drink with him. Joost got terrible mean 'less I took some. That booze is bad stuff, Jen," she warned. "You shooer start liking it. That's how it got Schwabby. Made him real happy at first, laughing and making everybody laugh with him." The chair creaked as Florrie shifted her bulk so she could lean back. Her eyelids drooped and for a moment Jen thought she was falling asleep.

"Schwabby, he didn't like my babies," she repeated abruptly. "They was always crying and puking. When Baby Jack come, Schwabby got terrible mean. He was always yelling at him to shut up. That's how come he started hitting me."

She lifted her hand and traced a scar near the hairline of her forehead. "Gosh, I don't know why I didn't hit him back," she said wonderingly. "He was a real small guy, but he shooer yelled loud. He yelled louder than our dad. And one time he got so terrible mad, he was gonna hurt Ben. That's when I started putting whisky in their bottles so's they wouldn't cry so much."

Jen stared at her. "How come you didn't just leave?"

Florrie lowered her hand. "I was going to. I told Schwabby I wanted to go back to the cove and he got so mad he come after me with a fish club. He joost hit me and hit me, 'til I couldn't see nutting. I t'ought he was gonna go after my babies, too."

Jen was horrified by the thought of anyone hurting Florrie. "Why didn't someone come and help you?"

"There wasn't nobody around. We was anchored up Jervis, fishing. He could'a killed us and nobody would'a knowed. But I t'ink he was too drunk. That's what Mag says, anyways. She come up the next day. I was half-dead and the babies was crying."

Florrie's voice dropped to a hush. "Mag said Schwabby must've fell off the boat and drowned befer she got there . . . but I heard her swearing at him. It was her who took Ben and Baby Jack to the Welfare to look after 'til I got better." She picked sadly at some crumbs on the table. "I told 'em why I give them babies the whisky, but they said I could'a killed them." Her expression grew perplexed. "They said I wasn't fit to raise babies."

Jen went around the table. "You're a great mother, Florrie," she said staunchly, giving her a hug.

As Mag had expected, the Saari kid had dulled her saw. Sharpening it took some time, but it also took the edge off her anger, and sawing up the remainder of the wood worked off the rest. By the time she went to the cabin, she was almost in a good mood. After all, she had fifty dollars in her pocket for doing almost nothing.

Florrie and Jen were at the table when she came in. "Well, I got her cut," she announced. "Now it's yer turn, girl."

Jen grabbed a hat and went out into the sun. For once she was glad to have work to do.

At the end of August, Jen made a trip to town by herself to use some of the money Sylvia had given her on a shopping spree. At the shoe store she bought a new pair of runners, then went to the thrift store and purchased two nearly-new pairs of jeans and three blouses. For once she took the time to try them on to make sure they fit. She ended up at the drugstore, where she bought her school supplies and had Florrie's prescription refilled.

That evening, as Jen paraded her purchases in front of Florrie, Mag watched with mixed emotions. The Evinrude she'd purchased for the Sangstercraft had given her seven years of good service, but in the past year it had developed problems that required costly repairs. The money Jen had wasted on her new clothes would have paid for the fuel pump Mag needed.

Sensing her sister's thoughts, Florrie cast a warning look at Mag and said enthusiastically, "Them t'ings are shooer nice, Jen."

"Humph!" Mag turned her back on both of them. *Money's spent anyways,* she thought as she massaged a foul-smelling liniment into her hands. Her knuckles were swollen and painful—a sure sign that the weather was going to change. "It's gonna rain soon," she predicted.

At breakfast the next morning she announced that she was going to repair the roof on the goat shed. As soon as she finished eating, she grabbed her hat and went out to search for some roofing material she'd stored in the shed.

Florrie felt dizzy when she got up from her chair and leaned against the table for a moment before straightening. "T'ink I'll joost lay down fer a spell," she said. Jen watched her limp to the bed.

Florrie hadn't had any more fainting spells, and her burn had long since healed, but there were times after cooking a meal that she looked so grey, Jen was afraid she *was* going to faint again. She wished it had been possible to slip a pill into her porridge, but there had been no way to do it without Mag seeing her.

"I'll go help Mag, then come back and make you an eggnog," Jen said.

"I'd like that," Florrie agreed sleepily.

Mag insisted that the old shingles had to be removed so the asphalt roofing would lie flat. Although the roof wasn't high above the ground, the shed was so old it seemed to shudder with every shingle they ripped away. Jen kept expecting the building to collapse beneath them, and was relieved when they tossed the last shingle to the ground.

"Shitah," Mag muttered, searching through the tools she'd brought to the shed. "Didn't bring the roofing nails."

"I'll get 'em," Jen offered, welcoming the chance to check on Florrie. "I'll take some of these scraps in for the fire."

"Don't be long," Mag warned. She hoisted a sheet of plywood to the roof. "Them clouds are getting darker."

Jen glanced at the sky. It was still a light grey over the cabin, but the cloud bank above Nagy Mountain was almost black, and it was heading their way.

Mag felt smug as she laid the plywood into position. She'd found it a few weeks earlier, stacked beside a dumpster near the marina in Sechelt. There was enough for the whole roof, and it hadn't cost her a cent.

"You kin hand me them nails now," she called down to Jen, then realized the girl hadn't returned from the cabin. "Probably having herself a coffee," she said irritably. She climbed painfully down the ladder and limped toward the house. "Maybe Florrie's fixed something good."

But when Mag entered the cabin it was Jen, not Florrie, who stood at the counter. The girl swung around. "Mag!"

"Yer supposed to be helping me," Mag scolded. "How come yer in here?"

"I'm just fixin' Florrie an eggnog," Jen said. Turning back to the counter, she brushed the crumbled pill off the breadboard and out of sight.

Mag limped over to the counter. Too late, Jen realized she hadn't hidden the pill bottle.

"What's this?" Mag grabbed the bottle and glared at Jen.

"They're for Florrie's heart," Jen said, adding with false bravado. "The doctor said she needs them."

"What doctor?"

From the bed where she was resting, Florrie said, "I seen him in town after I burned my hand."

"I never took you to town," Mag said.

"No, you was hunting, remember?"

"The doctor said Florrie will die if she doesn't take them," Jen said, fighting back tears.

"Them doctors don't know nutting about Florrie," Mag snorted furiously. "They killed our dad and they wrecked my leg. They're shooer not killing my sister!"

She emptied the container into the slop bucket.

"But, Mag . . ."

"Florrie don't need no doctoring!" Mag yelled. She stomped back outside.

Florrie winced as the door slammed shut. She understood why Mag was angry, but she wished her sister wouldn't yell at the girl. Jen was too young to know the harm doctors could do.

"Mag's got it right, Jen. I joost need to rest."

Jen went to the bed and sat on the edge of the mattress. She met Florrie's gaze with difficulty. "I'm sorry I didn't tell you I got the pills."

Florrie patted her hand. "You was joost trying to help."

Although Florrie didn't seem to get any worse after that, Jen couldn't forgive Mag for throwing the pills away.

"Don't you want her to get better?" she asked Mag one morning. They had taken the Sangster to Black Bear Bluff to fish for red snappers. Florrie wanted some for pickling.

"You should take the girl so you kin get more," Florrie told Mag. "Give you a chance to talk things out."

"Nutting to talk about," Mag had replied, but she had known better than to refuse when Florrie's chin was out. She nursed her line, lifting the rod and lowering it to swim the shiner she was using for bait. "Florrie joost needs some venison liver," she told Jen. "That always perks her up."

"Liver won't fix her heart," Jen argued. Her line jerked and she yanked her rod up. The shaft bent almost double from the weight of the fish she'd hooked.

"I t'ink you got a ling!" Mag said. She reeled in her own line. "Joost bring her in slow—don't let 'er go slack!"

"I know how to do it, Mag," Jen gasped as she alternately lifted the rod and reeled up the slack. Her arms soon ached from the strain of holding the line tight. "I don't think I can hang on much longer!" she panted.

"Oh, shooer, you kin do it, girl. Joost a little more. . . ."

The light leader line appeared, indicating that the fish was near the surface. Mag grabbed a large net from the bottom of the boat and leaned over the side. "Gosh, he's a big bugger!" she shouted. The fish thrashed violently as she slipped the net under it. "Uumph!" She used all of her strength to lift the net, but was only able to get it as far as the gunwale. The ling cod lunged and twisted close to her hand. Jen dropped her rod and grabbed the metal rim of the net. Together they hauled the rigging over the gunwale and into the boat.

"That's the biggest I ever caught!" Jen grinned happily at Mag. "Florrie'll have all the pickled fish she can eat!"

The cod almost filled the full-sized garbage can that Mag used as a catch box. "Put yer line down again, girl," she said cheerfully as she put the lid on the can. "Might catch another one!" There was camaraderie between them now, a sisterhood of victors. Although their subsequent catch was limited to a few small rock cod, they were both content when they headed home.

The *Squawk Box* chugged into the cove, while Mag and Jen were on the dock cleaning their fish.

Mag swore softly. At the start of summer she had secured an old outboard from Billy, thinking to fix it as a backup for her own. "I'll pay yer when I get some logs together," she'd promised. Then the logging camp had shut down, which meant there were few logs to be found on the inlet, and no one to buy those she did find. Now she was sure Billy was coming for his pay. "I'm not gonna use any 'joost in case' money," she said stubbornly "But it's too bad I took that motor all apart."

"Well, if it's in pieces, there's no way he can take it," Jen said.

Mag nodded. "Yer right. But that Billy can shooer be miserable when he gets mad."

However, it wasn't Mag's debt that brought the *Squawk Box* to their wharf. It was a small black puppy. Mag frowned as Billy climbed off his boat and dumped the wriggling black bundle into Jen's arms.

"Folks up Narrows was drowning it," Billy said. "Dey already got two dogs and no money to feed any more, so dey put the pups in a sack along with some rocks and tossed it off the dock. Only this one gets out and starts swimming, you know? I figured he was a seal at first 'til I seen his paws. He was pretty much done for when I hauled him in."

Mag's eyes narrowed. "So how come you brought him here?"

Billy scratched his head. "Well, see, I got dis idea. I don't got no room here for the dog, but I thinks, you know, dat Mag—she got lots of room and I don't think she got a dog."

Jen felt the puppy's warmth through her blouse. She turned her face as he tried to lick her nose. His dark, lively eyes stared up at her, filled with yearning. "We could keep him, couldn't we, Mag? I'll look after him, I promise."

Mag scowled, furious with Billy for bringing this on. "Got no place fer dogs here," she snapped, "and you'll joost spoil it. Next t'ing we'll have dead chickens, and goats being chased all over."

"Looks like he got a lot of Lab in him," Billy said persuasively. "Labs is real easy to train."

"I guess not," Mag retorted, then repeated, "We got no place fer dogs here."

Jen held the dog tight. "Maybe Sylvia will let me keep him there," she suggested.

Billy grabbed the opening. "Dat's a good idea, you know. You keep the dog here now and den take him to town."

Mag could feel herself being trapped. "No!" she said, but it wasn't as firm as before. "Sylvia won't be back fer months."

"Please, Mag?"

Billy spat on the ground, then rubbed his chin. "How you comin' with dat motor?" he asked meaningfully.

"It's coming," Mag said shortly, but she made no further protest about the dog.

He looked along the cove to the cascara grove. "Der's talk somebody's gonna log dis place," he said.

Mag felt a tightness in her chest. "Who?"

He shrugged. "Dey ain't sayin'. When dey do, I let you know." He climbed onto his boat. "You take good care of dat dog," he said to Jen.

She peered over the puppy's head. "Thanks, Billy."

As they walked up to the cabin, Mag said grumpily, "Dog kin stay in the shed. Don't want it peeing in the house."

In her heart, Jen truly intended to follow Mag's orders. But a storm came through that night, shaking the house frame and rattling the windows. Normally the sounds eased Jen into a deep sleep, but this time they were interspersed with a whimpering from the shed that kept her wide awake. Finally, taking care not to disturb Florrie, she went out to the shed. She meant just to soothe the puppy and return. She didn't count on him crawling onto her lap, or snuggling down against her tummy as he gratefully licked her hand. She shivered in the darkness as the wind penetrated the cracks in the shed walls. There was no way she could spend the night in the shed, but she couldn't bring herself to leave the puppy alone.

Mag won't know if I take him into my bed, she decided. *Especially if I get him back out here before she gets up.* A fresh blast of wind hammered against the shed. "Come on, little Rascal," she murmured, rising to her feet. "Let's go get warm."

In the bedroom, Mag heard the outer door open and close.

The puppy didn't move from Jen's side all night. A coughing from the bedroom the next morning warned her that Mag was about to rise. By the time she came into the kitchen, Rascal was safely back in the shed.

"It's starting already," Mag grumbled when Jen returned to the cabin. "Yer out there with that damned dog instead of lighting the fire and looking after the goats."

"Oh, gosh, leave her alone, Mag," Florrie scolded from her bed. "Yer the one said we had to use the camp stove this summer."

"Didn't say it today," Mag retorted as she shoved kindling into the firebox. She had spent most of the night trying to figure out who might be logging the cove and how she could stop them. She ladled water into the coffee pot. "I wish our dad never sold that land."

Florrie swung her feet to the floor. Then, overcome with dizziness, she sat on the edge of the bed. "He didn't have no choice," she said when the room stopped reeling. She heaved herself to her feet and limped to the table. "He needed that money fer Mother's funeral." She sat down, breathing heavily from the effort.

Jen finished dressing. "Can't you stop them from logging there?"

"I guess not," Mag snorted. "Not them big companies."

"Might joost be talk," Florrie said comfortingly. "They've talked befer, anyways."

Mag exhaled loudly. "Maybe," she agreed, but her sour mood didn't lift. It grew even worse when she tripped on a hole the pup had dug in the trail to the outhouse. "Shitah!" she yelled, regaining her balance. She yelled at Jen who was returning from the goat shed, "You'd best make a pen fer that dog if yer gonna keep him!" The pup was romping around Jen, but when Mag spoke he scampered toward her, barking enthusiastically. Mag kicked at him and missed.

"He doesn't know what he's doing," Jen said swiftly. She set her milk bucket on the ground and scooped the pup into her arms.

"Then you better get that pen made quick," Mag warned. She stomped into the outhouse, slamming the door behind her.

"I'll help Florrie make the pickled fish, then I'll do the pen," Jen promised. But with the start of school only two days away, she wasn't sure just how she was going to accomplish the job.

Jen wasn't looking forward to the first day of school. Although she hadn't seen Cal since the episode on the beach, they were sure to share some classes at the small high school. "He's probably blabbed about it to everyone," Jen confided to Marlene two days later, as they walked to their History 11 class.

"I never heard anything," Marlene said, more interested in their history teacher. "You hear we're getting Passmore this year?"

"Who?"

"He's a real hunk," Marlene grinned. She pushed a limp strand of hair away from her plump forehead.

As they entered the classroom, Jen suddenly felt queasy. Cal was leaning against a desk in the front row near the door. Sandra Cooper, Tracy Vanderpol, and Glee Aldrich formed a semicircle around him. He didn't seem to notice Jen as she squeezed past the group and found an empty desk three aisles away. *So far so good*, she thought.

Marlene slid into the desk on her right. "That's Passmore."

The tall, husky man who had just entered was wearing denim jeans, a blue cotton shirt, and a corduroy jacket. He met her gaze and smiled.

"I'm going to love history this year," Marlene said.

The students standing at the front of the class shuffled to their desks, and Cal claimed the desk immediately left of Jen's. He grinned. "Hey, Jenny Penny," he said, his tone friendly.

Jen ignored him, and Cal's grin deepened. "Hey, you're not still mad, are you?" When she still didn't answer, he made a tragic face.

166

"You gotta admit, I did sorta get the worst of it. I lost a brand new pair of shoes—unless you still have them."

Jen tried to ignore him by focusing on her history book.

"Do you have them?" he persisted.

"Mag shot them," she said finally, glaring at him. "Instead of you."

For a moment he paled. "I heard a couple of shots," he said. "I thought maybe she was shooting at you."

She looked at him levelly. "Nice of you to send help."

The teacher cleared his throat meaningfully. "If you two have finished your visit, perhaps we can get started," he said. Red-faced, Jen turned her attention to the lesson.

When the class was over, Sandra Cooper and the rest of her group surrounded Cal again, Sandra taking hold of his arm possessively. *Marking her territory,* Jen thought derisively. *Why doesn't she just piss on him?*

She was glad when school was out and she could escape to her boat. The hour-long journey up the inlet soothed the tumult within her. By the time she reached the cove she was feeling more like her usual self. The pup was on the wharf, barking excitedly as she pulled up.

"What's Rascal doin' out?" she asked when she entered the cabin. Florrie was at the counter adding flour to her sourdough starter. Mag was studying a catalogue at the kitchen table. There was a normalcy about them that reassured Jen.

"Florrie let him out," Mag grumbled. "She's spoiling him."

"Giving a pup somet'ing to eat won't spoil anyt'ing," Florrie retorted. "He's good company when yer both gone doing t'ings I can't."

Mag bit back a retort that if Florrie hadn't given up on working, she would still be able to move about. But there was no sense going over that again, she decided. What was done, was done. "I'm going into town tomorrow," she said instead. "Gotta order some new boots." She pushed the catalogue over to Jen. "You kin put the numbers down fer me. Them buggers at the post office won't help me."

Florrie put the lid on the sourdough starter, limped to the table, and sat heavily on her chair. "Maybe you kin order me some batteries," she said hopefully. "I'd shooer like to hear that radio again."

Jen deposited her backpack on the cot. "Thought you didn't have any money, Mag."

Mag grinned. "Someone's started Stevenson's old camp up," she said. "New boom man left the gate open, and there was logs all over. Rounded up five of 'em and he give me two hundred bucks."

After supper, Jen helped her make out the catalogue order form. The following morning, they left for town together, towing the Princecraft behind Mag's boat. The skies were clear and there was no wind, so they made good time. When they reached the dock, Jen helped tote the gas cans up the ramp before she went off to school. Mag left them outside of the café, then, while she waited for the taxi, she ordered a coffee and a slice of apple pie. She had just finished the treat when she heard a familiar voice behind her.

"How's dat dog doin'?" Billy Thom asked, settling into a seat opposite Mag.

"You bugger," Mag growled. "Florrie and the girl are spoiling that dog joost terrible. Next t'ing you know it'll be eating my chickens."

Billy nodded to the waitress who brought him a cup of coffee. "Yeah, but I bet he's made dem happy, you know?"

"Humph." Mag wasn't going to waste her time talking about a dog she never wanted. "You hear any more about that logging?"

"What I hear, you don't want to know. It's dat Pete Saari what's gonna log it. He got an outfit up Narrows what's just finishin' den he's comin' down to the cove. Dis Forestry guy told me all about it when I took him up Jervis last week."

Mag's eyes narrowed. "So that's what Saari and his kid was doing up at the cove this summer. That bugger don't miss nutting." She stared out the window, no longer appreciating the sun or its warmth. "Shitah." Having the cove logged was bad enough. Having Pete Saari do the logging was intolerable. "I gotta go to the post office," she muttered. She collected her pack and stomped out of the café, leaving Billy to pay for her coffee and pie.

Her mood was further soured when she collected her mail. Among the fliers was a letter with writing that was faintly familiar.

She stared at it for a long time before she remembered where she'd seen the script before, then she walked heavily into the main office to obtain a money order for her boots. When the clerk had completed the certificate, Mag handed her the letter.

"What's this say?" Mag made it a demand, rather than a question.

The woman was about to remark that her job was to deliver mail, not to read it, when she remembered what one of her co-workers had told her about Mag. "You're better off helping her because she'll make your life ten times more miserable if you don't." From the expression Mag wore this morning, the clerk decided the misery Mag exacted would be severe.

"I'll read it for you," she said grudgingly, "but only because there are no other customers right now." She took the letter and read aloud, "'Dear Mrs. Larson, You must think I'm terrible for never coming for Lisa. I did come once and watched her with you and your sister and you all seemed happy, so I figured there wasn't much sense dragging her along with me because I didn't have my shit together then. I'm doing better now. I'm not on drugs no more and I'm living with this guy and we've got three babies. Well, they aren't all babies now. Aimee is almost four and Selena's two, but Deek's still a baby. So I figure Lisa's old enough now she could come for a visit and get to know her real family. I'm trying to save enough for her bus fare, but if you was to give it to her I'd see you get it back when I can. Just send her up and tell her to go to the Bud Light Shack in Alert Bay. Everybody there can tell her how to get to the Quick Stop Motel where we're living and they'll probably even take her there. Only, tell her not to go with a guy called Whitey because he's bad news. Yours truly, Sue Drummond. PS I was gonna send a picture of the kids but I gotta wait 'til Sam gets paid before I can get them from the developers. They don't like to give credit in this hole.'"

The clerk looked at Mag in surprise. "I thought your girl's name was Jen Larson?"

"It is," Mag said curtly. She wished she'd waited until Sylvia returned to have the letter read.

The door to the post office opened and a man came in with a large parcel. Mag was happy to give him her place at the counter. She stowed the money order in the catalogue envelope, then shoved it into the mail slot. With the letter in her pocket, she trudged down the street to the grocery store.

That evening, while Jen was locking the goats in for the night, Mag told Florrie about the letter.

"You gonna show it to Jen?" Florrie asked anxiously. She was still upset over Mag's prediction that Jen would leave the cove when she was finished with high school.

"What fer? She joost wants the girl to look after her kids."

"She's better off here," Florrie agreed, her relief visible. "We kin show it to her when she's older."

"That's what I t'ink," Mag said. She tucked the letter beneath a pile of old magazines on the highest shelf in the cupboard. Then she glanced at the parts belonging to Billy Thom's motor that were scattered over the work bench below. "Gotta get that motor fixed," she muttered. "Old one's starting to act up somet'ing terrible."

It became a nightly routine for Jen to slip out and rescue Rascal from the shed. Mag might never have had to acknowledge that it was happening if it hadn't been for the war that erupted between a family of bushy-tailed wood rats that had settled under the house, and the visiting skunk that decided the large grey rodents would make a delectable meal.

The battle began one night, shortly after the sisters and Jen had gone to bed. It started with a faint musky odour and the rattle of debris, then escalated into a crashing and squealing under the floorboards. Mag was lost in a deep, dreamless sleep, unaware of the drama going on beneath her—until the pup started yipping. For a few moments she stared groggily through the darkness trying to identify the source of the disturbance. The skunk smell seemed stronger than before. *Skunk musta caught a rat*, she told herself. Suddenly there was a loud crash in the other room and she heard Jen hiss, "Rascal!"

Mag jumped out of bed. Groping in the dark she found her lamp and touched a match to the wick.

In the kitchen the din had increased. Lamp in hand, Mag opened the door just as a creature with a long, furry tail skittered across her workbench of motor parts, scattering them in all directions. Then it leaped onto the wall cupboard. Barking furiously, the pup jumped at the cupboard, dodging papers and boxes that the woodrat knocked off the shelves in its frantic effort to climb higher.

"What the hell's going on?" Mag thundered.

Jen lunged at the dog. "Rascal!" she yelled, but the dog was once again in hot pursuit of the rat, who had reached a ledge between the wall and the ceiling and was following it toward the cupboard where Florrie stored her dry goods.

Mag advanced into the room and set the lamp on the table, without glancing at Florrie, who was sitting up in bed looking thoroughly bemused. "What's happening?" Florrie managed as Jen chased the dog around the table.

"What's he doin' in here?" Mag bellowed just as plastic jar of raisins toppled off the top shelf of the dry goods cupboard.

"Watch out!" Jen warned.

Mag jumped out of the way and the jar crashed to the floor. "Shitah!" she swore, then headed for the gun rack on the opposite wall. She grabbed her .22 rifle and shoved a clip of bullets into the chamber.

Corralling the dog at last, Jen lifted him off the floor and held him close as Mag took aim at the rat, which at that moment ducked behind a box of icing sugar.

"You'll hit the roof," Florrie warned, cushioning her ears with a pillow, but Mag had already pulled the trigger. The discharge reverberated through the cabin, though the bullet went harmlessly into the wall. The rat's head appeared over the box of icing sugar just long enough for Mag to pull the trigger once more. The box exploded, showering the room with white powder, but the rat, now a furry-tailed ghost—and completely unscathed—leapt down to the counter. Startled by the shots, Jen loosened her hold on the now-panicked dog who jumped out of her arms and headed for the door.

"Shitah!" Mag swore, but before she could raise her rifle again, Jen ran to the door and opened it. As the cool night air swept into the room, the rat streaked toward the opening, followed by the now white-spotted Labrador pup. Mag swung her gun in that direction, but Jen slammed the door and leaned against it as silence filled the room.

"I better make sure Rascal comes back," she said finally.

Florrie leaned back against the pillows on her bed. "Gosh," she said wonderingly.

Jen put on her boots, not daring to look at either sister. When she did peek across the room, Mag was bent over her workbench, her back to the kitchen, her shoulders shaking.

"Are you okay?" Jen asked fearfully. But when she realized that Mag was laughing, Jen's relief erupted in a fit of laughter that doubled her over. She grabbed a chair for support. From the bed came the sound of Florrie's wheezing chortle.

Mag recovered her composure first. She went to the stove, stirred up the coals in the firebox, then added more wood. "I joost knew that dog would be trouble!" She dipped water from the bucket into the kettle. "When you find him, girl, you put him in the shed where he belongs. Then you kin gather up them parts the critter dumped all over."

It was while she was picking up the papers and magazines the skunk had knocked off the cupboard shelves, that Jen found the letter from her mother. She recognized the handwriting at once, having read and reread her mother's first letter a dozen times during her childhood.

"What's this?"

"It come last week," Mag said from the table where she sat drinking cocoa.

Jen brought the letter to the table. While she read, the kitchen was silent except for the crackling from the stove. At the end she looked up at Mag. "How come you never showed it to me?"

"What fer?" Mag demanded gruffly.

Florrie got out of bed and padded over to the table. Her face held a mixture of fear and apology. "You gonna go there?"

Jen read the letter once again. "I'd kind of like to meet her," she said, unaware of the panic on Florrie's face, "but I got school. And Rascal to look after."

"You kin go when yer grown, anyways," Florrie said happily. She didn't let herself consider the fact that Jen was almost grown already.

On the last Tuesday in October, Mag was manoeuvring a hemlock log into her boom when a tug passed by the cove. She pushed the log the rest of the way in, secured the gate, and positioned her boat so it would shield the logs from the tug's wake. "Shitah!" she exploded as the waves hit. She gripped the wheel, steadying herself. *What the hell they doin' so close?* Moments later she had her answer, as the long black barge that the tug was towing rounded Serpent Point. It was loaded with fuel drums, rolls of cable, a rusted bulldozer that might once have been orange, and a yellow grapple skidder. With a sickening feeling in her stomach, she watched the tug pass by the cove then nudge the barge into position off the beach below her cascara grove. The rattle of chains echoed across the cove as a deckhand on the barge dropped its anchor.

Mag steered the Sangstercraft back to her dock. She felt suddenly old as she trudged up the trail to the cabin, and she had an uncommon desire to return to bed as Florrie had done. But when she stepped inside, her sister was sitting at the table, the pup curled near her feet.

"Saari's moved his outfit in," Mag said as she hung her hat on the nail.

"I heard them when I was in the outhouse."

"I don't t'ink it's right," Mag said sourly. She poured herself some coffee and sat across from Florrie. "They joost shouldn't be able to come and take our trees."

"I guess they're not ours anymore," Florrie said. "Not since our dad sold 'em."

Jen was horrified when she returned late that afternoon to find the barge lying in wait like the vanguard of an invading army. She was even more appalled to find everything going on as usual in the cabin. Florrie was emptying a quart sealer of goat meat into a pot to make stew.

"Mag!" Jen exclaimed. "Your cascara trees are up there!"

Mag scowled at the motor parts she was trying to reassemble. "So's my shitty bark."

Jen stared at her. "You're not gonna let Saari take them, are you?"

"Humph!" Mag placed the carburetor on the head. In her experience, folks like Saari took what they wanted, and the law generally backed them up. "Should've shot the son of a bitch when I had the chance."

The following morning, they woke to the cranky growl of chainsaws. When Jen started for school, she saw a crew boat pulled up to the beach just beyond the mud flats, and as she motored out from the dock, she heard a dull thud as another tree crashed to the ground. "Shitah!" she swore, then revved her motor so she didn't have to hear any more.

In the cabin, Mag went back to fixing the motor. She had no desire to go outside.

On the Thursday after Saari's crew started cutting, Cob Junior escaped from the pen. Jen spent an hour roaming through the bush behind the animal sheds before she found him. Happy to have the unexpected gift of her company, Rascal romped at her feet as she pulled the recalcitrant goat back to the pen.

"Told yer I'd go looking fer him," Mag said when Jen returned to the cabin to change for school. She planned to butcher the billy in the next couple of weeks, but she'd learned it was easier to just do the job when Jen was at school and let her find out later. That way she didn't have to listen to the girl go on about animal rights or vegetable diets. Folks could starve to death that way.

"Yeah, right," Jen said. She was well aware of Mag's plans, but it made her feel better to give the billies as long a lifetime as she could. "This way I know he's safe."

After the girl left for school, Florrie returned to her bed. "I'll fix up the kitchen later," she wheezed.

"Yer starting to live in that sack," Mag said sternly. "You need to get outside and move yer bones befer they seize up fer good."

Florrie lay back against her pillows. "What I need is some fresh venison liver. That always fixes me up." She pulled the covers up around her chin. "It's cold in here," she complained.

Mag was thoughtful as she filled the firebox with wood. She had meant to go hunting for venison as soon as the season opened in September, but hadn't wanted to leave Florrie alone. Now, with Saari's crew working just across the bay, she was even more reluctant to be away. "I'll go up Narrows on Saturday and see what I kin do. Girl will be here then to look after the goats."

"Go tomorrow," Florrie said. "I kin watch things during the day and Jen'll be home early. She always is on Fridays."

Mag replaced the firebox lid. Of course, there would be less chance of anyone else being in the woods on Friday. She always felt nervous around weekend hunters, especially the ones who trampled through the brush like angry bears and shot at anything that moved.

"We'll see." She collected her hat and went outside to free the pup from his pen.

On the inlet, Jen pushed the Honda to top speed, thankful that the sea was calm. Arriving at the Sechelt Wharf just after nine o'clock, she moored the boat and jogged up the long hill to the secondary school. She reached her locker, breathless and dishevelled, and after collecting an armload of books, she headed for the math classroom. As she rounded the corner where the main hall joined a secondary corridor, she ran full tilt into Cal Saari.

"Whoa, girl!" He steadied her with his hands on her shoulders, then struggled to catch the books tumbling from her arms.

"Shitah," she muttered, and knelt down to pick up the papers that had spilled out of her binder. When she stood, Cal was standing so close she could smell salt and vinegar chips on his breath. Her stomach began to churn and she tried to move away, but he blocked her path. "I'm late, Cal."

"Who cares?" he scoffed. "So am I." He grinned. "Maybe we'll get a detention together."

"Like Sandra would put up with that," Jen snorted.

His grin disappeared. "I do what I want," he said stiffly.

"Yeah, right." She moved around him and walked toward the classroom at the end of the hall. Before she reached the door, he caught her arm. "You want to go to a party tomorrow night?"

Jen stared at him incredulously. "With you?"

He shuffled his feet. "Well, I sort of got a date, but I'll be around . . ."

She grasped the doorknob. "No, thanks," she said, then added bitterly, "I've got to go home and cut cascara bark before your old man chops down all our trees."

"There's a Halloween party at Sandra's place," he whispered hastily. "Her folks are out of town. Seven o'clock, if you change your mind."

That night, as Jen fried hamburgers for their dinner, Mag told her about the hunting trip she was planning. "You'll have to come home right from school," she said.

"Sure, Mag," Jen responded absently, her mind on the math test scheduled for the next day. Math had never been her strong subject, and this year was proving to be the hardest of all. "I just don't understand this stuff," she told Florrie later as they shared a cup of cocoa at the kitchen table.

Florrie was feeling good. She had managed to bake bread that day without stopping in the middle for a nap. She sipped her cocoa. "I joost never was any good with numbers," she said. "Not like Mag. She kin figure out anyt'ing with numbers."

"Not them kind of numbers," Mag said from the corner where she was cleaning her rifle. Jen had tried to explain geometry to her one day. Mag had looked hard at the textbook page filled with shapes and numbers that she'd never seen before, then suddenly remembered an urgent task outside. Now, as she pulled the oiled cloth from her gun barrel, she asked gruffly, "What you got to learn that stuff fer?"

"I need it to graduate," Jen said. She looked dolefully at the algebraic formulas she had yet to memorize. "And I need it to pass the test tomorrow."

She milked the goats at daylight the next morning. Rascal howled mournfully in his pen, but instead of letting him out, she paused just long enough to give him a good scratch. He howled mournfully when she left him. In the cabin, she set the milk bucket on the counter. "I'm going early," she said, "so I can get some help before the test." She grabbed her backpack and was gone before Mag remembered to remind her to come home early.

"Shitah." Mag poured herself a cup of coffee. On the back burner was the pot of porridge Jen had made, its scum congealed to a translucent crust. Mag spooned a helping into a bowl. Her gear was already stowed in the boat and, as she wolfed down her cereal, she planned the route she would follow up the mountain.

Florrie stirred in her bed and coughed. Her breathing was wheezy this morning.

"How come yer still here?" she gasped when the coughing passed.

"I was waiting 'til the girl left," Mag said. She emptied the rest of the porridge into another bowl, added sugar and milk to it and carried it over to the chair beside Florrie's bed.

"I put in lots of sugar," she said.

"I'm not real hungry," Florrie said weakly. "Joost leave it there. I'll eat it later."

Mag studied her carefully. Even in the dim light of the cabin, Florrie's face seemed greyer and more haggard than usual. "Maybe I'll go hunting tomorrow," Mag said reluctantly, although she hated to be steered away from a course already set.

Florrie shook her head. "Sooner you go, sooner you'll be back," she said. "Shooer nutting you kin do fer me here."

"I kin keep the fire going so yer warm," Mag argued. "I t'ink maybe you got one of them flu bugs the girl brings home."

Florrie had another coughing spasm. When it was over, she was too weak to speak for several minutes. Mag went to the nail where she kept her hat.

"I'm staying," she said. "I'll get them traps out and fix 'em up. Billy Thom says there's a guy up Jervis wants to buy some." She was opening the door when Florrie stopped her.

"Go hunting, Mag. It's what you want and it's what I want. Joost bring me some venison liver."

Mag peered at her. From the light of the open door it seemed as if the colour was returning to Florrie's cheeks. *Maybe she did too much yesterday*, she thought.

"Jen'll be home early," Florrie went on. "I'll stay in bed 'til she comes."

Mag stared at her a moment before she returned to the stove. "I'll fill her up fer you," she said. "Should last 'til past noon." By the time she closed the lid to the firebox and shut down the dampers, Florrie was snoring again, her breathing more natural. Mag collected the pup from the pen and set him inside the cabin. He stood uncertainly for a moment, then jumped onto Florrie's bed. When Mag left the cabin, he was curled up behind Florrie's knees.

"She'll be fine," Mag told herself as she made her way down to the boat. If all went well, she might get a deer early. She could be back even before the girl got home.

At school, everyone was talking about the party Sandra had planned. Jen was too relieved to have completed her math test to pay much attention to them. Having secured the teacher's help before class, she had done well on it. "I'll never be good at math," she told Marlene when she found her bent over the sink in the washroom at lunch time, "but I think I'm starting to figure it out." Marlene was splashing water on her face and suddenly Jen realized her friend was crying. "What's wrong?" she demanded.

"She told him," Marlene sobbed, stumbling to the towel dispenser.

"Who?"

"Passmore. Sandra told him I had a crush on him! Oh, God!" she moaned into the towel.

"I'll never go into his class again."

"Sandra's a bitch, Marlene. And Passmore probably didn't even believe her."

Marlene lifted her head. "Yes, he did. She stole a sketch of him. He was looking at it when I came in." She howled again, burying her face back into the towel. "What am I going to do?"

Jen turned her around. "You're going to get even," she said, so fiercely that Marlene lifted her face hopefully.

"How?"

Jen grinned. "You and I are going to a party."

Knowing she couldn't get home and back in time for the party, Jen decided to spend the night at Sylvia's cottage. She had stayed there several times since the beginning of term, when the wind was blowing too hard to make it safely to the cove, and she knew Florrie would understand if she didn't show up. It wasn't until she was scrambling herself some eggs for supper in Sylvia's kitchen that she remembered Mag's hunting trip. By then it was too dark to go up the inlet. *Florrie will be okay*, Jen told herself. *I'll go home first thing in the morning.*

It was late afternoon when Mag saw the buck. He was standing on the edge of a logging slash, his nose lifted to the breeze. Crouched downwind of him, on a rise just west of the clearing, she studied the terrain. *Guess I could pack him out to the road okay*, she thought. She knew it might be only a matter of minutes before he moved out of range. She checked her rifle, sighted on him, and fired. The sound exploded the silence of the clearing. The buck jumped high in the air before crashing down. Mag waited to see if he would rise again. When he didn't, she began picking her way down the hill, over mounds of tree butts and around the stumps left from the logging.

The buck lay where he'd fallen, a sturdy two point that would provide them with some fine steaks. She gutted him on the spot, carefully stowing the heart and liver in a plastic bag. By the time she finished, it was too late to get down the mountain before dark. She thought about Florrie being alone, then shrugged. The girl would be home by now.

She tossed a rope from her pack over the stout limb of nearby hemlock. Tying one end to the buck's hind legs, she used the other to hoist him high enough off the ground to discourage predators.

As she set her bedroll down in the shelter of a burned-out stump, closer to the logging slash, hunger pains gnawed at Mag's stomach, reminding her that she hadn't eaten since breakfast. She made a fire and cooked the venison heart by holding it over the flames on an alder spear. A slice of Florrie's bread and some coffee, made in a tin can she carried in her pack, completed her meal.

When she was full, she lay beneath the stars and watched the moon rise over the tree tops. It had been a long time since she had spent a night in the open. Too long, she decided. Then she rolled onto her side and slept.

When Marlene arrived at the cottage, Jen was on her hands and knees in Sylvia's garden.

"What are you doing?" Marlene asked. "I thought we were going to Sandra's party."

"We are," Jen said then held up a plastic bag of worms. "And we're going to get even."

"Ewww!" Marlene stepped back. "I'm not touching those!"

"You don't have to," Jen said confidently. "I've got it all planned." She tucked the bag into her pocket, rinsed her hands at the tap beside the cottage, and dried them on her jeans. "Let's go. The party was supposed to start an hour ago."

A full moon guided their steps as they walked along the road. By the time they reached the beach, Marlene was wavering between apprehension and excitement. "Sandra's going to be real choked when we show up," she fretted, shoving her hands into the pockets of the denim bib overalls she was wearing for the occasion. "They go to our church, Jen. What if her dad tells mine?"

When Jen assured her that Judge Cooper was out of town, Marlene's concern turned to the party itself. "Maybe they won't let us in," she worried.

Jen shrugged. "From what I've heard, half the school is going. They won't even notice us."

Her prediction was confirmed by the screeches, shouts, and deafening thump of rock music that greeted the girls long before they reached the Cooper's fashionable, two-storey home on the Trail Bay waterfront. From the cedar hedge that separated the property from the beach, they could see the patio surrounding a large swimming pool. Steam rose from the water and swirled about the noisy teenagers who seemed to be everywhere—in the pool, on the swing, dancing on the patio. Lounge chairs were occupied by couples so closely entwined they looked like single bodies with two heads. There were lights all around the patio and pool, and every window of the house was lit up.

"It looks like fun," Marlene said wistfully.

As they slipped through the hedge, they saw Cal Saari emerge from the house, brandishing a bottle of vodka over his head. "Who-oooh!" he shouted, "guess what I found?"

Jen led Marlene through the crowd to a poolside table overflowing with beer cans, a platter of chips and dip, and a large punch bowl into which several kids were dumping bottles of wine, vodka, and ginger ale. The worms would add a nice touch, Jen decided, if she could only figure a way to slip them in without being noticed. Marlene followed close behind her. "Look at Sandra," she whispered, pointing to the blond girl with a drink in her hand, dancing in front of Cal. "She's stoned."

Sandra laughed wildly as she danced. Occasionally she stumbled and clutched Cal's arm for support, which only made her laugh more. Cal steadied her, then watched her resume her dance.

"Hey, Marlene!" Trent Servant sidled up beside the two girls. A gangly youth with severe acne, he had an engaging smile and a sense of humour that had earned him the reputation of class clown. He was also Cal Saari's best friend.

Jen ignored him, but Marlene smiled. "Hey, Trent."

He handed her the beer he was carrying. "Want some?"

"No, she doesn't," Jen said sternly and tried to brush past him.

"No, she doesn't!" Trent mimicked in a high-pitched voice. He made a comical face at Marlene. "Is she your mother?" Marlene blushed and shook her head. "Then have some." He thrust the beer into her hands then nodded toward the patio. "You wanna dance?"

Marlene looked pleadingly at Jen. "Just one?"

"What do I care?" Jen asked sourly, but as Marlene followed Trent, and Jen was left standing by herself, she wished she had never started this caper. She wished so even more fervently when Cal spotted her.

"Hey, Jenny Penny! Come 'n' have a drink." He popped the tab from a can of beer and held it out to Jen.

"No, thanks," Jen said. He stood so close to her that she could smell his cologne—a nauseating, spicy smell that reminded her of the day on the beach. Suddenly Sandra pushed herself between them.

"What are *you* doing here?" she demanded. As Cal pulled Sandra against him and kissed her on the mouth, Jen turned away, only to be caught by his other arm to be included in the embrace. "Don't be jealous, babes," he soothed.

Jen and Sandra pushed away from him simultaneously. "Shove it, Saari!" Jen growled, while Sandra stormed across the patio to where Tracy and Glee were using rackets to toss ping pong balls at an upper story window. Cal grinned, but as he followed Sandra, Jen sensed that he wasn't as confident as he was trying to appear.

Marlene was still dancing with Trent, but when the song ended she suddenly reappeared beside Jen. "I have to pee," she said loudly. Jen took the beer can from her hands, dismayed to find it almost empty.

"Let's find the can," she said, leading the way through the patio doors. Inside the house the music was playing even louder than the stereo outside, and three teenagers were stomping to the beat on a polished wood coffee table. Others were investigating the cupboards behind an elaborate bar, and still more were seated on the floor in a circle, passing a joint from one to another. Jen had to shout to be heard as she asked one of the girls where the bathroom was, but she received only a vacant stare in response. Deciding to find it for herself, she grabbed Marlene and pulled her up an elaborately carved staircase filled with more kids.

Marlene giggled. "This is fun!"

"You're drunk," Jen said accusingly, which caused her friend to giggle even harder.

"Am not," she insisted, but her weaving gait, as they made their way along an upper hallway, said otherwise.

"God," Jen gasped as she opened the bathroom door, "look at this—even the can has carpet!" She pushed Marlene inside and went on to peek into the next room, where a half-naked couple were entwined, too absorbed to notice her. The next room held a wall full of books and Jen couldn't help but venture inside. Next to a sturdy oak desk, a large window overlooked the patio and pool, and beyond that, Trail Bay. She stared at the shimmering path of moonlight that stretched shoreward from the dark shadows of the islands. In garish contrast below her Sandra and Cal were performing a striptease, encircled by a crowd of teenagers who clapped and shrieked in unison, "More! More!"

Jen turned away. Beside her, the desk was strewn with legal-looking documents, books and letter writing materials, and in their midst, a camera. Jen picked it up and peered through the viewfinder. It was just like the one she had used in photography class the previous term.

"What are you doing?" Marlene demanded from the doorway.

Jen grinned. "I don't think we're going to need those worms after all!" She carried the camera to the window and began snapping pictures. "The judge is going to get a surprise when he develops these." When the roll was finished, she returned the camera to the desk. "Now let's go home and get you sobered up," she said.

"But I wanna dance some more," Marlene pouted. "Trent likes me."

"Well, I don't like him," Jen retorted. "You can stay if you want, but I'm going home."

Still grumbling, Marlene followed her down the stairs and back out onto the patio. They were just passing the pool when someone shouted, "Cops!"

In an instant, everyone except Sandra was running away, pouring out of the house and climbing out of the pool. Jen grabbed Marlene's arm. "Let's go!"

"My dad's gonna kill me!" Marlene sobbed.

They ran through the opening in the hedge, then scrambled over a pile of driftwood on the beach.

"He's not gonna find out," Jen panted, half-dragging Marlene toward a rocky outcrop. Behind them, flashlights splayed across the darkness as the police approached the beach. Jen ducked low, forcing Marlene down with her. Half-crouched, they clambered over the rocks then dropped down on to the beach and slipped into the shadow of a large, overhanging ledge. When the tide came in, this part of the beach would be underwater, but for the moment it was dry. They were joined by four of the other teenagers and they crouched together, listening to the shouts as more kids ran further up the beach.

Then suddenly there were running footsteps on the rocks above them. "They're coming!" Marlene whispered hysterically. Jen covered her friend's mouth with her hand as someone jumped off the ledge and squeezed into the shadows. The air filled with the masculine scent of spice cologne.

"Who's here?" Cal whispered, and six mouths shushed him as boots crunched the gravel above them.

"You see where the little bastard went?" a loud male voice demanded. He was answered by a second man. "Too cold for swimming. Must've ducked into the woods."

"I'm going after him."

"Nah. We broke up the party. That's all Cooper'd want."

As the voices and footsteps retreated, Jen removed her hand from Marlene's mouth. When there had been silence outside for several minutes, Cal stepped out of the shadows and held up his bottle of vodka. "Anyone want a drink?" One of the boys grabbed the bottle from him and began circulating it.

"Guess the party's over," Trent Servant grumbled.

In the darkness, Jen didn't see Marlene take the bottle and put it to her lips, but she heard her choking a moment later.

"Hey! Don't waste it," Cal protested. He pried the bottle from her grip and took a long swallow from it before handing it to Trent. "Let's go someplace else," he suggested, and though no one knew where that "someplace else" might be, they started down the beach. They were soon joined by other kids who had been hiding behind logs and in the shadows of cottages that lined the shore. Some carried six-packs of beer they'd grabbed from the Cooper house, while others toted bottles of wine.

Trent had taken Marlene's hand and she stumbled along between him and Cal. Reluctant to leave her friend alone, Jen followed behind them.

"All's we need is music and a place to dance," Cal said.

"We can go to Jen's place," Marlene offered. "Sylvia's not there."

"No way!" Jen exploded, but her protest was lost in the delighted hoots of the others.

"All ri-i-ight! Let's party on!" Cal whooped. While he and Trent walked ahead, Marlene dropped back to plead with Jen.

"Aw, come on, Jen. Jus' for a while."

"No way," Jen snapped. "It's not my house!"

"But Trent likes me," Marlene wailed.

"He just wants a place to party," Jen said coldly.

"You're jus' jealous," Marlene snapped.

"Yeah, right," Jen scoffed, but she knew Marlene wasn't entirely wrong. A part of Jen would have liked to share in the fun the others seemed to be having.

"Well, I'm goin' with 'em anyways," Marlene said thickly, and suddenly Jen was faced with a new dilemma. Marlene was already half-drunk. If she went with the other kids, she could end up pregnant or worse and Jen knew it would be her fault because she had thought up the whole stupid scheme in the first place.

"All right," she said finally. "They can come to my place. But just for a while. And you gotta promise not to drink anything else."

"I promise!" Marlene swore.

Mag woke at daylight. Her body ached as if every joint was being pulled apart. For a moment she wasn't even sure where she was. Then she remembered the deer. She crawled painfully out of the stump. The deer was still hanging from the hemlock limb and, as far as she could tell, nothing had touched it in the night.

She stirred the ashes in her firepit. A few embers still glowed and, with the help of some dry shavings, they soon flamed to life. Mag fed them some of the wood she'd gathered the previous evening.

Hot coffee and more of Florrie's bread finally warmed Mag's limbs so she could move. She doused the fire, loosened the rope holding the deer, and lowered the animal onto her shoulders. Bent almost double, she started down the deer trail to the beach.

By early afternoon, she was guiding the Sangstercraft into Serpent Cove. *Soon as I look after the goats,* she decided, *I'll cook Florrie up some of that liver.* She pulled alongside the dock. There was no sign of the girl's boat. Nor was the dog barking on shore.

Jen opened her eyes a crack and squinted at the floor strewn with her clothes, then glanced at her watch. It was almost nine o'clock. Florrie would be wondering where she was.

She heard a noise in the kitchen and felt suddenly nervous. Had the police come back? She pushed herself up on her elbow. "Is someone there?"

Footsteps sounded in the hall and Sylvia appeared in the doorway. Her expression was grim.

Jen stared at her. "Sylvia! I didn't think you were coming 'til Monday!"

Sylvia looked at the clutter on the floor. "That's rather obvious." She shook her head. "You'd better get dressed. There's a mess to be cleaned up." Before Jen could respond, Sylvia stepped back into the hall and closed the door. Jen scrambled out of bed. Quickly she changed into jeans and a T-shirt, gathered the clothes from her floor, and dumped them into the hamper near her bed. Then she went to the kitchen where Sylvia stood, arms folded across her chest, surveying a burn mark on the counter. *Trent's toke*, Jen remembered. The living room was even worse. Sylvia's favourite Haida mask sat in a pool of spilled beer on the teak table.

Jen closed her eyes. *It's a nightmare*, she told herself. *I'll wake up and it will all go away!* Nothing had changed when she opened them again. The concern that had compelled her to look after Marlene had vanished. Standing among the ruins of Sylvia's beautiful room, Jen could summon no justification for her behaviour.

"Here." Sylvia thrust a cup of coffee into her hands.

Jen mumbled her thanks. She brought the steaming cup to her lips and let the hot liquid burn her mouth and throat. Punishing herself. "I didn't mean this to happen," she managed finally. "They said they just wanted someplace to dance. Then everyone started throwing things. I told them to stop, but they wouldn't. Not until the police came . . . and Mrs. Greystone."

"Your behaviour is inexcusable, Jen." Her voice was cold. "I can't remember when I've ever been so disappointed in someone." She collected her purse and car keys from the counter. "I have to go down to the police station and prove that I had no involvement in this . . . this insanity. I expect you to have my home cleaned up before I get back." The door slammed behind her.

Jen set the coffee cup down, went into the living room, and began picking up garbage. She was unable to remove the imprint of two moisture circles on the teak table. She cleaned the bathroom where Glee had thrown up, and mopped the kitchen floor. Sylvia still hadn't returned when she finished, although it was long past lunchtime. Jen waited a while longer, then scribbled a note of apology and headed for the dock.

Even the neoprene lining of Jen's floater coat could not protect her from the icy northeast wind that stirred the inlet into a rough chop. Her attention, however, was not on the cold, but on the water as she struggled to keep the Princecraft on course. Not until she rounded Chum Point did the chop subside. Thrusting the throttle ahead, she sped past Serpent Point and entered the cove.

Mag's boat was moored beside the dock. *She must not have gone hunting after all,* Jen thought with relief. Still, something wasn't right. The afternoon sun was already close to disappearing behind the hills; its lingering rays touched the cabin roof, turning the mossy shingles to gold. But it wasn't the colour of the roof that Jen noticed. There should have been smoke.

She glanced over at the barge near Saari's landing. The crew boat wasn't there, and the woods were still. She pulled up beside the dock, then quickly cut the engine. Securing her bow rope only, she hurried up the ramp. In the grass along the path she saw drops of fresh blood. As she walked further, she realized there was a strange stillness in the air. Even the roosters weren't crowing.

Why isn't there smoke coming from the chimney? And where's Rascal?

She pushed the cabin door open and peered into the darkness. "Florrie? Mag? Rascal?"

Florrie was huddled on the bed. Jen felt a surge of relief as she removed her pack and dumped it on her own cot. But something was still wrong. The cabin was too quiet. And too cold. She crossed the room. "Florrie?"

There was no response. Suddenly, Jen realized that Florrie wasn't snoring or wheezing as she usually did when she slept. Jen touched her arm and found it cold. "Oh, no. Florrie, no!" Jen's throat constricted as she tried to roll Florrie onto her back. But her body was stiff, and Jen didn't have the strength to lift her. She clutched the unyielding shoulder and buried her face in the fabric of Florrie's shirt, unconsciously searching for the warmth that would never be again. Pain cut through her chest as she sobbed uncontrollably.

In the tool shed it was almost dark. Mag could barely see the bits of hide she was trimming from the deer. Her arms were coated with dried blood. The buck's severed head rested on the floor, its large ebony eyes staring at nothing. Beside it lay the pup. He had whimpered at the sound of Jen's motor but hadn't moved.

Don't want to leave his dinner, Mag surmised. She wasn't willing to delve further into the matter. It was better to keep trimming.

She didn't stop working when Jen stepped into the shed, only complained, "Yer blocking the light."

Jen moved to one side. She watched the gnarled hands guide the knife along the red flesh, trimming it, smoothing it. She thought of Florrie's hands, stiff and cold.

"You said you'd come home," Mag said suddenly, "last night."

Jen met her gaze and flinched inwardly. Mag's eyes were hard.

The girl's throat ached. "I didn't mean . . ." She lowered her gaze, squeezed back tears. "I . . ." she tried once more but the words wouldn't come. Mag turned back to the deer. The crisp sound of her knife slicing through flesh filled the shed. Jen began to shake uncontrollably as she stumbled out of the shed's darkness into the cold twilight.

Rascal raised his head, hesitated a moment, then followed her outside. She scooped him into her arms, and he licked her face as she made her way down to the dock.

CHAPTER ELEVEN

*M*ag was exhausted when she finished skinning the deer. The girl and the pup had both disappeared. Vaguely, she remembered hearing the Princecraft's motor, but she couldn't decide if it was before or after Jen came to the shed. One of the nannies bleated from the goat yard. *Why hadn't the girl looked after them?* Mag wondered. But it was easier to feed the animals herself than to figure out the answer. It also delayed the moment when she had to return to the cabin.

She was shivering by the time she did go inside. She lit a lamp, then went to the stove and shoved paper and kindling into the firebox.

"Gonna be cold tonight," she said, but didn't light the fire. "I'll start it in the morning." She avoided looking at Florrie's bed. There was a loaf of bread on the counter. Mag had not eaten since morning. Although she had no appetite, her belly demanded food. She broke the bread into a bowl, poured milk and sprinkled sugar over the pieces, and ate it without any sense of taste. Then weariness got the best of her. Blowing out the lamp, she made her way to her bedroom. She lay down with her clothes and boots still on, and pulled the covers over herself. *Tomorrow,* she thought as she drifted off to sleep—tomorrow she would find the jars so she and Florrie and Jen could can the venison.

Rascal perched on the Princecraft's tiny bow, his face turned to the breeze. Jen steered close to the western shore as she made her way down Salmon Inlet in the darkness. She felt numb inside, impervious to the frost-tinged air, unable to think clearly enough to plan what she should do. Return to Sechelt? *What for?* Then she remembered the letter she'd found from her mother. *Maybe I could go there,* she thought miserably, *and be like Marlene, always looking after little brothers and sisters.* Inexplicably, she also remembered the English composition on Elizabethan theatre that she was supposed to write this weekend. She had already done the research and was looking forward to completing the project. Now she felt a wave of despair. *I've ruined everything!* She had lost Florrie. Mag and Sylvia hated her. And now she couldn't even go back to school.

She rounded Mid Point, where the lights of a fish farm anchored near the Kunechin Islands guided her into Sechelt Inlet. As she drove on, she realized how tired she was and thought of the boat that had pulled into Serpent Cove the previous summer. A young couple with three small children had walked up to the cabin. Mag had been away in Sechelt, but Florrie had been there, sitting on her rocker outside. She had Jen make some coffee for them and bring out a bag of Oreo cookies for the children. The visitors said they were from a fish farm up Narrows Inlet, and now Jen wondered if they were still at that farm. It couldn't be that far, just around the next point and a mile or so inside Narrows. She could probably tie up there for the night.

The moon was rising over the eastern mountains, tinting the water with a satiny glow. The same moon, Jen thought dismally, that had guided her along the Trail Bay beach the night before, when everything went wrong. She looked longingly at the distant lights of Sechelt, then lifted her chin and turned the boat northward. The Cheekeye power line towers, outlined in green and red lights, rose from promontories on either side of Sechelt Inlet, at the point where it began tapering toward the Skookumchuck Rapids. She knew the entrance to Narrows Inlet was just beyond the tower on the east side, safely south of the rapids. It took another fifteen minutes before she passed under the power lines, but a few moments later when she looked back to confirm her position by the tower lights, she could no longer see them.

"That's not right," she muttered. Glancing up at the sky, she realized with a shock that the stars and moon had also disappeared. She felt a dampness on her cheeks. Fog. Even the dog had been swallowed by the darkness.

"Rascal?" she called, her voice edged with panic. The boat rocked and his nails clicked against the metal hull as he made his way to the stern. His coat blended with the night, but she suddenly felt the warmth of his body against her leg. "Good boy," she murmured, putting one hand on his head.

She slowed the motor, but after ten minutes of creeping blindly through the mist, she shifted into neutral. *What do I do now?* The dog wriggled in behind her legs. She stroked his fur, calming herself as she reviewed her options: continue heading for the fish farm, which must be only a few miles to what she guessed was the east, or turn back to what she thought was Sechelt and hope the fog didn't follow. Because it was closer, the fish farm won the argument. *Even if I miss the farm, we can go on to the wilderness camp at Tzoonie, she reasoned.*

Her mouth dry with fear, she accelerated, inching the Princecraft forward. She squinted into the blackness, trying to distinguish even the faintest of shapes. At the same time she strained to listen for a sound that might guide her. All she heard was the smooth, steady throb of her Honda engine.

A dark mound loomed on her right. *Tzoonie Point*, she thought. With considerable relief she advanced the throttle.

"Guess we missed the fish farm," she told Rascal, "but the wilderness camp's just ahead." As the dog licked her hand in response, she heard a muffled roar over the putta-putta-putt of the motor. *A waterfall?* Jen knew there were no waterfalls near the point. "Oh, shitah!" She sucked in her breath as the boat swung in a different direction than she was steering. The land form she'd just passed was not Tzoonie Point—it was Skookum Island! Instead of travelling up Narrows Inlet, she had been steering a direct course to the Skookumchuck Rapids!

The whirlpool spun the Princecraft in circles, completely destroying any sense of direction she had left. Rascal slid away from her, whimpering as he banged into the side of the boat. She clutched the handle of the outboard and accelerated to top speed. The engine roared. Slowly, the boat pulled away from the grip of the pool. Still, it took all of the little engine's power to keep from being sucked in again. Rascal crept back behind her legs. *Which way?* Frantically she twisted in her seat. *Which way?* The sound was the same no matter what direction she faced.

A cool gust of air pushed a lock of hair away from her forehead. Wind! It was really little more than a breeze, but the occasional gusts swept patches of fog away from the water. Jen cut her speed and peered hard at the rippled surface. *Is that a whirlpool? Or is it a rock?* The boat began to spin again. Accelerating, she escaped the eddy as fog patches closed and opened around her. Now she felt a resistance separate from the whirlpools. *The tide.* She had been so upset when she left the cove that she hadn't paid attention to the tide. Quickly calculating, she decided this had to be the ebb tide, so she must be travelling south, toward Sechelt.

Suddenly the motor coughed. She accelerated and it ran smooth again, but she faced a new worry. *How much gas do I have?* Although she'd filled the tank before leaving Sechelt, it had to be running low, especially using the extra power. She bent to lift the gas can just as the Princecraft hit another whirlpool and began spinning like a cumbersome top. She struggled to regain control as dizziness and nausea swept over her. *I can't stop it!* Desperately, she twisted the throttle wide open, and at last the boat surged away from the whirlpool. At the same time, land forms emerged around her, revealing that she was in a narrow channel, and as it gradually widened, she saw lights glinting in the night. *That's not Sechelt. It's Egmont!*

Egmont. She pictured the tiny community that clustered around Secret Bay, just north of the rapids. Her whole body shook as she steered toward the light, past a buoy and into a small bay where a well-lit wharf beckoned. Jen throttled down. There were no vacant berths visible, so when the boat bumped gently against the side of a cabin cruiser, she cut the engine and grabbed the cruiser's gunwale. With stiff fingers, she tied the Princecraft's stern line to the cruiser, then crawled forward and secured the bow. Then she crept into the centre of the boat and lay down on the floorboards. Holding Rascal against her chest, she closed her eyes and fell into an exhausted slumber.

Mag slept restlessly. Her joints ached, but she refused to go into the kitchen for the liniment that would soothe them. Instead, she searched through the bags at the foot of her bed until she found a quilt she had purchased that summer in the thrift store. With the extra warmth from the quilt, she drifted back into a sleep filled with dreams of herself and Florrie when they were children. Each dream ended with Florrie disappearing into a dark chasm.

In the early dawn, Rascal whimpered and scratched at side of the Princecraft, waking Jen. Two men were quarreling on the other side of the cabin cruiser. One of the voices belonged to Billy Thom.

"Goddamn it, Billy," the other voice shouted. "I've got ten men waiting for breakfast and no cook!"

"Well, I know dat, Gus," Billy agreed, "but the guy couldn't help dat his wife is having the baby. He say he come Wednesday for sure."

Jen crawled to her feet, holding onto the cruiser's gunwale for support. The two men were standing on the dock beside the *Squawk Box*. Jen recognized Gus Stevenson from years before when he had operated a logging camp near Serpent Cove. Rascal barked and leapt from the Princecraft onto the cruiser, and from there onto the dock.

"So what the hell am I going to do without a cook for the next two days?" Gus ranted.

Jen scrambled after the dog. "I can cook," she said stepping onto the dock as Rascal, barking excitedly, threw himself at Billy's legs.

Both men turned to stare as if she were an apparition. "What're you doin' here, Jen?" Billy asked, bending to scratch the dog's ears. Gus forestalled her answer.

"You're the Larson girl, aren't you?"

Jen nodded. "You said you need a cook," she said, not looking at Billy. "I need a job."

Gus turned to Billy. "You ever tasted her cooking?"

Billy nodded, his expression still perplexed. "She make the biscuits when I hauled a load of hay for Mag."

It was enough to satisfy Gus. "Can you start this morning?" When Jen nodded, he said, "Then get your gear. Billy will take you to camp and show you the cookhouse. Job includes cleaning the bunkhouses. We'll see how you handle breakfast. If the boys haven't tossed you out by the time I get back this afternoon, you'll have yourself a job." He stomped away before Jen or Billy could say anything.

"I don't have any gear," Jen told Billy. "Just my boat."

"I knew dat Princecraft look familiar," he said. "Well, pull it around dem boats and we hitch 'er to the tow bar. Den you can tell me what the hell you're doin' here."

The sun had already reached the cabin when Mag crawled out of bed. In the kitchen she cut a fat slice of bread and some of the goat cheese Florrie had made a week earlier. "Be needing some more soon," she told the mound on the bed. She ate at the table with her back to Florrie, washing the dry food down with goat's milk. "Girl hasn't come back yet." She didn't let herself think about why Florrie wasn't answering. "Gotta look after the animals."

She felt better when she got outside. The sun warmed her, as it was warming the roofs of the cabin and sheds. Mist rose from the shingles and was absorbed by the warmer air above. The dog wasn't in his pen. He hadn't been there last night either, she remembered. *Girl must have took him.* She walked past the shed where the deer hung. *She better get back soon so we kin can that meat.* Jen had been doing the job ever since Florrie started getting tired spells.

The goats were unusually quiet, as if they sensed something amiss. Mag milked them, then let them out into their pen and forked fresh hay over the fence. She carried the milk to the cabin, but set it on the porch instead of taking it inside. *Got other things to do*, she told herself. *Girl can take care of it when she gets back.* She went into the shed and rummaged through the gear until she found a mound of netting and a roll of nylon cord. Hauling it to the chicken yard, she began to patch some holes she'd found in the mesh that surrounded the pen. The chickens scattered when she first started working, then gradually came back to peck at the grain

195

she had strewn on the ground, and she was soothed by the normalcy of their soft clucking and scratching.

"Gotta check the outboard when I'm through here," she told them, determined to keep her mind busy, so it didn't drift to places she wasn't ready for. "Plugs need cleaning and adjusting. Maybe needs a new filter."

By mid-afternoon she had finished with the fence and she headed for the dock. She hadn't stopped for lunch or gone near the cabin.

Jen's boat was still missing. *Maybe Sylvia's come back,* Mag thought. *They're probably joost yakking like they do.* She boarded the Sangster, unfastened the motor cover, and set it aside. The plugs were splattered with oil. One at a time she removed them, carefully cleaned the surface with a rag, then shortened the gap between the points. She was just returning the last plug to its socket when the *Squawk Box* entered the cove. Mag didn't acknowledge its presence. She removed the air filter from her motor and set it aside. While Billy docked, she dug a new filter from the shelf in the bow of the boat. She was securing it in place when Billy walked over to the Sangster. For a moment he stood silent, scratching his head.

"I saw your girl," he said finally.

"Oh, shooer?" Mag positioned a screw and fastened it into place.

"She got a job for the weekend. Cooking for Gus Stevenson up Jervis."

For the first time Mag looked at him. "What she doing that fer?"

"She got in some kind of trouble with Sylvia. And she figures you don't want her around no more."

Mag sat back onto the stern seat. She couldn't make sense out of anything Billy was saying. She didn't even want to try to make sense of it. There was too much else going on. Too much that she didn't want to think about. Her shoulders slumped and she let out a long breath. "I t'ink this should work now," she said. She picked up the motor cover and replaced it.

"She tol' me about Florrie," Billy continued. "I'm sorry, Mag."

Mag picked up the rag. She slowly wiped the grease from her hands.

"Police come and get her?" Billy persisted.

Mag stared down at the rag. It was stained from other jobs she'd done. She tried to think which stain belonged to each job.

"Dey did take her, right, Mag?"

There was the time she ran over that stick and broke the sheer pin. She'd replaced it and greased the fittings. That had caused the big stain in the middle. There was some dried blood near it. She remembered skinning her knuckles putting the pin in place.

"Jesus, Mag. Florrie's still here, ain't she?"

Billy Thom made a lot of noise, Mag decided. Just like his boat. She climbed onto the dock. "I gotta get some firewood. Deer meat needs canning." She walked slowly up the ramp. Billy Thom watched her climb the trail, then turned and went aboard the *Squawk Box*. Picking up the headset on his radio, he punched in 9-1-1.

Jen was cleaning the toilet stalls in the last bunkhouse when Gus returned to the camp. Rascal was sleeping in the doorway, and Gus knelt down to scratch the dog behind the ears. "The boys said the breakfast was edible," he commented.

"Billy showed me what to do," she said. "He helped me put out stuff for the lunches before he left."

He raised one eyebrow. "And tonight?"

"I've got steaks out thawing, and potatoes peeled, and greens cut up for salad." She rinsed the mop in the bucket and squeezed it dry with the mop press.

"What about dessert?" he asked as she pulled the bucket out into the hallway.

"There were some pies in the freezer, and ice cream."

He nodded approvingly and straightened. "You'll do," he said.

Jen let out a shaky breath as he strode from the bunkhouse. She was finding it almost impossible to talk without crying—as if talking pulled something out of her that was so connected to Florrie that Jen felt she was losing her over and over again. Gritting her teeth against the pain, she grabbed a broom and began sweeping the floor.

Billy Thom came into camp Monday morning with fresh groceries. He told Jen that Sylvia had arranged for Florrie's funeral to be held on Wednesday.

"I'll come an' take you der," he said, as Jen walked with him back to his boat. "I already godda bring dat cook here."

She shook her head, and though still finding it difficult to speak, she said, "I'm not going, Billy."

Billy stopped. "To the funeral?" he demanded, then said harshly, "Dat Florrie, she be like your muther."

"I know that!" Jen snapped. She swiped angrily at the tears flooding her eyes. "I just don't belong there anymore. Not after what I did."

He spat on the ground. "Florrie, she wouldn't care no matter what you done." He untied the mooring ropes and climbed aboard the boat. "I pick you up after breakfast. You be ready."

"I'm not going, Billy."

"You be ready," he said again. He disappeared into the cabin. A moment later the engine roared to life.

Mag was surprised by all the people who came to the graveside service. They said nice things about Florrie. How she was an example of courage and endurance. How, when they'd stopped in at Serpent Cove, she had made them welcome. Mag listened, bewildered. Florrie never mentioned folks stopping by. Billy told a story of Florrie chasing a bear that had stolen some goat cheese she had set on a plate near the cabin's open window. Florrie, he said, was so mad she had grabbed a broom instead of her rifle. He said he didn't like to think of the bear's fate if she'd ever caught up with him. Everybody laughed at the story, but not Mag. The things they were saying made her throat hurt.

She peered out from beneath her old hat. Sylvia stood nearby, pale and haggard, her hair falling grey and limp on her shoulders. She was there to help if Mag needed her. *She's the one needs help*, Mag decided. But she had no help to offer.

The girl stood beside Billy. They'd come after the service started so Mag didn't have a chance to talk to her. Not that Mag had anything to say. She wouldn't have been here herself if Billy hadn't insisted it was what Florrie would have wanted.

What did he know about Florrie? she thought now. She stared at the large wooden coffin resting beside the open grave. The sun had risen above the mountain behind them, and its first rays touched the yellow cedar lid, giving it a golden hue. Florrie's body was in there. Mag had seen her, all white and cold. But there was nothing of Florrie herself in the body, or the box. No warmth. No laughter. *Florrie shooer wouldn't like this place of dead folks. Not even to listen to the stories.*

"I'm going home," Mag said suddenly, interrupting a tale John Duncan was telling about Florrie catching the biggest salmon he'd ever seen. An awkward silence followed, but as Mag stomped away John continued with his story.

That was up in Jervis, Mag remembered. *When Florrie was living with Jedson.* She reached Sylvia's car and sat sideways, half inside the front passenger seat, so her back was toward the graveyard. *Florrie was happy with Jedson,* she mused. *Happiest she ever was, 'til Jen come.* She looked across the road to where a faint trail penetrated the far edge of a grove of alder trees. *Deer been coming through here,* she thought.

Jen felt such a great heaviness inside, that even a polite smile became a Herculean feat. She hadn't been able to look in the coffin, and she felt as awkward as Mag among the mourners. She'd never been to a funeral before and she hadn't known what to expect. Certainly not all the sympathy people were giving her. Sympathy she had no right to. When Mag walked away, Jen stole a glance at Sylvia. She nodded briefly, before turning back to Florrie's coffin. A fresh wave of remorse washed over Jen. Sylvia wasn't that close to Florrie, but it was plain that she was hurting badly. *What do you expect?* Jen derided herself. *You wrecked her things. Broke her trust. Shitah.*

She walked over to the car where Mag sat staring at the trees. Jen leaned against the back door. The trees were like ghostly skeletons. It had been cold the night before and the ground was moist from rain. As the sun warmed the soil, a mist formed, and a light breeze sent it wafting up through the bare branches to the open sky.

"Deer trail over there," Mag said.

Jen followed her gaze. "How do you know it's not a people trail?"

"Too low fer folks. See how them branches cross over it? Folks would've broke them off."

A late robin warbled in the brush beside the road. A car drove slowly past, its occupants peering curiously at the graveyard. Mag took off her hat and scratched her scalp, rubbing her eyes briefly against her forearm. Then she looked at Jen. Her dark blue eyes seemed to penetrate the girl's soul. "How come you run off?"

"I didn't think you wanted me around," Jen said in a low voice.

"Humph." Mag looked down at the hat in her hand. "Venison needs canning," she said finally.

Jen wasn't sure what Mag meant by the remark. She hadn't considered going back to the cove, hadn't let herself think of it. She wondered if she could even bear going back to the cabin without Florrie.

"I got a job," she said finally. "Cooking for Gus Stevenson."

Mag nodded. "I heard."

"Your job is to go to school," a familiar voice said behind her. But before Sylvia could say any more, they were surrounded by other people returning to their cars. John Duncan, and a few others, walked over to Mag to express their sympathies. When at last they were all gone, Mag turned to Sylvia. "I got to get back to my boat now."

Sylvia nodded. "I have some refreshments ready at the cottage," she offered, but Mag shook her head. "I'm going home." She swung her legs into the car and shut the door. Sylvia turned to Jen. "You must finish high school, Jen. You're far too bright to turn your back on an education."

"You listen to her," Billy Thom advised Jen as he led the way to his pickup. "Dat school, she wasn't right for me and she wasn't right for Mag. But she's right for you."

"Humph." Jen opened the door to the truck. Rascal jumped

out and ran into the bushes before Jen could grab him. She coaxed him back with a piece of sandwich meat.

"Dat dog need to know who's boss," Billy said. Jen didn't answer. They drove along the highway in silence, following Sylvia's car down to the public wharf. When they pulled up to his parking space, Billy switched off the engine. "Mag, she don't say it, but she needs you, Jen."

Jen didn't move for several minutes. Then she turned to him. "Why do you care?" she asked levelly. "Mag's never even been nice to you."

Billy shrugged. "Law of the sea—boat in trouble, you go help. Today, Mag need help. Tomorrow, maybe Billy Thom need help."

Mag felt old as she hauled the newly-filled gas can down the ramp to her boat. Old and cold, and deathly tired. She climbed over the gunwales, then lifted the can into the boat. As she connected the fitting, she contemplated crawling under the bow cover and having a sleep. The dock swayed slightly. She looked up as Rascal hopped into the stern.

"Can we get a ride?" Jen asked.

Mag moved to the passenger seat. "You take it," she said wearily. She leaned her head against the canvas top and closed her eyes. Jen watched her anxiously. She'd never known Mag to relinquish control of her boat before.

"Sure . . ." she said. She pushed the motor leg into the water, then went forward to the controls and pressed the starter. The motor rumbled to life. She let it idle while she untied the mooring ropes. Mag didn't move, even when Jen steered away from the dock and opened the throttle. Rascal stood uncertainly in the aisle between the two seats. Finally, he tucked himself down beside Mag, leaning his warm body against her legs.

CHAPTER TWELVE

The cabin was cold and damp. Mag hadn't lit the fire since the morning she left on her hunting trip. The table was still littered with dishes from the breakfast they'd shared that morning. To avoid dealing with the mess, Mag had been living on goat's milk for the past week. Now she hung her hat on the hook by the door and made her way to the bedroom. There she crawled under the quilts piled on her bed. The girl could start the fire, she decided. Or not. May didn't really care. All she wanted to do was sleep.

Some of the heaviness left Jen as she followed Rascal from the boat to the goat yard. The nannies greeted her at the fence, eagerly nibbling her fingers.

"You're hungry!" she cried, growing more alarmed. Mag had never before neglected her goats. But when Jen opened the door to their shed, she was overpowered by the stench of urine and goat manure. Hastily she closed the door.

She took as long as she could to feed the goats and chickens, and clean out their sheds. When she finished, and there was nothing left for her to do, she reluctantly climbed the steps to the cabin.

"Jesus, Mag!"

She stared at the mess on the table and counter. Then slowly she turned to Florrie's bed. She clenched her teeth against the fresh wave of pain that surged through her chest.

It's not right! Why Florrie? She never hurt nobody. She was always laughing. Shit!

She stumbled back outside, half-blinded by tears that she was damned if she would shed. As if sensing her distress, the pup didn't frolic as he followed her down to the dock. He stood silently by as she stared at Pete Saari's barge. Everything that had happened to her in the past week seemed centred on that barge. If it hadn't been for Cal Saari, she would have been here when Florrie needed her. She wouldn't have hurt Sylvia. She scowled at the black, monolithic structure and her chin came up.

"Come on, Rascal," she snapped. In the cabin, she retrieved Mag's rifle from its perch above the workbench. She loaded the empty chamber with .22 longs she found in a box on the shelves.

"Don't ever load yer gun 'less yer gonna use it," Mag had told Jen once when she was giving her a shooting lesson. Now, as she pushed the copper-coloured shells into the chamber, Jen's lips tightened. Damned right she was going to use it.

Mag lay on her bed in the gathering dusk. She stared at a wet spot on the ceiling. The roof had leaked badly during the last big rainstorm. A bucket still stood on the floor where she had placed it to catch the drips. She had planned to repair the roof the next day. Instead, she had let Florrie persuade her to go hunting.

Don't matter now, she thought dismally. *Whole damned place kin rot away.*

She closed her eyes, but the sleep that she craved eluded her. Instead, she heard her dad's stern voice. "Got no business sulking, girl, joost 'cause life don't go yer way."

She turned her face to the window. It was darkened with cobwebs. Outside, salmonberry bushes scraped against the glass whenever the weather was stormy.

What do you know, anyways? she argued sullenly. *Now there's nobody but me.*

The crack of a rifle exploded the silence of the cabin. Mag leaped out of bed. "Shitah!" She stumbled over the bucket as a second shot rang out.

The shooting came from Saari's landing. As she charged along the beach trail, Mag met the panicked pup racing for home. On the beach, Jen was taking aim at the skidder parked at the base of a road the cat had roughed into the woods.

"Hold up, girl!" Mag shouted, but her voice was drowned by another blast from the rifle.

"Shitah."

Jen emptied the used cartridge and advanced the next bullet into the chamber.

"What you t'ink yer doin'?" Mag demanded.

Jen wiped at her eyes with her arm. "I'm stopping those assholes!" She took aim again.

"Yer gonna kill yerself from the ricochet," Mag snorted.

Jen squeezed the trigger. The gun cracked, and a puff of gravel burst from the ground near the skidder's tire.

"You figure on plowing up the beach?" Mag asked mildly.

"At least I'm doing something," Jen snapped. She reloaded and aimed once more, this time raising the barrel. "I'm not just letting them take our bush, like you."

Mag scratched her forehead. In her haste to leave the cabin, she'd forgotten her hat. "Nutting fer us to do," she said quietly. "You kin shoot all the holes you want into them tires. They'll joost buy new ones. And send the cops to lock you up."

Jen swallowed a sob and lowered the rifle. She turned to Mag. "Why, Mag? Why are we letting them do this? Why do we always let them hurt us?"

There was desperation in the girl's face—a hurting that matched the pain in Mag's own gut. She looked into the angry eyes and saw herself forty years earlier, when Florrie had told her she had a baby in her belly and Erik Saari was the father. Erik denied ever having touched her. He had said she was just "a loggers' whore" and the kid could belong to anybody. Mag had started after him with that same rifle, but their dad had stopped her. He'd said she couldn't mind his trapline if she was in jail for murder. Erik Saari was long dead from a tree falling on him, but there was a bitterness in her now that she had never felt before toward her father. She should have been the one to kill Saari.

"Why, Mag?" Jen asked again.

Mag looked out at the cove. "It don't matter what they do to us," she said slowly. "It's what we do fer ourselves after that counts." She walked back toward the cabin. "You get the fire going," she said over her shoulder. "I'll cut us some deer steaks."

The next day, Jen canned the venison. Then she helped Mag

dismantle Florrie's bed. Its absence left an emptiness in the cabin that both of them felt, but neither spoke of. The corner would fill, eventually, as every corner of the room had filled. But for now it was a void that had to be borne.

Jen returned to school on Monday. Sandra and Cal were both absent, and Marlene was jubilant when Jen met her in the hallway at the end of the day.

"My dad said Sandra's been sent to a private school that's really, really strict," Marlene said. "And Cal's gone to his uncle's place in Merritt. The cops caught him breaking into one of the beach cottages, looking for more booze. Trent was with him, but he escaped out of a window before the cops saw him." She added smugly, "We're going to a movie this weekend—if my dad lets me."

Jen felt inexplicably sorry for Cal. It was the same kind of pity she felt for the animals caught in Mag's traps. But she had little time to dwell on the feeling. An east wind had come up, which meant a rough trip home. She wished now that she had accepted Mag's offer of a ride to and from school.

It was dark when Mag heard the girl's motor. She grabbed a flashlight and hurried down to the dock. The beam was just strong enough to guide Jen in. The pup barked as she drew up, and licked her face when she grabbed the deck.

"I had to pull in behind the bluff for a while," Jen told her. "Wind was blowing too hard."

"You should'a stayed in town," Mag scolded, tying the bow line.

Jen secured the stern line and crawled out of the boat. "I blew that privilege last weekend," she said bitterly. She followed Mag up to the cabin. She was cold and hungry and, for the first time since Florrie died, she was glad to be home where it was warm. Still, she longed for Florrie's welcoming smile and the smell of fresh bread that had greeted her so many times before.

The following morning, Sylvia was working on a crossword puzzle at the kitchen table when Mag knocked on the door. She called for Mag to come in, but didn't get up to greet her.

Mag was surprised to find her in a housecoat. "You sick?" Mag asked suspiciously, keeping her distance.

Sylvia shook her head. "Just had no reason to get dressed," she said.

Mag stayed near the door. "Weather's shooer getting bad, anyways," she said.

Sylvia looked at the rain pelting the kitchen window. "Yes, I suppose it is."

"It's hard to come in everyday when it's like this. And my motor's running terrible." When Sylvia didn't respond, Mag ventured further into the room. She sat on a chair at the opposite end of the table. "Florrie shooer wanted the girl to have schooling."

Sylvia met her gaze. "So what are you getting at, Mag?"

"She t'inks you don't want her to come here."

"She thinks right," Sylvia agreed. "The fact is, Mag, I'm not sure if I'm even going to be here much longer."

"Is that so?" Mag removed her hat and placed it on her knee. "Are you going to look fer more of them old garbage dumps?"

Sylvia frowned. She pushed the crossword puzzle aside. "No," she said shortly. "The doctor I've been working with has chosen to continue with underwater research. So we've decided to end our . . . association."

"But I guess you don't need him to look fer garbage," Mag said philosophically. "There's lots of that stuff right close to here."

Sylvia remained silent, but Mag thought she saw a gleam of interest in the other woman's eyes. Pressing what she perceived to be an advantage, Mag said, "You should finish what you started with the girl."

"That *girl* practically destroyed my home," Sylvia said harshly, pointing to the burn mark on the counter.

Mag shrugged. "I guess everybody makes mistakes sometimes." When Sylvia didn't respond, Mag continued coldly, "Yer the one let Jen get attached to you, anyways. Buying her all them things. Making her into a town kid."

"I was kind to her. That doesn't make me responsible for her."

"When you change a critter's ways," Mag went on, as if Sylvia hadn't spoken, "there's joost two t'ings you kin do. One's to shoot it. The other's to look after it." She replaced her hat and got to her feet. "Guess you need to figure which one yer gonna do." She slammed the door on her way outside. As she started down the trail, she heard the door open, but she didn't turn around. The Sangstercraft bumped gently against the dock when Mag climbed inside, aware that Sylvia was watching her from the head of the trail. She started the engine, released the bow line, and was about to untie the stern line when she saw Sylvia walking down the hill. Mag waited until the woman was on the dock.

"Tell her to bring some goat's milk," Sylvia said.

Mag nodded. She untied the stern line, went forward and shifted into gear, then gently guided the Sangstercraft away from the dock.

Saari's landing had been quiet all week. On Friday after school, Jen found out why when she met Billy on the wharf as she was preparing to set off for the cove.

"Dat Saari's having trouble with his crew boat," he said happily. "He want me to haul dem guys in der, but I got too much other stuff to do."

Mag just grunted when Jen relayed the news later that evening. "Saari'll get it fixed," she said. "He always does." She surveyed the pup Jen was feeding under the table. "He dug himself outta his pen while you was gone. Guess you better fix her up tomorrow."

"He only does it because he misses me," Jen protested.

"Well, I'm tired of him digging his damned holes all over the place."

"But, Mag . . ."

"You kin start after you feed the goats. Unless," she added grumpily, "you want to take the dog back to Billy, where he should'a stayed in the first place!"

The following day was cloudy. A brisk wind had the trees swaying restlessly. Jen shivered as she rummaged behind the goat pen for fencing material. Rascal scampered around her, dashing into the bushes, then lunging out and attacking the wires she pulled free from the dead grass. When he tired of that game, he started digging another hole under the remains of an old log. "Rascal! No!" Jen shovelled the dirt back into the hole.

"He's shooer not missing you now," Mag observed as she walked past the clearing. She stared thoughtfully at the log Rascal had been excavating. "That's where you found that rock."

Jen looked up from the wire she was trying to free. "What rock?"

"That Indian thing," Mag said. "Where'd you hide it?"

Jen sat on the grass as she tried to figure out what Mag was talking about. "Indian thing?" Then she remembered the artifact she had found so many years before. "You mean the hammer?"

"I guess so," Mag said. "You still got it, don't you?"

For the first time since Florrie's death, Jen laughed. So Mag had always known she'd hidden it. "Yeah," she said. She hadn't visited the hollow stump for years. Now, with Rascal following close behind, she headed for the clearing by the creek. Only, it wasn't a clearing any longer because salal and salmonberry bushes had grown up, obscuring the old trail—but Mag brought a machete, and they soon had a path cleared to the stump. Jen barely fit inside. In the dimness she could see the metal coffee cans that held her childhood treasures. Beside one was a dark stone object with a smooth shaft about three inches thick. One end of the shaft was round, the other end fashioned into a hammerhead.

Outside of the stump, Mag waited impatiently. "Is it there?"

Jen crawled out with the stone in her hand. "Since when did you get interested in archaeology?" she asked.

"Joost give me that rock and keep quiet about finding it."

Jen hesitated. She would probably never see the hammer again if she gave it to Mag. On the other hand, living with Mag would be pure hell if she didn't hand it over. Reluctantly, she held it out. "It should go in a museum."

"Yer right," Mag said. She grabbed the stone and hurried down the trail to the cabin. When Jen saw her again about an hour later, Mag was wearing her backpack.

"Where you going?" Jen called

"Up the beach," Mag said. "You keep working on that pen."

Mag returned long after dark, but all she would say about where she had been was that she had checked on Saari's survey ribbons. The following morning she rose early. "I'm going to town," she told Jen, who was just waking.

Billy Thom hadn't started his daily run. He was still tied up to the dock in Sechelt when Mag climbed aboard. "You got any coffee worth drinking?" she asked.

"I got the *only* coffee worth drinkin'," Billy responded. He grabbed a cup from a hook on the wall and poured some of his thick, black brew into it.

"Yer cousin Louis—he still looking fer shitty bark?" Mag asked as he handed her the cup.

Billy eyed her warily. "Yeah. He gets it when he can find it. Not much left now."

Mag grimaced at the bitter taste of the coffee. She set the cup down. "I t'ink if Saari gets his crew boat fixed, he's about one day away from hitting my shitty bark trees."

"Yeah?"

"Oh, shooer," Mag said, her voice sorrowful. "Too bad I can't get the bark off 'em befer he does."

Billy's eyes narrowed suspiciously. "How come you can't?"

Mag rubbed her leg near the site of her old fracture. "Leg's too bad fer me to go up there," she complained. "Couldn't go up last year, neither." She shook her head regretfully. "Tried to send the girl up, but she's got too much school work. Says she can't do it, anyways."

"Two years, no cuttin'. . . . dat means the bark gonna be real good."

"I guess so." Mag took a final drink of coffee, then got to her feet. "You tell yer cousin Louis, if he wants that bark he better come fer it soon." She left the cabin and climbed down onto the dock. She knew Billy would be a while figuring out her invitation. But he would come. And Louis Paul would come with him.

Two days later, the *Squawk Box* appeared in the cove and anchored close to Saari's barge. Jen had just finished milking the goats and was heading for the cabin to change for school. She stopped to watch curiously as Billy and Louis John climbed into a small skiff. They paddled to Saari's landing, then disappeared into the timber. "What do you think they're doing?" she asked Mag as she walked past with a bucket of eggs.

"And joost how am I supposed to know what Billy Thom's up to?" Mag demanded crossly.

The following morning, the silence of the inlet was broken once more by the cranky whine of chainsaws, and the sickening crash of falling timber. The bulldozer roared as it snorted its way deeper into the woods.

"It's not fair," Jen stormed, slamming pots about as she prepared breakfast. She was still angry when she steered away from the dock on her way to school.

Less than an hour later, Mag was walking toward the storage shed when a grey Zodiac pulled up beside Saari's crew boat. She smiled smugly as she rummaged through the shed for material to patch the leak above her bedroom. Later, from the roof of the cabin, she watched the Zodiac leave. Then, as a tall, dark figure marched along the beach trail toward her, Mag climbed down from the roof. While the dog barked frantically outside, she stood beside the table in the cabin loading her rifle.

"Larson!" Pete Saari's voice thundered.

Mag opened the door. She stepped onto the porch and pointed her rifle at the ground. "Yer trespassing, Saari."

Rascal nipped at the man's heels, dodging the kicks Saari aimed at him. Saari's face was contorted with fury. "You done this, Larson," he snarled.

"Don't know what yer talking about," Mag said with feigned innocence.

He shook his fist at her. "Bullshit, you don't. Louis John says you told him where to look for the damned rock. I wouldn't put it past you to have planted it there, you bitch."

Mag stared at him coolly. She raised her rifle so the end of the barrel was pointed at his chest. "You know, I've been wanting to shoot me a Saari since me and Florrie was girls."

When Pete's fist remained in the air, Mag lifted the gun higher and fired. The bullet lodged in an alder behind him. He drew back his arm. "You'll go to jail for this," he snarled as Mag reloaded. "That timber's mine. I got a right." He swung on his heel and stomped back to the beach. Mag waited until he was out of sight before lowering her rifle. "Some folks t'ink they got more rights than others," she muttered.

On Friday, Mag quit work early. She lit a fire so the cabin was warm when Jen returned from school. The aroma of freshly brewed coffee greeted the girl when she opened the door. Tossing her pack onto the cot, she went to the table and dropped the local paper in front of Mag.

"Interesting story on the front page." She pointed to the two headline pictures—one of a Sechelt Indian Band leader holding up a stone maul, and another of a grim-faced Pete Saari. She read the article out loud: "Ancient artifact stops inlet logging. Local contractor Pete Saari had just started to log his lease at Serpent Cove last week when the artifact was found by Louis John of Sechelt, who was cutting cascara. Wednesday morning, Judge Cooper granted an injunction against further logging, until both environmental and archaeological studies have been completed. 'I've invested everything I have in this venture,' Mr. Saari said. 'And it's going to take years for those studies to be done.' Mr. Saari has sought legal council, claiming the artifact was planted. Louis John said the hammer was found tangled in the roots of a cascara tree. Cedric Portman, a local archaeologist, has confirmed that the stone maul had been buried for hundreds of years. 'The cascara roots must have grown around it and lifted it from the ground as they grew,' he said. 'It is a remarkable discovery and probably indicates that more will be found in the same vicinity.'"

While Mag studied the pictures, Jen went to the counter and poured a cup of coffee. "Strange," she said, returning to the table. "That hammer looks just like the one I found."

"Humph," Mag said. She bit into the goat cheese sandwich she'd made and chewed slowly, savouring the flavour.

EPILOGUE

Mag let the girl sleep on Saturday morning. The sky was dark and seagulls swooped and screamed in the wind, high above the cabin, while the evergreens moaned in unison. In the chicken yard, the rooster crowed. The pup barked imperiously, throwing himself against the wire of his pen. They were good sounds, Mag decided. Sounds Florrie had loved.

Best let that dog out or there'll be no peace all day. She trudged to the pen Jen had made.

"Oh, shooer, joost quit yer yapping," she scolded. She unfastened the rope that secured the gate. The puppy bounded out of the kennel, ran around the yard, then launched himself on Mag, almost toppling her. "Scat!" She shooed him away, but he was back underfoot a moment later. "Yer gonna be the death of me, Dog!"

The hens were still scratching the oats Jen had spilled on her way to feed the goats the previous evening. She had tripped on one of the dog's holes and the bucket had gone flying into the chicken yard. The girl had laughed like a fool. *She'll find out. When we run out of feed and it's too stormy to get more, she'll find out then about wasting.*

A nanny came to the opening of the goat shed. Her sad dark eyes surveyed Mag solemnly. Mag held out her hand. The nanny licked her fingers but found nothing worth digesting. She raised her head and looked at Mag expectantly.

"You got fed enough last night," Mag scolded. "I seen how much oats she put in yer bucket when she t'ought I wasn't looking."

When she finished milking, Mag walked back to the cabin. Setting the bucket in the old refrigerator, out of the dog's reach, she lowered herself onto Florrie's rocker. The pup lay down at her feet and closed his eyes.

Mag rocked gently as she stared out at the inlet. The wind had died away while she milked. Now the water was flat calm and dark, like the hills around it. She had always loved the pause after a storm,

213

when everything was at peace. She thought of Florrie sitting there day after day. And the girl. They'd loved each other, Florrie and the girl. Like they was real kin. Started that first day when Mag handed the baby over to her sister. Didn't work out too bad, neither.

She closed her eyes and felt her sister's presence.

"I'll join you soon enough," Mag said. "But not joost yet. My girl needs me a while longer."

She was answered by the yodel of a loon far across the cove.

ROSELLA LESLIE was born in Edmonton, Alberta, and grew up in small towns throughout Alberta and British Columbia. She worked in Merritt and Vancouver, before moving to a floathouse at Clowhom Falls on Salmon Inlet to focus on her writing career in 1980. In 1991, Leslie moved with her husband and son to Sechelt. Leslie's hobbies include gardening, pulling up crab traps, and early morning mountain walks with her golden retriever. She is also the author of *The Sunshine Coast: A Place to Be*, and has co-authored *Bright Seas, Pioneer Spirits: The Sunshine Coast*, and *Sea Silver: Inside British Columbia's Salmon-Farming Industry* with Betty Keller. Leslie is also one of the authors of *Stain Upon the Sea: West Coast Salmon Fishing*, which won *The Roderick Haig-Brown Regional Prize* at the 2005 British Columbia Book Awards.